Readers love R

Dirty Kiss

"…a nail-biting, stay-up-late, page-turner of a book."

—Top2Bottom Reviews

"This is a great romantic suspense novel with a gritty film noir atmosphere and a sexy, heartfelt romance."

—The Book Vixen

"I didn't catch who the killer (was)… kudos to the author."

—Elisa's Reviews and Ramblings

Dirty Secret

"The obstacles and the twists and turns in this action-packed tale kept me glued until the last page."

—Top2Bottom Reviews

"The exciting sequel to *Dirty Kiss* packs a solid, seductive, and bloody punch."

—Joyfully Reviewed

Sinner's Gin

"It was jaw-dropping and reeled me into this equally amazing book from the get-go."

—Under the Covers

By RHYS FORD

NOVELS

Sinner's Gin

COLE MCGINNIS MYSTERIES
Dirty Kiss
Dirty Secret
Dirty Laundry

Published by DREAMSPINNER PRESS
http://www.dreamspinnerpress.com

DIRTY LAUNDRY

RHYS FORD

Dreamspinner Press

Published by
Dreamspinner Press
5032 Capital Circle SW
Ste 2, PMB# 279
Tallahassee, FL 32305-7886
USA
http://www.dreamspinnerpress.com/

Dirty Laundry

Cover Art by Reece Notley
reece@vitaenoir.com

ISBN: 978-1-62380-631-6
Digital ISBN: 978-1-62380-632-3

Printed in the United States of America
First Edition
April 2013

Dirty Laundry is dedicated to Charles and Joyce Howell, a second set of parents I hold in such high esteem. May all your lychee be juicy and your fish fins crispy. And also to their daughter, Jacque, who endures my random nature and forgetfulness.

Every bit of cat in this book goes to Denise Ruiz, my darling Star and kin. Much love and purrs.

ACKNOWLEDGMENTS

TO THE FIVE, or rather the other four. Dearest Penn, Lea, Tamm, and Jenn, always here in the words, be they ink or digital. And to my darling sisters, Ren and Ree. Eat more and stay happy.

On the business side, a hearty thanks to Elizabeth North for letting me ramble. *Huge* thanks to the Dreamspinner Press staff who make me look damned good: Lynn, Julianne, Ginnifer, Anne, Brian, Mara, Julili, and everyone else who varnished and polished.

A hearty shout out to my beta readers and the Dirty Ford Guinea Pigs. They are in random order and are listed as they are to be known: Reetoditee "Didi" Mazumdar, Bianca "Bubbles" Janian, Tiffany "Coffee Bunneh" Tran, Lisa "Shoes" Horan, VJ Summers, Christy Duke, My Pants Losing Friend DarienMoya, CC Hunt, Camiele White, Crissy Morris, The Grand Princess Heather Cook, Sue N., Lea Walker, Jess B., Nikyta I Am A Rocking Princess Jenkins, Lisa "Lakerkat" L., Sadonna, Verena M., Sey, Amy Peterson, Aniko, Whitney Watkins, and Patricia Grayson.

GLOSSARY

All words are Korean unless otherwise noted.

Agi: Baby, as in infant. This word is used between Jae and Cole as a teasing affectionate term, referencing to when Cole called Jae baby in English.

Aish: Common Asian-centric sound denoting exasperation or disbelief.

Ajumma: Older middle-aged woman. Sometimes considered to be an insult in some circles as it denotes the woman has aged enough for it to be noticeable.

An nyoung ha seh yo: A general greeting. Can be used at any time of the day.

Beom joe ja: Criminal or criminal element.

Bulgogi: Thinly sliced steak marinated in a sweet, soy sauce mixture.

Char siu bao (Chinese): A steamed or baked bun made of bread and stuffed with a sweet, barbequed pork mixture.

Chigae: A stew-like Korean dish, made with kimchi and other ingredients, such as scallions, onions, diced tofu, pork, and seafood,

Dongseongaeja: Homosexual

Enceinte (Latin/French origins): To be pregnant

Halmeoni: Grandmother

Hangul: Korean alphabet / lettering system

Hanzi / kanji: Logogram characters used in Chinese (hanzi) and Japanese (kanji) writing. Sometimes used in Korea but less frequently as hangul replaced it as Korea's formal writing system centuries past.

Harabeoji / abeoji: Grandfather

Hyung: Honorific used by a younger male towards an older male he's close to.

Ibanin / iban : A different type person, a lingual play on the Korean word *ilban-in*, meaning normal person.

Jagiya: A term of endearment similar to baby or darling.

Kalbi: A sweet, soy sauce marinated short rib dish.

Kimchi / kim chee: A fermented Korean side dish made of vegetables with a variety of seasonings. Usually refers to the standard cabbage variation which is the most common form of kim chee. If another vegetable is used, the dish will be referred to by the vegetable used, such as cucumber kim chee.

Kimchijeon / kimchi buchimgae: A griddle pancake made from kim chee and flour. Sometimes, other vegetables or meats are mixed in as well.

Kretek (Indonesian): A clove and tobacco blended cigarette originating from Java. The word comes from the sound the cloves make when burning.

Kuieo: Korean slang for queer.

Mandu: Fried or steamed dumplings made of rice or wheat flour wrappers and stuffed with a variety of ingredients.

Musang (Filipino): Wild cat, most commonly used to refer to a civet.

Ne / de: Yes

Nuna: Hyung: Honorific used by a younger male toward an older female he's close to.

Omo: Common Asian-centric sound denoting disbelief.

Oniisan (Japanese): Older brother

Oppa: Honorific used by a younger female toward an older male she's close to.

Panchan / banchan: Small dishes of food served along with cooked rice at Korean meals. Traditionally, the more formal the meal, the greater the amount of panchan.

Papas (Hispanic usage): Fries. Preferably covered with carne asada, cheese and sour cream but plain is okay too.

Saranghae: I love you

Sunbae: Senior or teacher. Someone who is considered a mentor.

Tatami (Japanese): Flooring mats either made of straw or other materials covered with straw rushes.

Unnie / eonni: Honorific used by a younger female toward an older female she's close to.

CAST OF CHARACTERS

Madame Hyuna Sun, a Korean female fortune-teller
James Bahn, Madame Sun's son
Madame Sun's deceased clients:
     May Choi, car jacking
     Eun Joon Lee, murdered during burglary
     Bhak Bong Chol, apparent heart attack
Vivian Na, Madame Sun's assistant
Joon Eun Yi, Eun Joon Lee's neighbor
Gangjun Gyong-Si, rival fortune-teller/Madame Sun's former colleague
Terry Yi, Gyong-Si's assistant
JoJo, owner of JoJo's Boxing and Gym
Stan Jenkins, LAPD detective
Hong Chul Park, Bhak Bong Chol's grandson
Abby Park, Hong Chul Park's daughter
Darren Shim, a former friend of Hong Chul Park

MCGINNIS FAMILY
Cole Kenjiro McGinnis
James Michael McGinnis (father)
Barbara McGinnis (step-mother)
Colin Mikio McGinnis (older brother)
Madeline "Maddy / Mad Dog" McGinnis (sister-in-law)
Tasha "Tazzie" McGinnis (sister)

Bianca "Bi" McGinnis (sister)
Melissa "Mellie" McGinnis (sister)

Bobby Dawson (Cole's best friend)

KIM FAMILY
Kim Jae-Min (Cole's lover)
Kim Jae-Su (older brother)
Kim Tiffany (younger sister)
Kim Ree (Serena) (younger sister)
Neko-chan (Jae's cat)

SCARLET'S CIRCLE
Scarlet (Crisanto Songcuya Seong)
Seong Min-Ho (Scarlet's lover)

DUPREE FAMILY
Claudia Dupree
Sons in order of birth:
        Martin (kids: Mo, Sissy)
        Marcel (Korean girlfriend, Hyunae)
        Malcolm
        Mace
        Morris
        Marcus (gay son)
        Matthew

TOKUGAWA FAMILY
Tokugawa Ryoko (Cole's biological mother)
Tokugawa Masahiro (Ryoko's husband)
Tokugawa Ichiro (Son, Cole's half-brother)

PINELLI FAMILY
Ben Pinelli (Cole's deceased partner)
Sheila Pinelli (wife)
Jennifer (daughter)
Benji (Ben Jr.) (son)
Michelle (daughter)

SEONG MIN-HO'S FAMILY
Shim Min-Cha (Seong's wife)
Sons in order of birth:
    Seong Ji-Chin
    Seong Ji-Hei
    Seong Ji-Moon (twin)
    Seong Ji-Sung (twin)

LOS ANGELES POLICE OFFICERS
Detective Dell O'Byrne
Detective Lynn Brookes
Detective Dexter Wong

CHAPTER ONE

I HATE little girls.

Hands down, they are secret vessels of Satan and probably rule their own special circle of hell reserved for people who abandon dogs by the side of the road and assholes who molest innocent children.

Or it could be that I was bitter about running my fucking ass off down a back alley with a rabid poodle slung in a baby carrier across my belly while a pack of frothing fighting dogs ripped the shit out of my jeans.

While I didn't *really* hate little girls—particularly the little girl who'd hired me to rescue her dog—I was getting kind of sick of learning to navigate through Los Angeles's back alleys.

I knew she was trouble as soon as she walked through my door. Wearing a deep red velvet dress with more white ruffles on its hem and sleeves than a wedding cake, Ava Hernandez was an angelic portrait of sweet innocence with fine mahogany hair, luminous, liquid brown eyes, and a chipped front tooth. In about ten years, her father probably would be sitting out on the porch guarding his daughter's virtue with a double-barreled shotgun.

Actually, he should have been there with that damned shotgun to take out the asshole who made her cry, because her face was wet with tears when she placed a chipped pink porcelain pig on my desk and declared she was there to hire me.

And if the pig wasn't enough, it was joined by a slightly melted chocolate bar and a bright purple toy unicorn with a curled rainbow mane.

I was doomed from the start.

She had a sad tale to tell, and I was the only guy man enough to help her. A couple of gangbangers stole Ava's poodle mix, Pookie, and she was determined to get her dog back. She knew where they lived, a bad section of street a little bit away from her house, but the cops weren't too interested and Animal Control'd been less than helpful. Loaded for bear with her bus pass and her entire savings, she'd dug through the Internet for a private investigator, dressed in her Sunday best, and rode the Metro to hire me.

Not bad for a nine year old with a net worth of three dollars and fifty-one cents. I admired her bravado. Then I dialed her mother to come pick her up.

I took the case. For the cost of the chocolate bar. I gave Ava back the pig and unicorn. It seemed like the right thing to do at the time. Now, in the middle of a warm Los Angeles night and being herded by the savage growls behind me, I was beginning to think I should have held onto the unicorn.

"Bobby! Where the fuck are you?" I was shouting to the air. Fucker was nowhere to be seen.

He was supposed to have stayed behind the house so I'd have an easy escape. Climbing over the rickety wooden-slat fence, I'd spotted Pookie, holed up in a small plastic kennel, the type someone would use to cart a small cat back and forth to the vet. There were other broken plastic transport boxes keeping her company on the patio, but what worried me was across the yard—a more substantial bank of kennels made of chain-link fences and concrete floors.

And each bay was occupied by a thick-necked, over-muscled fighting dog.

People who raise dogs to fight should be shot. Men who steal a little girl's dog to bait a fighting dog should die the slowest, most torturous death possible. Their skin should be separated from their flesh with an air hose through minute slits and then have water from the

Salton Sea injected slowly into the cavities while someone rips off strips of duct tape from their balls.

But that's just off the top of my head. I was sure I could come up with something more concrete if given a little time. Okay, I might have borrowed that death from Jae's overactive imagination, but it popped into my head once I saw the dogs. Whoever turned them into vicious animals needed killing.

If Pookie didn't get us killed first.

Before my partner, Ben, killed my lover, Rick, and shattered my life and body in a hail of bullets, I shared a townhouse with Rick's small dog. He'd been a quiet, fluffy thing with bulging eyes and a discerning palate. We'd come to an agreement of sorts. I wouldn't let Rick put bows on the top of his head and he didn't chew up anything I owned. I called him Ragmop too often to remember his real name.

He'd been one of the many things Rick's parents took with them while I was lying on a hospital bed fighting for my life. Well, what I had left of my life after they removed any sign of his existence from our place. It was bad enough that Ben killed him. I could have done without them erasing him completely.

Now, I'd be lucky if the dognappers' mutts didn't finish the job Ben started.

But at least, I'd fulfill the promise I made to my current lover, Jae. I wasn't getting shot at.

Or I'd planned on fulfilling that promise until the shooting started.

There was a hell of a lot of shooting going on, and the popping noises I was beginning to hear were loud, rapping sounds bouncing through the streets.

Somewhere, I'd taken a wrong turn. Pookie wasn't helping. Her ears flew up and hit my face with every stride I took, sometimes blinding me with white fuzz. Circling through the neighborhood led me back to the wide street where I'd expected to find Bobby's truck. The dogs skittered around the corner, their claws scrabbling to gain purchase on the broken sidewalk. A rough cinder block wall held promise. If anything, it was solid enough to keep the mutts from chewing my ass off.

My knees struck the wall as I swung up, my muscles going numb when I hit. The uneven blocks dug through my jeans and scraped my skin, turning my knees into hamburger. I'd take inventory later. Between the dog struggling against my chest and the bloodthirsty howls at my back, I had better things to worry about than whether or not I'd look like a piece of road rash once I got out of there.

The wall was covered in dank black lichen along its prickly flat surface and thick with Los Angeles traffic dust. The mold made it difficult to get a purchase on the wall, and more than once I felt my sneakers slip when I tried to get a better hold on the ridge. Someone'd begun to shout, and it was getting louder and more incessant. Ignoring everything but the dog strapped to my chest, I heaved myself up and bit through the pain arcing through my shoulders. Heaving my weight up, I finally got a foot on the wall's lip and balanced precariously on the wide cinder block ledge.

Pookie twisted in her holder, throwing me off balance, and I fell, right through the thick plastic sheeting draped down over a ramshackle carport's support beams. Pookie yelped her displeasure and tried to snatch my nose off my face, but I kept her steady, cupping her wriggling body against my chest with one hand.

I'd already eaten the chocolate bar, or I'd have been sorely tempted to toss her back into the garage and let her work out her own escape.

The dogs barking furiously on the other side of the wall were the least of my problems. I knew the smell coming up from the thick foliage. It was a sweet, sticky odor reminiscent of days I'd spent in college trying to clear my head after a long day of classes. Whatever strain the grower was producing, it was epic in its sugary scent, and the plants were practically opaque with resin-rich clusters. My sneakers stuck to the floor when I began threading through the pot plants toward the torn plastic I'd come in through. Working my body through the opening, I spotted a gate and sprinted through a barricade of cast-off household items blocking my path down the side yard. My fingers were on the latch when my luck ran out.

Lights flared on in the house and poured through the grime of closed louvers. To make matters worse, flares of red and blue lights were sparkling the sky, casting up an ominous fireworks show. The bottoms of my sneakers were now covered in enough resin to make a hashball, and I had a white poodle mix dangling from a baby carrier across my belly.

If I were still a cop, I'd haul me in just on principle.

Things got worse when a bullet went whizzing by my head and the wooden gate in front of me grew an extra peephole near my shoulder. Another few pops and bullets hit the supporting cinder block post, sending rocky shards into my face. Not being overly stupid, I didn't need to see who was shooting at me. Not when valuable seconds could be spent getting behind a thick cement wall that could take a blast from any street-legal weapon.

The latch was locked, but I was motivated. Wrenching it open, I tore it from its hinges. I slammed the gate open and rushed through, hoping the piles of discarded toilets, engine blocks, and furniture would keep my pursuer occupied for a few minutes. Or at least enough time for me to disappear down the street. Still, I wasn't all that convinced I was free and clear of getting shot that night.

Jae would have my damned dick for *chigae* if I got shot again. He'd all but threatened to skin me if I came home with more holes than I'd left with.

Pookie twisted halfway around in her harness when I broke through and her snapping tiny teeth were hell-bent on piercing my nostrils.

"Come, dog, I'm trying to rescue you here. Give me a fucking break." I took a few strides forward when a gruff voice screamed at me in a rough Spanish I couldn't understand. I didn't know him but judging by his pissed-off face, I guess he owned the lush greenery I'd trampled through. While my Spanish was failing me, I did however understand the semi-automatic he pointed at my face. With only a couple of feet separating us, chances were, even if he was the shittiest shot in the world, I was going to lose my face.

He came up to my upper arm and sported an impressive thatch poking out from under each armpit. The rest of him was shorn clean of hair, with only a whimper of a scrawny mustache over his pierced upper lip. Dressed in the odd combination of bright white socks, flip-flops and long cargo shorts barely hanging onto his skinny hips, his attire was made less laughable by the badly inked off-blue tattoos scrawled over his torso, neck and face.

He was a snarling bantam. The kind of man who really deserved to own Pookie since they seemed to share the same personality. If it wasn't for the fact that I was pretty sure he would use Ava's white poof of doom as a silencer for the enormous gun he held in his hand, I'd have handed the mutt over and wished him the best.

But he had other plans. Apparently he didn't need no stinking silencer, poodle or not.

"I'm a'gonna shoot you, mother...."

Guys always have to talk when they're trying to shoot you. There are some exceptions. My police partner, Ben, did no talking when he riddled me and my lover, Rick, with bullets from his service piece as we left a restaurant. I'm sure he did plenty of talking at some point. Just not to me. Since he ate his own gun shortly after killing Rick and damning me to a life of nerve-seizing scar tissue, I never did get the chance to ask him why. In the case of the shaven-head, hairy-pit rooster with a handgun masquerading as a cannon, I wasn't going to stick around to listen to his threats or reasons on why I should let him fill me full of holes.

Besides, there was that promise to Jae that I wouldn't get shot again, and I had a serious ass-kicking to give Bobby once I found him. It was one thing to jack a friend by leaving him in a club. It's quite another to ditch him while he was nipple deep in a pot farm after pulling a poodle out of death-row solitary.

Not getting shot seemed like my first priority. However, ass-kicking seemed like it would be more fun.

No one really expects another guy to kick them in the balls. It's a time-honored agreement between men. Thou shalt not emasculate the cock and scrotum. I, however, never claimed to be a gentleman, so my foot went up and scored a long goal shot down center field.

Then I did the sensible thing.

I ran. Unfortunately for me and Pookie, running seemed to come with a new complication—one of the biggest shepherds I'd ever seen outside of a horror flick.

Sadly, even though my Lilliputian terrorist was writhing on the floor cupping his own goods and I thought I was possibly home free, the large canine had other plans. It was huge, much larger than the ones I'd avoided in the alleyway. I could have stayed and admired it. Sleek and wolfish, the dog was a masterful specimen of whatever hellhound breed it belonged to. It also seemed more than willing to take up the task of riddling me full of holes, using his teeth instead of the mutant ninja pygmy's gun.

I ran harder.

By no means am I graceful. Not ballet graceful and certainly not the slinky, bend-in-half-backward graceful Jae seems to be able to pull off, but in situations like these, grace hardly mattered. Stamina. I had stamina. I could go rounds with Bobby in a boxing ring, mostly dodging his cement-like fists before they pounded into my body, but still, I had stamina. It was the name of the game, outlasting one's opponent.

Also speed. That's never something to laugh at. Speed was key. Whoever said knowledge is half the battle did not have a 'roided up wolf dog chewing on their ass. Knowledge gave me jack shit in this instance. Fucking jack shit.

My heart pounded, and for some reason, the scar tissue along my rib cage decided right then and there it needed to perform an origami maneuver to curl itself into a crane. Or maybe it was a bunny. Either way, it was starting to hurt, and Pookie chose that moment to begin twisting around to break free of the harness.

Sharp teeth on the back of my thigh tore straight through my jeans, giving me further incentive to quicken my pace. My back pocket went next, along with a piece of skin. The ripping pain under the rise of my ass ached more than my side, and I kicked out, breaking my stride long enough to fight the dog off. I heard a yelp and kept running, praying my knees would hold out despite the angry, stabbing pangs kicking up my thighs.

Mister Bald Rooster must have recovered somewhat, because a trash can next to me sparked and shot backward, a smoking black hole through its battered metal walls. Another blast took out a piece of wooden fence, and I ducked, only catching a few of the wooden shards across my neck and face. Pookie screamed her defiance at the dog chasing me, speaking in an ancient Poodle tongue that I'd have liked to imagine insulted its mother and possibly cursed its shriveled dick. Then she bit my chest, scoring a hit through my T-shirt, and I knew she was only egging the dog on to take me down.

A few feet in front of me lay a desert of tarmac, and a tremor of fear tickled my balls. The tight alley broke apart into a double lane of black asphalt, and I'd be out in the open where the dog could maneuver around and circle me. My only hope was to hug the fences along the sidewalk and pray to get hit by a bus or possibly by a falling satellite. I'd take either one since it would mean I'd be taking Pookie with me.

I was a little bitter about the blood trickling down my belly.

My daring escape came to a screeching halt when the street I'd turned down lit up in a dance of red and blue. Slamming to a stop, my hands caught air just as the dog behind me caught up with me. Its teeth found their mark again, digging into my thigh, and I howled, drowning out the cop ordering me to my knees. I recognized Bobby and his truck silhouetted against the patrol cars' headlights, and from the way his hands were pulled behind his back, he seemed to have a halfway decent enough excuse for not being where I left him.

Rough hands grabbed my shoulders and forced me down, jostling Pookie. She snapped at a cop's hands, raking her teeth over his fingers. Screaming obscenities at my head, the cop backhanded me like I'd been the one to bite him, and I sensibly fell over. The asphalt grabbed my naked thigh and hip, scraping me raw.

As if auditioning for a talent show, Pookie popped out of the harness like a greased pig, shooting out and landing a few feet away.

Barking happily, she squatted in the middle of the road and peed, wagging her tail at the dog who'd been chasing me down the alleyway.

The same dog I'd kicked straight in the head apparently seemed to be wearing an LAPD K-9 unit jacket.

It was still huge, more fur, teeth and muscle than should be allowed on a dog, and he trotted over to sit attentively at another cop's side, no sign of his previous aggression apparent in his relaxed wiggling as the cop petted him. Within seconds, my arms were twisted behind my back and cuffs were snapped over my wrists before I could protest. A gust of cool wind blasted up the crack of my ass, and I could have sworn the dog's muzzle curled into a wicked grin as he dropped what looked like pieces of my underwear right at Pookie's fluffy white feet.

The bitten cop leaned over and spoke, his words a malevolent curdle of a whisper filled with an awe-inspiring disgust I would have admired if I hadn't been the one on my knees. "What kind of sick fuck steals a little dog?"

CHAPTER TWO

SOME men are sexier when they're angry. Apparently, my lover, Jae, was one of those men. My calling him down to a police station at four in the morning to bail out his boyfriend and said boyfriend's best friend should have been considered a favor to all of the women and gay men who were in the station that night.

I know I certainly enjoyed the sight of him stalking back and forth as I was being led into the holding bay. I wasn't going to like what he had to say to me, but still, I'd have to be a dead man not to enjoy the view.

His black hair was rumpled, sticking up slightly in front, and his sleepy, hooded brown gaze flirted between sensual fire and feral iciness. His toes were bare, sticking out of a pair of black flip-flops, and the white T-shirt he wore looked like one of mine, a bit too large for his slender frame. A pair of ratty jeans, barely held together by a whisper and a few threads, were stretched tight across his ass when he shoved his hands into his front pockets. I should have gotten a Get Out of Jail Free card just for getting that ass into the station. His face, like his ass, was a thing of beauty, a plump, succulent mouth set beneath high cheekbones and long-lashed almond eyes. The sight of his canines chewing on his lower lip evoked a lot of memories of that mouth and those teeth gnawing on sensitive stretches of my body.

More than one pair of eyes followed his progress back and forth in the waiting area, and I caught a very macho-looking cop dropping his gaze to the tight plumpness of Jae's rear. The cop bristled when I grinned at him, and a red flush crept up from his cheeks and over his ears. Jae saw my smirk, and his mouth thinned into a disapproving line.

No, my hot, sexy boyfriend was not amused. Not in the slightest.

A wall of bars separated us from the waiting area, and there was only one other man in line with us. The guy's suit was wrinkled and he smelled like burnt vodka. A thick brush of gray whiskers covered his movie-star chiseled chin and cheekbones. He looked like someone I should know, but I couldn't place his face. Blustering, he shoved past us and stomped over to the outtake clerk. Whoever he was, he was one of three reasons the outtake window was open.

Bobby and I were the other two. Sometimes, it's good to be an ex-cop. Even if most of the boys in blue weren't too happy about us waving the rainbow flag, we were still their brothers. Okay, Bobby was still their brother. I was that second cousin once removed everyone had to invite to the wedding or else there'd be talk.

The outtake window was manned by a foul-tempered bear of a civil servant who seemed to take great delight in very slowly handing over the man's personal effects. I didn't have high hopes he would be any happier to see us when we finally got to the window. It was too early in the morning for him to be there, and by the sounds of his terse, biting questions to the man in the suit, we were all lucky he hadn't come to work with a bottle of water for each of us and a hyped-up Taser.

"Hey, your boy's here." Like me, Bobby'd retired from the force. Unlike me, he'd not done it openly gay and in a hail of bullets but served out his time before coming out of the closet. It'd shocked me to find out he played on my team. Muscular and rugged, he'd seemed like the proto-cop when he'd worn the badge. With it off, he was making up for lost time, cutting a swath through the hordes of twinks who liked an older man with a bit of silver at his temples and enough bulk to arm curl a couple of industrial microwaves.

He'd also been my sanity while I recovered from my partner's shooting and now seemed to be cruising my boyfriend.

"Stop checking out Jae's ass." I didn't fear Bobby poaching Jae. They had a decent enough relationship, prickly at times but mostly solid. Still, I had to give at least a token protest of Bobby's lechery.

"You sure you're ready to get out of here?" Bobby nudged me with his shoulder, inching me forward. "Could have made some new friends in there."

We'd been given a separate cell, farther away from the general riffraff, but there were still grumbles when we'd been led down the row toward our freedom. A skinny crackhead dressed in a purple spangled dress seemed mighty interested in seeing if he could suck my jeans off of me, but since the police dog already took care of that, I graciously declined.

"You'll be lucky if you get to keep the one friend you have now, asshole," I grumbled. Shuffling forward, I approached the window when a rookie buzzed the other guy out.

"Which one are you?" the guy behind the window growled at me. "McGinnis or Dawson?"

"McGinnis." I took the manila envelope he handed me, opened it, and signed off on the line assuring the LAPD I was getting back everything I'd had in my possession when the cops brought me in.

The bag held everything I'd come with except for the dog. She'd been sprung nearly as soon as we crossed the threshold of the police station. All I had left of her was Ava's smile, gashes on my hands, and the baby carrier I'd borrowed from Claudia's daughter-in-law. If I'd had a lint brush on me, I could have gathered up all the fur Pookie left behind and made another dog. Luckily, the carrier was machine washable.

Passing through the gated door, I was glad to reenter the real world, and suddenly the fatigue hit me. My legs were rubbery, overextended from the long sprint down the alleyway, and then the punctures in my skin began to ache. I wanted to get home, crawl into bed, and pull Jae on top of me, preferably to be woken up sometime in the afternoon by the promise of a cold beer and a hot pizza.

Or maybe a cold beer and hot sex.

It would all depend on what Jae's schedule looked like. From the look on his face, I'd be lucky if he still gave me a ride home.

"Are you okay?" Jae looked like he was hovering between punching me for getting hauled into the station and giving me a kiss, something he'd never have done in public a few months ago. Either would cause a scene, and Kim Jae-Min wasn't one for scenes. He also had a wicked right hook, and I was pretty certain that would have won out if we'd been alone.

"Yeah, I'm okay." I touched his arm lightly, twisting to show him the gauze and tape covering my thigh. "I got all my shots and everything."

My jeans were a loss, and I'd tossed out my underwear. There was nothing much left of them after the K-9 cop got through with them, and they'd begun to bunch up against my balls. I asked the dog's handler if he wanted them as a trophy, and he'd laughed, saying I wasn't the first one Draven had given a reverse wedgie. I had to wear my torn jeans out, hoping the bandages gave me enough cover to hide anything I'd get arrested for.

The bantam gangster hadn't been so lucky. One of Draven's coworkers had taken him down in the alleyway, ripping him down to the bone. Considering he'd tried to empty his gun into my head, I wasn't going to send him a get-well card.

"I'm glad you're fine." Jae leaned in so he could whisper into my ear. "Because I'm going to fucking kill you when we get home. What the hell were you two thinking?"

"I know... this wasn't the smartest thing...." I stole a look at Bobby, who was still in the outtake cell. "We didn't think it would get so... big."

"Cole, how many police stations do you have to get dragged to?" Sarcasm cuts deep when sharpened with disgust, and in the hour between me calling Jae and being released, he'd taken his to a whetstone of mammoth proportions. "Is it like some quest the two of you have? Do they give those... what are those called... badges? They give those out for this?"

"Jae, we didn't mean for this to happen." We were getting sidelong glances from the clusters of cops around us. "Swear to God, it was supposed to be a simple go in and grab the dog."

"Yeah, I know." He rattled the keys in his palm and nodded toward my back. The clang of the barred door was ominous, a rattling metal screech announcing Dawson's release. His heavy tread squeaked across the linoleum floor toward us, and Jae shot him a watery grin over my shoulder. "Bobby's done. Let's go home."

It was still pitch black outside, but the liquid stink of a Los Angeles morning was already rising up from the streets. A rotary cleaner chugged past us, spurting out lukewarm suds to wash oil and soot from the road. The foam slunk down to the curbside, a frothy curl of dirt and black specks. Jae chirped open my Rover and dangled the keys over my hand, letting them drop into my palm when I opened my fingers for them.

"Hey, I want to see if I can get my truck back. That's the detective there. Give me a few minutes to schmooze him." Bobby looped an arm over Jae's shoulders and gave him a quick half hug. "Thanks for coming to get us, man. I appreciate it."

I answered for us both. "Sure, no problem. We'll be by the car."

I was already talking to Bobby's back, a broad wall of muscle built up from years of kicking bad guys' asses and knocking lesser mortals about in a boxing ring. Jae walked over to my Rover. His long legs ate up the distance to the car with a few strides, and I hurried to catch up with him, wincing when my leg protested at the rapid movement. The tape tugged on what little leg hair I had, and the gauze stuck to my wound ripped off of my skin, starting a slow, seeping leak into my bandage.

"Hey." I caught up with him at the Rover's passenger side and placed my arms on either side of his waist, trapping him against the car. "I'm *sorry*. I am. It really wasn't supposed to go down like this. How were we supposed to know we were walking into a drug sting tonight? It just got… out of control, okay?"

He tilted his head back and exhaled, pursing his lips to kiss the air above him. He scrubbed at his face with his hands, and when he lowered his chin to look at me, there was a shimmer of wet in his eyes. He wouldn't cry. Not here. Not out in the open. But it was there, lingering on the razor edge of his control. There was a break in his voice when he spoke, a painful crack of emotion in his sultry rasp.

"I get scared when the phone rings and the ID says it's a police station." His voice was breaking, and my heart shattered under the grief and fear in his words. "There's been too many times… too much blood for me not to think something bad has happened. So can you please… not do this again? *Please?*"

I shouldn't have taken him in my arms, not with his aversion to showing affection and his fear of being outed as a gay man, but in the middle of the parking lot, listening to Bobby try to charm his truck out of impound, it seemed like the right thing to do. Typically, he fought me, a minor struggle to break free and somehow hide from my affection, but I refused to let him go.

It was selfish of me. I knew it. Our sensibilities warred with one another. His instincts fought me, driven by an ingrained fear of his family's shunning. I'd already been ostracized, thrown aside by my father and the only woman I'd ever called mom. I wanted to pull him over to my way of thinking, nearly begging him to turn his back on the single most important thing that defined a Korean man—his family.

Whereas I'd just found out my mother… the woman who supposedly died giving birth to me… actually went back to Japan to have another family before dying five years ago. My brother Mike and I had differing opinions on that matter. He was willing to forgive and reach out to the man who called himself our half brother. I was pretty much pissed off at everyone except for my sister-in-law, but then Maddy endorsed my father being drawn and quartered for lying to us all these years.

So I wasn't exactly thrilled by the whole concept of family at the moment.

I wanted Jae to be my family. I wanted both of us to go home, close the door, and lock everyone else and everything outside. Maybe just open it up for takeaway delivery and possibly to throw out the trash. I'd yet to master tossing a full bag into the dumpster behind my carport. Close, but I couldn't get enough swing to clear the arc, and the weight varied too much.

That particular nirvana was never going to happen. Jae needed to roam, stretching himself out in dark places to capture them on film, and it would be impossible to keep him contained. He also knew, once he came out of the closet, he would have no one left… no one but me, and he wasn't quite ready to trust that I'd be with him to the end of time. So

I held him, smelling the sweetness of his hair and the citrus soap he used on his skin, then resigned myself to having to let him go.

"*I am sorry.*" Repeating it seemed to help. Ghosting a kiss over his mouth, I caught the sigh he exhaled, taking his hot anger inside of me with a press of my lips. "I really am."

"I know," he murmured back. Laying his forehead against my chest, Jae exhaled again. This time his shoulders relaxed, and the tension slid from his spine. "You just don't know… how fucking scary it is to think something's happened to you. Even if it's just for that one second. It *hurts* so much, Cole-ah. I can't… take it. I don't want to take it. It's too much to ask."

Leaning back slightly, I cupped his face with my hands and pressed a light kiss onto the end of his nose. "I promise I am not trying to get killed. Okay?"

"Hey, you two quit sucking face so I can get a ride home." Bobby's shout pulled Jae back, and he stumbled, pushing at my hands when I tried to catch him. Trotting up to the Rover, Bobby growled a few curse words at the detective walking up the steps to the station. "Asshole won't let my truck go. Says it's evidence."

"Kind of is." My shrugging at him didn't help his temper, and Bobby's nostrils flared at me. "They tossed bricks of hash into the back of your truck, and then you took off."

"Shit, I thought it was you jumping in," he groused. "How the fuck was I supposed to know it wasn't?"

"You could have looked?" Jae snorted, opening the car door. "Get in. The sooner we get you home, the sooner I can go back to bed. And, Cole-ah, Mike's starting to call me now. I am staying out of it, so when you wake up, call your brother. Or I'll tie you to the bed while you're asleep and tell him to come over so he can beat some sense into you."

IN THE end, I didn't call Mike. I'd meant to. It was on my mental list of things to do first thing in the morning. However, by the time I woke up it was about noon and I was late in opening up the office. Jae was already gone, and Neko, his wicked black cat, already laid claim to his empty pillow. From the fishy stench of her breath when she meeped at me to wake up, I guessed Jae fed her before he headed out for his morning assignment.

It'd been only a few weeks since Claudia, my office manager, was laid up by a gunshot meant for me. The doctors were giving her a two-month recovery time. Her family gave it five more days before she showed up at the office with a pillbox hat and a stir-crazy look in her eye.

I was under strict orders to turn her back around and send her home. All bets were off if she showed up with pie. Claudia's homemade pies were delicious enough to outweigh any potential damage her sons might do to me if I didn't call them immediately.

Since I wasn't planning on doing anything more strenuous than sitting on a pillow to ease the ache in my thigh, I found the most comfortable pair of jeans I owned. The bite seemed healed over enough to leave off a wrapping of gauze, especially since I didn't trust myself not to tape up my leg. The canine left only light punctures, but they hurt enough to sting when the shower spray hit them. Promising myself coffee when I got the office opened up, I grabbed a couple of Jae's Choco Pies and headed to the front of the building.

Judging by the frowning, tiny older Korean woman standing on the porch of my investigation office, paperwork was going to have to wait a little while.

I'd been around Jae long enough to recognize the type of woman he called an *ajumma*. I'd originally thought it was a term of respect, like calling Scarlet *nuna*. I learned that lesson quickly when I used the *A* word in her presence, and the look I got in return would have fried me like a piece of bacon if Jae hadn't laughed it off and pushed me out the door. I was then schooled on the proper use of the word, preferably when the woman in question couldn't hear it being said.

One did not call a sleek, elegant transvestite like Scarlet an *ajumma*. No, that word was reserved for the squat cherub of a woman peering imperiously down at me from the top step of the porch. A pair of black rhinestone-studded glasses were perched low on her nose, secured from falling to the ground by a silvery crystal leash looped around her neck. More than a few strands at her temples were bright silver, but the majority of her curled helmet of hair was inky black, the same color as her heavily made up eyes.

Even through her thick glasses, I could see a hefty dose of crazy lurking in those eyes, but I opened the door for her anyway. I'd been accused more than once of having more than my own share of crazy. She might have been a bit close to the off-kilter side of mental, but by all appearances, she seemed to be holding her own.

Polyester seemed to be her preferred fabric. Her bright pink pants were a few inches shorter than they needed to be, and her floral chiffon blouse was tight across her midsection, flattening her breasts until they were almost square in shape on her torso. From the wrinkles near her eyes and the grooves along her mouth, I'd have put her age at late sixties. Judging mostly by the sucking hiss of disappointment she gave me when I approached, she could have been Methuselah, and I was the reincarnation of her worthless grandson who'd forgotten to get the dinosaurs and unicorns on the fucking ark.

"Are you the detective?" Her words were rounded with a soft Korean accent, much like Jae had when he was sleepy or angry. Another telling sniff and she glanced at the thick gold watch on her wrist. "It is bad for business to open so late."

"Sorry, ma'am, I had a late case last night." It's funny how an angry elderly woman immediately upped my manners to high alert. "Let me get you inside and make some tea."

I didn't like tea. The only reason there was tea in the office was because Jae and Scarlet drank it when they came to visit. Other than that, it was a coffee kind of place, furnished in massive vintage desks and comfortable chairs. I'd stripped down the years of paint from the wood half-wall paneling when I'd bought the building and stained it a dark cherry, varnishing it until Claudia could put her lipstick on in its shine. It was a vast open space with a separate conference room. I liked it a lot. Claudia said it reminded her of a men's club. Scarlet, who actually sang at a gentlemen's club, agreed with her. Since I was the one paying the bills, I wasn't going to change one damned thing about it.

"Coffee would be better," she muttered at me, her eyes skittering around as she took the office in. "This is suitable. It looks more like a detective than you do."

Counting to ten worked. So did using instant Vietnamese 3-in-1 and the hot water from the spigot on the coffeemaker. I made myself a double batch, filling up my mug, and carefully walked a smaller mug over to the couch where she'd taken roost. I placed the steaming mug on the table in front of her and sat down in the leather wingchair opposite the couch.

Sipping my coffee, I let the caffeine hit my system before I felt ready enough to take her on. She had no such reservations. After tanking down a mouthful of the scalding liquid as if it were tap water, she set the mug down with a fierce thump and looked me square in the eye.

"My name is Madame Sun." She drew out the *U* until it was almost a ghostly sound. "You should know that you are in the presence of the best fortune-teller in Los Angeles, possibly even Korea, now that my *sunbae* has retired."

I ranked fortune-tellers up there with people who came to my door insisting on dumping a pile of dirt on my carpet to show me the vacuum they're selling will pick it up. I couldn't have faked being impressed if she'd dropped her pants and unfurled a foot-long dick that danced and sang "Hello, My Baby."

I went with a murmuring sound of mild awe. "What can I help you with, ma'am?"

"Someone is killing my clients. Three have died so far, and from what I have seen, more will die." The *ajumma* stabbed at my arm with a bony finger, demanding my attention. "And I want to hire you to stop them."

CHAPTER THREE

THERE are an infinite number of things I know nothing about. From the existence of God to why they can't figure out a better wrapper for American cheese so I can get it all out without leaving that small strip behind. The world is a mysterious and awesome place. With this philosophy, it makes it pretty easy to be a private investigator. Usually, I push the *I believe* button when someone asks me to prove their beloved husband or wife is faithful to them, but it worked just as well for clairvoyants. At the very least, I could show her no one was dying because of her.

I made Madame Park Hyuna Sun another cup of instant Vietnamese coffee and encouraged her to continue.

"It all started with May Choi. She is… was… one of my regulars. Young woman. Very pretty and married to a good man." Madame Sun's rings flashed as she wove her hand about to tell her story. "I'd just had a consultation with May. It was good news, but there was a blackness around her. I didn't say anything at the time, but after she left, I was filled with a cold feeling. The next day, I saw on the news she'd been killed by a man who wanted her car."

"That's unfortunate, ma'am," I said as gently as I could. "But that's not your fault."

"I could have warned her." Madame Sun slammed her open hand on the coffee table, rattling our cups. "I felt something lingering over her. I should have known. She left my salon at noon and died twenty minutes later. What kind of man would kill a woman in the daylight for her car? The policeman I spoke to on the phone told me I was crazy."

There was not a whisper from me that *crazy* had been my first reaction. My second too. Instead, I jotted down a note in my steno pad to follow up on the Choi investigation. "It sounds like an accident, Madame Sun. I'll be glad to ask the police about what they're doing, but I don't know how—"

"There have been two others." She leaned forward and pinned me in place with a hard look over her glasses. "Both dying after leaving my salon. May's death might have been unfortunate, but the others right after her? *That* is something dark moving against me."

I got details out of her concerning the other two deaths. Unlike May Choi, who'd come from Seoul a year ago, the others were Koreans who'd lived in America for many years. The second of Madame Sun's clients to die was Eun Joon Lee, a housewife killed during an afternoon home invasion. Following her a few days later, Bhak Bong Chol, an elderly businessman, died of an apparent heart attack in his own office. Madame Sun gave me as many details as she could, including their addresses and how long they'd been her clients.

"Have you heard anything—from anyone—that might lead you to believe any of your other clients are in danger?" I didn't want to open that Pandora's box, but on the far off chance that she actually had concrete evidence of something going on, I had to ask.

"No, no, you cannot say anything. I don't want to alarm anyone." She shook her head, and not a single strand of her hair moved, although the beads on her glasses' leash jingled pleasantly. "But yes, I have *felt* that more death is coming. It is all connected to me. I know it inside of me. Please, Mr. McGinnis, these people do not deserve to die because they come to me for advice."

"No one deserves to die like that, Madame Sun," I assured her. "And no, I won't speak to any of your current clients. I just want to know if you've had anything concrete I could chase down."

"My premonitions *are* concrete, but I understand what you think. You are not the first one I've met who does not believe. I don't need you to believe, Mr. McGinnis. I just need… to make sure that the people I advise are safe. Will you need money to begin?" She reached into her bright pink alligator purse, and I stopped her with a shake of my head.

"No. Let's see if I have something to investigate first. If I have something to chase after, I'll call you and tell you what it'll cost."

I had no intention of charging her. It didn't sound like a conspiracy or curse, just unfortunate circumstances arriving too close together for comfort. The case was going to be as profitable as Ava's case but without the chocolate bar. It wouldn't cost me anything to ring up a few cops and shake out some information, and at the end of the time I spent, Madame Sun would at least feel better. Time was a small price to pay for an older woman's peace of mind, and time was something I had a lot of.

"Vivian—she helps me—call her if you need more information." She stood up, creakily rubbing at her knee when she stepped out from around the table. "Her number is written there, *ne*? My son, James, is outside. I do not want to make him wait too long."

"I'll call you after I speak to the police and they have something I can share." I saw her to the door, holding the screened panel open for her to pass through. She gave me a mumbled thank you, and I nodded at the middle-aged man waiting by the sedan parked at the curb.

Cops don't like it when private investigators call them up and question them about their cases. Actually, no cop really likes having someone else's nose peeking over their shoulder, but a follow-up wouldn't be too out of the ordinary if I couched it as trying to calm a concerned elderly woman.

It took me about half an hour and more than a few transfers before I found myself speaking to Dexter Wong, a detective I'd become friends with. Wong'd handled the cleanup following my last case and caught the Choi investigation. When he answered the phone, he sounded slightly bemused to hear from me.

"A fortune-teller, huh?" I heard Wong tapping something against his desk. "My mother goes to one. She swears the old man helps her. I figure, if my mom wants to consult the I Ching, that's her business. I wear my lucky socks when I play ball. Like I can throw stones? What can I help you with?"

I gave him what details I had, and Wong hummed over the line at me. "I'm not looking for much. Even if you guys don't have any leads, I can tell her I spoke to you. She seemed nice enough, worried about her people. I thought I'd chat you up and maybe ease some of the pressure she's feeling."

"No, no... totally get that. I'll tell you, but the details stay between us, McGinnis." He continued after I murmured an agreement, "It's down as a carjacking, but really, it's a straight-up homicide. She was shot through the open window of her Beemer while at a light. Her purse was grabbed but dumped a few feet away. Guy left the car. Shooter did it in broad daylight. Witnesses say he was average height, wearing a black tank top and jeans. Ski mask so no one saw his face, but skin tone was tanned. Could be Asian or Hispanic descent. Happened off of Vermont, right at the edge of K-Town, so no one's talking and no one's pointing fingers. You know how that is."

"Yeah, I worked areas like that in patrol. Seems kind of over the top just to grab a purse. How old was the Beemer?"

"New. It still had dealer plates on it. She was known for carrying large amounts of cash but not enough to get two bullets in her face." Wong tsked. "I got a picture here. She was really pretty. Her husband's tight-lipped, but he seemed upset by it when we talked to him. Still, he hasn't called me up to ask how the case is going."

"Could be he knows you don't have a lot to go on." I chewed on the end of my pen, then pulled it out of my mouth as if Claudia was next to me admonishing me not to get ink on my lip. The office was too quiet without her, and I was beginning to slip into the bad habit of opening up late.

"Maybe. But if I had a young, pretty wife shot to death, I'd be riding the cops' asses until they gave me the name of the guy I could beat the shit out of for it."

"What do you think? Was their marriage good?" I poked a hole at the husband's grief. It was easier without him standing in front of me, a faceless man who possibly ordered his wife's death.

"Seems like it," Wong surmised. "Once again, hard to tell. Both came from Seoul. He's older than she is by about eleven years, and she was young—barely twenty. He works the American end of his family's import business. Choi's lived here for about three years but went back over to Korea to get married."

"Choi? She took his name?" I frowned when Wong confirmed it. "That's odd. Thought most Korean women kept their names."

"Could be because she's living over here? Acclimating and all that," he replied. "Her maiden name was Gangjun. That's about it. If I get a break in this, I'll let you know, but nothing much else to tell you."

"Got anything on the other one? Eun Joon Lee?" I flipped through my notes. "The third name I got is Bhak, but he was a heart attack."

"Someone else caught Eun Joon Lee." Wong's keyboard sounded like it was getting a workout. "There's not much there either. Home invasion a few blocks away from Choi's carjacking. They got some small electronics but no cash, and they left the jewelry. Husband thinks she walked in on them. We don't have ballistics yet, but it looks like the same caliber as Choi's. A nine millimeter, but that's common."

"Think anyone would look at you funny if you asked for a cross-reference between Choi and Lee?" It was a long shot. There were a lot of 9 mm handguns out on the streets of Los Angeles, and the odds of them being the same weapon were very slim.

"Wouldn't hurt to ask. The lab usually looks out for that kind of thing for us, but it's hit and miss. They're overloaded." Wong cleared his throat. "Look, I've got to bail. If you hear anything on your end, give me a call. If these two are connected, then we'll have something to go on. I'll look at the Madame Sun angle from my end, okay?"

"Thanks. I owe you a dinner."

"Can I bring my girlfriend?" Wong teased. "You know, so you don't get any ideas that it's a date."

"Sure, so long as I can bring Jae. You know, so you don't get any ideas that you actually have a chance with me," I countered.

"Great, now I'm going to really be the ugliest one at the table."

"I'll pick up the tab and buy you a beer." I hung up after we made tentative plans for Korean barbeque. I sent Jae a text asking him about what days he was free, promising him he could pick the restaurant, so long as it was Korean.

Oddly enough, I wasn't quite ready to put a pin in Madame Sun's paranoid butterfly. The three deaths occurred in quick succession, spaced out over a few days, and from what I could see on an area map, very close together. It was odd for the jacker to leave a new BMW behind, and I wondered if he'd not planned on killing Choi. Wong's eyewitness reports were pretty clear. The shooter walked up and shot Choi nearly point blank, then booked it through K-Town's jungle of buildings.

"He knew she'd be there," I mused, wheeling over to the coffee machine. "Someone knew her schedule. It feels more like a hit than something random."

Not wanting to make a whole pot, I doctored up another cup of instant Vietnamese, then scooted across the floor to my desk. I was only able to wheel around the office when Claudia wasn't there. I'd have to break the habit before she came back or I'd feel the flat side of her hand on the back of my head when I rolled past.

"Okay, so we've got a carjacking that leaves the car and takes only a purse." The back of my leg began to itch, and I lifted my leg to lightly scratch at the denim over the bandaged area. "And a home invasion that leaves behind a shitload of jewelry but takes what's out in the front rooms. Something stinks here, McGinnis."

It got even stinkier when I heard my older brother Mike yelling my name as he came up the walk toward the office door. The porch rattled a bit from his stomping feet, and the screen door screeched in protest when he yanked it open. As usual, his hair was a prickly cactus of black spikes, and the glower on his face was an impressive display of curved lines and gritted teeth. Much like my feelings on Madame Sun predicting the future and telling fortunes, I wasn't that impressed by my older brother's displeasure.

Only a few years separated us. Well, a few years and quite a few inches. Mike took after our mother, a small Japanese woman named Ryoko our father met while stationed overseas. Stocky and broad shouldered, Mike fended off any short jokes growing up with hard fists and an even harder head. I simply grew taller, had longer legs, and could outrun him until he gave up. I might have been the only one of us to get my dad's brown hair and green eyes, but we'd both inherited his hot temper.

Since I wasn't going to be running any time soon with the punctures in my thigh, Mike was going to have a distinct advantage, even if I wanted to walk away from his shit. I took the easy way out and stood up, using my height to intimidate my ruffled brother. Picking up Madame Sun's coffee cup, I turned my back on him, then hobbled over to the sink to wash up.

He followed, an infuriated duckling trailing behind me.

"Why didn't you call me?" Mike came up about a head short of being able to stare me down, but his nostrils flared with the intensity of rabid sunspots. "I *told* Jae—"

"Let's agree on something, brother. You don't *tell* Jae anything." I shook off the excess water from my hands and wiped them on my jeans. I'd forgotten about the dog bite on the back of my thigh, and the press of my fingers on the thin bandage nearly made me yelp. "He was nice enough to pass along the message, but he's not one of your peons. Neither am I. I'll call you when I call you."

"I wouldn't have to contact Jae if you'd returned any of my calls." Mike circled around me and helped himself to a tea bag and a cup. He filled the cup with hot water and turned around to find me already at my desk. "We need to talk."

"We don't need to talk." Finally turning on my computer, I waited a few seconds for it to boot up so I could begin a case file for Madame Sun. Sure, she was a free ride, but that didn't mean her case deserved any less attention. Also, Claudia would ship me to Siberia if she came back and the files weren't in order.

After setting his mug down on Claudia's computer table—well out of my reach—Mike hitched himself up onto the edge of my desk and poked me in the shoulder. I flinched, the residual pain from a gunshot wound pulsing along the point of his finger, and he had the good grace to look slightly apologetic.

"I talked to Ichiro again this morning. He wants to know how you're doing." Mike offered up a shrug. "I didn't know what to tell him."

"Dude, we've gone over this." I wasn't in the mood to go a round with Mike. My night'd run long, and my sleep was too often disturbed by the aching skin on my thigh. "Why do you have to tell him anything?"

"Because he asked about you. He's our brother, remember?"

Ichiro. Our half brother. The one our mother raised in Japan after she supposedly died while giving birth to me.

Jesus had *nothing* on Ryoko McGinnis Tokugawa.

Mike'd been trying to shoehorn me into a relationship with Ichiro ever since we'd found out he existed. I wasn't interested. Not now. Maybe not ever. I needed time to wrap my head around being tossed out by not just one mother but two. It hurt too much to think about, so I did what I usually did when I didn't want to get hurt.

I avoided thinking about it.

"I'm working a case here, Mike. Do I bunny rage into your office whenever I feel like it?"

"Bunny rage?"

"Never piss off a jackrabbit," I said, turning back to the mess of papers I'd left on my desk. "They'll cut you."

"Cole, Ichiro—"

"Mike, do you know what Ichiro means?" I turned in my chair and glared at him. "You follow enough baseball to know. It means *first son*. That's what he was to her. She *left* us, Mike. She fucking left us with our asshole father and walked away."

"We don't know what happened between them." It was a weak protest but the best one Mike had. Neither one of us knew what went on between our parents. Ichiro might, but he wasn't on my buddy list at the moment.

"*We* happened between them." I shoved the chair back, its wheels squealing across the floor. "Her *sons*. And now you want me to go sit around a fire and make s'mores with the kid she had after us? The kid she raised but couldn't be bothered to drop us a fucking letter about?"

"That wasn't his fault." Mike's chin came up, thrusting forward to challenge me. "He's our *brother*, Cole."

"Don't want the one you got? I'm not good enough? Too gay? Too fucked-up?" I shot back. "So you're going to go with the new one? What? He's straight? Got kids? Has his shit together? Maybe he plays golf and can hook you up with some connections in Tokyo."

I'd gone too far. Even as the words left my fucking mouth, I knew I'd gone too far. Mike reeled back a step, as if I'd punched him in the stomach, and all of the emotion drained from his face.

"Fuck you, Cole," he said, not without some heat. His words were a calm, thin line, drawing something firm between us. "I didn't deserve that."

"No, you... fuck. Mike...." I reached for my brother and winced when he pulled away. "Dude, I'm sorry. Fuck, I just... this is too fucking much for me to deal with. You *knew* her. All I got were a couple of fucking pictures and a middle name I couldn't pronounce. What the hell am I supposed to do with a guy who had her around? Especially after—"

"Barbara? Our stepmother?" Mike crossed the distance between us and placed his hands on my shoulders. Pushing me back down into my chair, he leaned over to look me in the eyes. "Baby brother, I know what she did was shitty and Dad fucked you up something bad, but none of that's Ichiro's fault. He didn't know we thought Mom was dead."

"I have a hard time believing that, man."

"Cole, it's true. He's as pissed off about this as we are. He wanted to reach out to the brothers no one would talk about. You're the one who's always on my case to be more tolerant. Why can't you find some of that shit for him?"

"Maybe." I ground my teeth. "I'm just not fucking ready for this. For him. I need some time, Mike. Just some fucking time."

"Time I can give." Mike slapped me lightly on the face, stinging my cheek. "Just stop being a damned asshole about it."

CHAPTER FOUR

I GOT nowhere closer on the Madame Sun case, having only the shreds of information I'd gleaned through what I could find on the computer. Until Wong could e-mail me a few reports on the sly, I wasn't going to find a connection between May Choi and Eun Joon Lee on the Internet. Setting aside my notes, I stared at Claudia's empty chair and chewed on my lip.

She'd insisted I hire someone to cover the phones for the few more weeks she'd be out, but seeing someone else in her chair would feel like a betrayal of some sort. But, I needed someone in that chair if I was going to hit the streets or needed to go on a run.

But I wanted that person to be Claudia. I *needed* that person to be Claudia.

Lacking that, I reached for the phone and dialed up the next best thing, her oldest son, Martin.

"Hey, man," Martin's voice rumbled, lightening slightly when he realized it was me. "Mama's asleep. I got her to take one of those pain meds."

"Actually, I called to talk to you. I need some help." I outlined what I needed, and he listened, murmuring every once in a while. "I'm hoping someone in your family might want to answer phones for me. Maybe even a couple of the kids? Even if just in the afternoon."

Halfway through the conversation, I realized Martin might have reservations on sending another of his family to the exact same spot his mother'd been shot. Something with sharp teeth began to gnaw on the inside of my stomach. I'd be lucky if *Claudia* wanted to return.

"It'll just have to be until Mama feels better." Martin interrupted my panic attack. "She's going to come back to work. You can lay money on that."

"I'd understand if she—" I couldn't get the words out. The bossy woman who'd moved into my life was too big a presence for me to let go. I'd bribe her with more money and a hot limousine driver if I had to, to get her back, but I couldn't be certain she'd be safe. Swallowing my reluctance, I said as much to Martin.

Martin was definitely his mother's son. "Bullshit, Cole. No one's ever safe. You did your damned best for Mama, and she's coming back. She'd kick my ass out of the way if I ever even tried to stop her. If any of the kids want to work for you, we're okay with it. You hear me?"

"Got it," I murmured, rubbing at my face. "Just until she comes back, then?"

"Just until she can come back," he reassured me. "Let me see what everyone's schedule is. I'll get back to you later, okay?"

I hung up and leaned back in my chair. It squeaked once, then again when I rocked back and forth. It took me about five seconds before I was stir-crazy. My phone still didn't have any messages from Jae, but that wasn't unusual. If I wanted some attention, I was going to have to beard the lion in his den.

"'Course, I probably want to do things to my lion that never crossed David's mind," I mumbled to myself. It was too early to drop in on Jae. He'd growl and shove me back out the door if I crawled into his space this early in the afternoon. Armed with addresses of the crime scenes, I made the decision to sniff around the areas in case someone felt like talking. Even after a couple of weeks, something like a shooting was juicy gossip for a neighborhood.

I closed up the office, made a quick stop into the house, where Neko was appropriately worshiped, then left with a helping of tuna and egg. The arrival of cat food rendered me useless in her eyes, and she ate noisily, growling over her food.

"You're welcome," I said to the cat.

She did not deign to give me a reply I could understand, but it was pretty clear from the abrasive snarl she gave me, a coarse *fuck off* was somewhere in there. I locked the door behind me, leaving her eyebrow deep in the stench.

THE City of Angels operated mostly on a grid pattern, with a few winding streets tossed in to fuck up a tourist trying to get from Hollywood to downtown. Adding to the confusion are three of the worst intersected freeways known to mankind. An innocent stranger to the molasses gridlock around the downtown exits could unsuspectingly take the wrong course among the five hundred options available amid the endless construction and find himself circling the area, hopelessly lost until he either ran out of gas or went mad from the hell he couldn't escape.

Bobby was dead certain many of the street people trudging through downtown muttering to themselves were actually motorists who finally abandoned their cars and set to walking the cement and steel desert until the end of their days. I wasn't all together certain he was wrong.

With this in mind, I kept to surface streets to head to Koreatown. The Wilshire area is ringed by a predominantly Hispanic zone on three sides with an affluent upper-class district to the North. Unlike most of LA's neighborhoods, where the lines of demarcation were clear, rich on one side, poor on the other, Koreatown is a mishmash of middle class and poor, dotted with high-end stores and fantastic restaurants. The best hole-in-the-wall food can be found in the oddest corners, but getting there is always tricky.

I cut through Beverly Boulevard, turned down Western, and hunted down the address closest to me, the townhouse where Eun Joon Lee allegedly surprised her murderers. The townhouse was located near an all-you-can-gorge Korean barbeque place Jae took me to once to meet his friends. A space opened up and I parked on the street then strolled down to get a feeling of the place. Like much of Koreatown, residences ran mostly to apartment buildings, with the occasional complex of condos to ease the monotony. The Lees lived in one such rabbit warren.

It was a sans-serif U-shaped beige building formed around a garden courtyard with tall trees, thick flowering bushes, and spots of lawn mounds green enough to look fake. To call the place condos was misleading. They were converted apartments sold as individual homes and probably now governed by a rabid homeowners' association to dictate the height of the greenscaping. From the looks of the courtyard, someone on the HOA was hoping someone would stop by and film a scene of *Jurassic Park V* in its murky green depths.

The Lees purchased a corner unit, giving them the spacious view of the complex's parking lot. It was one of the places farthest from the archway entrance I'd walked through, and I got halfway past the courtyard before I was apprehended by a plump, older Korean woman wearing a floral housedress bright enough to blind someone wearing a pair of night-vision goggles. Her short salt-and-pepper hair was permed into loose curls around her mischievous face, and I gave her a short head nod to greet her.

"*An nyoung ha seh yo, nuna.*" I slaughtered the hello, but she dipped her head down and grinned at me. Jae at least would have been proud I tried, even as he winced and tried not to throw up at my pronunciation.

"*Aish, halmeoni* more like it." I didn't know the word but murmured something negative, and she tittered. She glanced toward the Lee place, then back to me. "You are another policeman?"

"No, *nuna*. I'm a private investigator. I was asked to look into what happened here." Schooled by Jae's admonishments, I avoided saying the word murder or death, letting my new companion lead the conversation. "You lived near to her?"

"Over one. Next door." She nodded toward an orange and yellow door. "We have almost the same names, so sometimes it confused people. She was Eun Joon Lee but I'm Joon Eun Yi. The postman always gets our mail wrong. My sister is scared the thieves were looking for me, but I told her she was silly. What do I have? No, Eun Joon had much more to take, and that is why they were there."

"Have the police been back since… the first time?"

"Pfah, the police do nothing. Just like when that crazy man down the street blew up all the garbage cans." Ms. Yi made a face. "She was nice, and her husband … Dong-Ju Lee…worked hard for her. It is very sad."

"Her husband's last name is Lee?" I checked my notes. Eun Joon was in her early forties, but I had no information on her spouse. I was guessing they were similar in age or he was older. "Same last name, then?"

"They were cousins but no children. That's a shame. Now, he is alone." A calculating look briefly flitted over her smiling face. "Did he hire you?"

"Someone was concerned about the incident. Were you close to Mrs. Lee?"

"Eun Joon was—not to say anything bad—"

I nodded so both of us could silently agree that, while Eun Joon Lee was a saint, her ignoble death necessitated at least a modicum of gossip to be shared.

"Her family has money, more than her husband's, and she never complained about where they were living…."

"But?" I seeded the conversation. There was always a *but* to gossip. It's what made talking behind a neighbor's back so delicious.

"Always high class, you know?" Ms. Yi sniffed the air, her neck wattle flapping back and forth under her chin. "She lived here like us, but she was very picky. Everything had to be just so, very Korean. Hardly anything from here. Even the music she listened to, very old. I was older than her, but her music was too old for me, more like my mother's."

I took it as an avenue to slide the conversation to where I needed it to go. "So she did a lot of things here that she'd do in Korea? Like a fortune-teller?"

"*Omo*, she wasted so much money on those people she went to. Not just one but two!" Ms. Yi made a disgusted face that rivaled anything Neko gave me when I put chilled cat food in front of her.

"Let's see, she saw Madame Sun and Gangjun Gyong-Si. I don't go to either one of them. Too rich for me. What is wrong with Madame Hae-jung? Nothing! So she is younger! We were all younger before."

"She went to two fortune-tellers?" I frowned. "Did they know about Mrs. Lee seeing both of them?"

"Hah!" Ms. Yi wrinkled her nose and slapped my arm. It stung, but nothing like being shot. I was thankful for that small favor. "You don't tell something like that. Especially to those two. Sun and Gyong-Si butt heads all the time. If they see each other on the street, you watch them, because one might start screaming at the other. Madame Sun is a better fortune-teller, but some of the women, they like going to Gyong-Si. He says he likes men so women like talking to him, but I don't know. I don't believe that. I know better."

"They're rivals?" I frowned, trying to make sense of what she was saying, and she scowled back, not understanding me. "Sun and Gyong-Si? How come?"

"Madame Sun and Gyong-Si always fight for people. One says something bad will happen to you and the other says something good. You go to the one that is right most of the time until you get an answer you do not like. Then some people switch." She shrugged, her shoulders a wave of purple and pink hibiscus flowers.

"Do they tell fortunes a different way?" I had no idea what qualifications made a good fortune-teller or even how to go about choosing one. It wasn't anything I'd ever thought about, but I had a feeling I was going to get a crash course in it soon.

"No, the same way… Sun and Gyong-Si came from the same teacher, a very famous fortune-teller in Seoul, Kung Choong-Hoon. Gyong-Si was here first. Then Madame Sun moved to LA with her son. Stole a lot of his clients." Ms. Yi scowled, obviously disgusted by their behavior. "Gyong-Si wasn't happy when she came. Everyone knows they fight, digging into each other like centipedes. Why would you go to someone like that to tell you how to live your life?"

Madame Sun having a rival changed things. I couldn't imagine anyone killing a couple of women to warn clients off of another fortune-teller, but people have done crazier things. "Do you know if they gave her conflicting information? Maybe she was going to choose one over the other?"

"If they were so good, why didn't either one of them tell her not to get murdered?" The woman flattened her lips further into a thin line. "No, she needed to see both of them, in case one had information the other one didn't. I don't know if they knew she was seeing the other. Probably, no? If they knew, they would have made her choose. Neither one shares. They refuse."

"Do you know where I can find Gyong-Si?" I pressed lightly. "Maybe he spoke to Eun Joon before she died? I know she had an appointment with Madame Sun that morning."

"He is easy to find, easier than Madame Sun, but I don't know his address. *She* says she only takes people who know one of her clients, but that is a lie. She takes everyone. She is just trying to hide that her place is in a bad area. Gyong-Si sees people in his home. He has a front room he uses to greet people. You can find him there."

I extracted myself as quickly as I could. Walking around the building, I cased the place as if I were a burglar. Situated on the second floor, the Lees' home wouldn't have been my first choice if I was looking for quick cash.

"The cops thought they saw no sign of forced entry at the front door." I recalled what Wong told me but I wanted to check things out for myself. "Only other way in and out would be to go over the balcony."

A pass-through walkway connected the central area to the parking lot behind the building, and its cool darkness was a balm after the muggy dampness of the courtyard. The Lees' balcony was in reality more of a high-walled burp of a cement outcropping, a typical feature in California's mid-80s apartment architecture. Since the apartment overlooked the parking lot, anyone climbing up onto the second floor would have been spotted in the daylight hours by anyone coming or going. Covered in thin stucco and painted a light sand, the walls were chipped and white where stones probably flew up from a lawnmower and struck the coating.

Pressing my sneaker against the wall, I tested its grip on the stucco. The sprayed-on faux mud crumbled under my weight, streaking the paint white where my shoe dug in too deep. Crouching, I examined the wear of another mark in the coating. From the sharp angle, it appeared to have been made by something hard rather than spongy like the sole of a shoe, but its edges were weathered, softer than the scrapes I'd gouged into the stucco surface.

The walls around and near the Lees' balcony showed no sign of being scraped or gouged. The stucco coating above me was the same weathered hue as the rest of the building, and I couldn't see any sign of powdery debris beneath the balcony. From the appearance of other abrasions, it didn't look like the building's maintenance man would have rushed to repair the damage.

"Whoever the cops sent out here was a fricking idiot. No one climbed up there. It had to be the front door." I climbed out of the agapanthus planted around the edge of the building, shaking a stray purple bloom off my T-shirt. "So either they picked the lock or they had a key, because no way in hell they got in this way. Wong's going to be pissed."

I'd have to check out Gangjun Gyong-Si and whether or not May Choi was as much of a double dipper into the fortune well as Eun Joon Lee. I double-checked my notes. The psychic's name was familiar. Other than sounding like a district in Seoul, I'd heard that name before. Recently, if the whispering in my mind could be believed.

"Son of a bitch, Gangjun was May Choi's maiden name." I jotted down the connection, drawing a dotted line between Choi and Gyong-Si.

It could be a coincidence since there were only about two hundred and fifty Korean surnames, and while not Park, Kim, or Lee, the three used by nearly half of all Koreans, Gangjun could be one of the more commonly used. If Gyong-Si was related to Choi, then there was my connection to Mrs. Lee.

I pulled my phone out and found there were a hell of a lot of fortune-tellers in Koreatown. It seemed like everyone's nutty Aunt Esmeralda dried a bunch of newt eyes and hung up her shingle to peer into a cup of tea leaves. I found Gyong-Si by accident, using a phonetic spelling of Gangjun and praying for the best. I was memorizing his address when I noticed a missed text from Jae. Frowning, I scrolled through the message, wishing Jae'd called so I could have heard his voice.

Busy. I'll try to call you later. In the middle of something big, he'd sent. *Might not be home. Please feed the cat.*

"Hah, cat's been fed, and if I know you, you haven't been." I gave myself a fist pump. Looking at the time, I figured I'd give him a couple of hours before I descended on him with some food. I messaged back that I'd bring him *kalbi* and rice then slid my phone back into my pocket before he replied with an argument. With the phone out of sight, I could plead ignorance. "I'll drop by once I'm done talking to Gyong-Si the Magnificent."

TRYING to get anywhere in Koreatown is solely dependent on parking. Street spots are an urban legend. Usually, tantalizing openings turn out to be driveways or painted red by the evil SoCal parking gnome for no reason other than to thwart people looking for a place to put their car for a few hours. After circling the block for five minutes, I gave in to the inevitable and pulled into a garage structure. The last time I'd left the Rover in such a structure, I'd been shot at by a client's deranged ex-lover and forced to use an old metal hubcap as a Frisbee to bring him down.

With that in mind, I paid a valet extra to park the Rover and told him I'd be back in an hour or so.

Gyong-Si's place was a rarity in the district, a stand-alone bungalow tucked into the back of a stack of quad-plexes. The one-story, flat-roofed structure appeared to have once served as the rental office before being converted to a residence. More of that thin stucco covered the outer walls, this time painted that curious shade of salmon pink some idiot decided looked Southern Californian. It was a color used by many large housing developments, saturating the landscape with its bromide and vomit hue until common sense prevailed and construction companies went back to a more reasonable sandy brown.

At some point, an enterprising owner stretched a wide covered porch across the front of the place, painting it a sharp white. It did little to mute the pink. If anything, it made the bungalow look like a bonus stop in a game of Candy Land. A few metal wind chimes hung from the porch's supporting beam. The dull singing coins were alternated by wind socks made of rainbow threads and a couple of spinning-wing flamingoes, the afternoon's light breeze turning them about in a slow waltz.

A large sign above the steps announced to any visitor that they were in the presence of the famed Gangjun Gyong-Si, blessed fortune-teller and purveyor of futures. I assumed the Korean below extolled Gyong-Si's virtues. This assumption continued when I was further inundated with a magazine rack full of leaflets, all printed in a now familiar circle and hash mark writing Jae used to mark his projects.

An OPEN placard hung behind one of the glass-paned windows framing the front door. A bell clanged when I stepped in, bringing my arrival to the attention of an overly pretty young man sitting behind the receptionist's desk. Gyong-Si's reception area ran the entire front length of the bungalow, with only a single doorway covered with a beaded curtain leading off to the shadowy cool in the back. Painted a muted bamboo green, the front room was decorated in modern California Zen, with the prerequisite water fountain sitting on a side table and motivational, artsy posters urging readers to release their inner child and embrace their peace.

Judging by the receptionist's youthful appearance, Gyong-Si also liked to embrace hot, sexy twinks.

Dressed in blood-red skinny jeans and an overlarge T-shirt artfully draped off of one golden shoulder, he slinked around to greet me. He was cute, a perfectly packaged sip of Korean beauty. Poems could have been written about limpid pools or windswept mahogany locks, all with him in mind, and he certainly was confident in his sexuality, especially when his thigh brushed across the front of my jeans.

Surprisingly, nothing in me tingled, not even when he slid his hand up my upper arm and squeezed. My cock seemed to be off doing sudoku, and the only growling response my body had was my stomach not so politely informing me that my sole meal that day had been coffee and two purloined Choco Pies. If there was any question, it'd been answered. Apparently, I was so deeply in love with Jae, the young man with his soulful brown eyes and plump mouth did *absolutely* nothing for me.

"Uh, hi." I was a master of conversation, mostly with myself, but *still* a master. "I'm looking for Gangjun Gyong-Si. I'm an investigator. I was hoping I could ask him a few questions."

"Oh, I was hoping you were a new client. It would be nice to see someone in here besides dried up *ajumma*." Mr. Fluttering Eyes' smile waned. "Do you have an appointment with *sunbae?*"

"No, I was hoping he could fit me in." I ignored his snigger. "Does Mr. Gangjun have an opening?"

It was an entrance any drag queen would have been proud of. The beads were flung back for effect, their clatter a soft drumroll to herald his arrival. I don't know what I was expecting. Perhaps someone as coolly elegant as Scarlet or even maybe a warm grandfather dressed in a cardigan and singing about neighbors. Instead, I got a plump Korean man dressed in an orange silk shirt, tan jodhpurs, and a red beret set at a jaunty tilt on his balding head. I'd always wondered exactly what angle *jaunty* was set at, and now I knew.

He gave me a once-over that had me wondering if I was about to board a flight or was suspected of smuggling heroin balloons up my ass. I wouldn't have been surprised if he snapped on a pair of pink rubber gloves and told me to bend over.

Gangjun Gyong-Si was the true-to-life, breathing embodiment of every gay stereotype I'd ever heard of, so it certainly was no surprise to me when he dipped into his magic bag of double entendres and purred, "Oh, dear boy, for someone as beautiful as you, any opening I have is all yours."

CHAPTER FIVE

"DOES that line ever work for you?" Being sarcastic to a fortune-teller didn't earn me a lightning bolt from the heavens, so the man definitely didn't deal out instant karma. I smirked, giving Gyong-Si a once-over.

He smirked back and winked. Up close, he looked both older and smoother than I expected. I thought he used makeup to achieve his youthful appearance, a suspicion verified by the thin dusting of foundation and powder on the collar of his shirt.

"No, it never does." He threw his head back and laughed, exposing his very white teeth. "But I keep hoping someday it will. Come, come. Let me take you some place more comfortable, Detective. Terry, make us some coffee, please." Gyong-Si gave me a sly look from under his lashes. "Unless you'd like something… sweeter?"

"Actually, nothing. I'm good." I thanked Terry and followed a pouting Gyong-Si through the beads.

A small, dim hallway led to the back of the bungalow. Gyong-Si turned right at the first door, but I could see the hall continued down a few steps to open up into his private quarters. I couldn't see much beyond the half-door fabric curtain, but from what I could make out, the man *really* liked eye-bleaching colors. If I thought the outside of the bungalow was spasm-inducing, the yellow-green walls peeking out from between the slit in the fabric were sharp enough to cut.

The mediation area, or whatever it was the room was called, mimicked the front room, with a cool wash of soothing sea grass walls and enormous chairs. They were cut low, and while comfortable, when

I sat down, my knees struck the edge of the teak coffee table the man probably used for his readings. Gyong-Si smiled apologetically as he sat across from me, reaching over to pat my arm when I grabbed at a pair of candles before they fell over.

"I am so sorry," he murmured, stroking at the back of my hand. "Most of my customers are shorter. Their legs… they are not so long. Maybe you would like to go into my living room instead?"

"No, no. I'm good." The last thing I wanted to do at the moment was cross that fabric barrier, even if it meant I could get a better look at the man's living space. I wasn't sure what I was more scared of, being put into a compromising position on the man's couch or my eyes bursting from the flood of color leaking off the walls. "I only have a few questions. I don't want to take up too much of your time."

"Anything for the police." Gyong-Si inclined his head.

Again, I didn't correct him. People often told the cops more than they'd share with a private investigator, Ms. Yi aside, and I'd take any advantage I had in getting Gyong-Si to talk. I used to wear a badge. I kept telling my conscience that, but it snickered back at me.

"I'm here about Eun Joon Lee." As I spoke, his face turned tragic, a mask of sorrow so deeply carved into his skin, I was afraid it would stick that way. "I imagine that you've heard of her passing."

"I did hear. Bad news always travels fast." He made a steeple with his fingers. If it was supposed to make him look wise, I wasn't seeing it. "Terry, my assistant, lives near to Eun Joon. He informed me of the troubles visited upon her family. I sent her husband my regrets. I am sorry to say that I saw nothing in her fortune that told me of her death. I divined the I Ching for answers, but so far, nothing has been revealed to me. I'm not sure what I can tell you."

It was easier to just lay my metaphorical cards on the table, especially since my knees seemed to hone in on the one in front of them. "Mostly, I was wondering if you knew Mrs. Lee was also seeing Madame Sun? Did she share that with you?"

There was the barest flicker of his eyelid, so faint I would have missed it if I hadn't been looking for it. Nothing else in the man's face changed, not even the beatific smile he'd plastered on his face. The light in his eyes dimmed and his nostrils twitched before he tightened his grin further and shook his head.

"No, I did not know that," Gyong-Si murmured. His hand shook when he withdrew it from my arm. "She must have been troubled far more than I thought."

"How often did she see you? Can you share with me what was she troubled about?"

"Normally, I would say no, because anything a client says to me is in confidence, but she is... no longer with us. I will do anything to help." He wiped the spare beads of sweat forming on his forehead, nearly knocking his beret off. "I would see her once or twice a month, but we spoke of so many things."

"Anything you can tell me is fine. What did she speak to you about mostly?"

"She would come to me to talk about her marriage, sometimes. Eun Joon's husband felt she spent too much money. They did not have children, and she sometimes would shop to make herself feel better. She felt it was her fault they did not have a son. He wanted her to be more frugal. He would get angry at her sometimes"

As a cop, I'd seen women and some men beaten to almost a pulp turn around and swear they loved their spouses too much to press charges. The "reasons" for the beatings ranged from overcooked food to a new dress. Many of the arguments were started about money, and a few ended in death. It wouldn't be beyond belief that Mrs. Lee's murder came at the hands of her own husband.

"Did he... hurt her? Did she tell you anything like that?"

"No, he loved her. He would never do that. She might have spent too much money than he liked, but he would only scold her lightly. She had a good husband. He would yell, but it wouldn't go beyond that," Gyong-Si insisted. "Wasn't it decided that it was a robbery? That's what I was told."

"Nothing's been ruled out." That was the truth. I didn't want to rule out anything until I was sure the deaths were merely a coincidence. "Just want to make sure every base has been covered.

"Tell me about Madame Sun... what you can, I mean." I brought my employer into the conversation. If the two were rivals, he'd want to dish dirt about her, but Gyong-Si wasn't taking the bait. Shaking his head, his frown turned to an apologetic, almost bashful smile.

"I have no quarrel with Madame Sun. We both were students of a great man, Kung Choong-Hoon. She is a sister to me."

"So you're not bothered Eun Joon was seeing her as well?"

Gyong-Si gave me another practiced saintly smile. "Of course not. Sometimes a person can discover so much about themselves by seeing another fortune-teller. Eun Joon sought out Madame Sun for some reason. I am certain she would have told me about it if she needed to."

His entire livelihood was based on his ability to read people and present them with the image they wanted to see. If anyone was skilled at packaging himself, it was Gyong-Si. From his appearance to his mannerisms, he projected the friendly and safe wise counselor. I wasn't seeing the real man. I was sure of that.

I played the one card I hoped would shake off the man's mask.

"Are we almost done?" Gyong-Si glanced at a clock on the wall. "I have an appointment soon."

"Almost done." I decided to play the trick I had up my sleeve. It wasn't an ace, but if it made him flinch, then at least it was a face card. "Did you know a woman named May Choi? She was a victim of a carjacking. You might have seen her as a client—"

He cut me off before I could finish. "No, I don't think so...."

"I thought maybe you would, since her maiden name was Gangjun." I shrugged as if it weren't important. "I thought maybe she was a relative or something."

This time, there was no hiding his flinch. It rattled his face, a visual tic undulating across his cheeks and down to his mouth, rippling his powdered flesh. Gyong-Si fought to control his features, but the rattle spread, widening his eyes and bringing a gasp to his lips. This time, his perky beret lost its battle against gravity and tumbled to the floor, a spread of red felt on the woven tatami mat beneath the coffee table.

"It's a common name. Koreans… we have so many of the same names. Who is to say if we were related? Now, excuse me. I need to meditate before my next appointment," he sputtered, but his eyes remained wild at the edges, even as he regained his placid mask. He stood, taking more than a few steps to the door before I could even get out of my chair. "Terry will see you out. Please feel free to contact me again if you have any more questions."

Oh yeah, there was definitely something there.

I couldn't push. I wasn't actually a cop, so threatening to drag him down to the station would have been just that, a threat. I picked up his beret and paused at the threshold before he could fully shove me out, his hand on the door to close it behind me.

Handing Gyong-Si's hat back, I leaned closer, as if to gain his confidence. "Anything you tell me, I can promise to keep confidential. Is there something you'd like to tell me? Are you afraid of someone? Maybe whoever killed Eun Joon… or May Choi?"

"Good-bye, Detective," Gyong-Si hissed as he lightly pushed me out of the door. "Give Terry your number, please. Please excuse me. I have to… prepare."

Finding Terry seemed like a good idea. Gyong-Si needed to protect his interests, but Terry looked like the kind of guy who was only interested in protecting himself. There was a good chance I'd get more out of him than I did his boss.

The problem was, Terry was nowhere to be seen when I walked out into the front room. I caught a whiff of cigarette smoke coming through one of the side windows, descended the steps, and sought out its source, assuming it was Gyong-Si's receptionist getting a drag in before the divine Mr. G came out to look for him. All I had to do was follow the smell and I found Terry huddled up against a storm drain spout, inhaling as much of a menthol cigarette as he could in one pull.

What Gyong-Si coughed up wasn't much on the surface, but there was definitely something brewing under the man's skin. May Choi hit a nerve, but only after I revealed her maiden name. Strange I'd get a bigger hit from May Choi's name than his rival's. It was something I'd have to chase after. As soon as I shook Terry down for information and hit Jae up for some loving.

There's a split second when walking up on someone when their face is bare of all artifice. What I saw in Terry's appealing face was cynicism and a weariness I'd only seen on whores way past their prime. There was a tightness to his face, a thin layer of disgust with his job... his life... hell, maybe his underwear chafed, but something was ruffling Terry's perfectly gelled feathers.

His dark eyes were hooded, and he tilted his head back slightly so a swirl of smoke obscured his lips when he exhaled. It was erotic and obviously staged so often it'd become a habit. He must have used that gesture countless times to pick up guys at a club. If I'd met him a few months ago, I would have bitten on his lure, but a checkup on my cock told me it had apparently moved on to reading *War and Peace* or watching *Wheel of Fortune*. Either way, it couldn't be less interested in the lean, handsome young man draped against the wall in front of me.

"This in-love thing kind of sucks," I muttered, stalking up to Terry. "Hey, can I borrow you a second?"

Terry straightened up, stubbed out his cigarette on the sidewalk, and tucked the butt into a sun-bleached soda can. Giving me a nod, he pulled his pretty Asian boy act on, slithering it over his face and body like it was a one-piece bathing suit and he was about to be painted on a WWII bomber.

"Hello again." From the raspy come-hither in his voice, I expected him to wend his body around my legs, demanding to be scritched behind his ears. "What can I... do for you?"

Having been eyefucked before, I had my *thanks-but-no-thanks* smile on the deck. Pitching it out, it hit home and deflated Terry's ego gently. He wasn't really interested. I was just the only warm-blooded male in his orbit, and since he'd figured out I played on his team, I should have been a sure bet.

I wasn't. But it didn't mean I didn't appreciate the mental reach around.

"Hey, Gyong-Si said I should leave my card with you." I made a show of patting my pants and grimaced. "But I think I left them at my desk. How about if I give you my cell and you can call me if he remembers something about Eun Joon Lee that might be of interest?"

"That would be great." Terry wasn't taking the no-thank-you to heart, sidling up to press as much of his body against me as he could. His hand brushed dangerously close to my inseam, and I ducked, slapping at the air as if a bee were buzzing by me. Moving away a few steps, I put enough distance between my uninterested dick and Terry's wandering fingers.

"Thanks. Really, anything you guys can tell us would be great." I tore a page out of my mini-notebook, scribbled down the number to my office, and handed it to him. I waited a heartbeat, then looked down into Terry's face. "Between you and me? I wished Gyong-Si told me more. I got the feeling he knew a lot more than he said."

Terry rolled his eyes and tapped a cigarette out of his pack. He stopped and glanced at me. "Do you mind if I...?"

"No, go ahead," I assured him. Resting my shoulder against the outer wall of the bungalow, I glanced back to the front door as if I expected Gyong-Si to come barreling out. Dropping my voice down to a whisper, I said in what I hoped was my most seductive voice, "Anything *you* want to tell me?"

I didn't have much hope for my seductive voice. I couldn't get the cat to come to me even when I held an open can of white albacore, so I nearly choked on my tongue when Terry began to sing.

"About Gyong-Si or Eun Joon?" Terry brushed a bit of ash from his arm. "Because I can tell you a *lot* about him."

"If you want to talk about him, I'm happy to listen," I promised.

If someone asked Claudia to roll over on me, she'd knife the guy before he could finish his sentence. Apparently, Gyong-Si didn't inspire the same loyalty. It said much more about Claudia than it did about me, but I wasn't going to argue about Terry's lack of commitment.

"You're not a cop, are you?" He assessed me again, the blatant sexual interest in his eyes changing to something more cunning, more suspicious. "Now that I think about it, you don't dress like a cop. And your hair's too long."

"No, I'm not a cop, but I *am* a private investigator," I admitted. "I was hired to look into Mrs. Lee's death. Gyong-Si's name came up, so I thought I'd come by to ask questions. Sometimes someone knows something they think is really small but it's the missing piece to a puzzle. I was hoping Gyong-Si might have heard or seen something that could help."

Terry spat on the grass, aiming away from my feet. "Shit, he doesn't see anything but himself. He's an ass. I can't believe my mom told me to take this job.

"Hell, I don't care who knows what I think. There's a job I might get. Pays more, and I don't have to deal with his shit every day," Terry scoffed. "He's not even gay! You know that? He fakes it because the old ladies like it. He even screws some of them too. Someone who knew him back in Korea told me he said it's to release their inner beauty. It's all bullshit. I'm glad my mom sees someone else. I don't want her around him."

"Was Eun Joon one of the women he hit on?"

Terry's teeth worried at the tender skin of his lip, and I had my answer.

I prodded gently. "Did her husband know?"

"No, I don't think so. I'm not really sure if they were doing it," he said, shaking his head. "She didn't do anything with him last time, but she was pissed off. She ran out of her last appointment. Gyong-Si came out of the back after her. He had a big handprint on his face. I guess she decked him."

"Did he try to stop her? Say anything to threaten her?"

"No, he saw me and stopped." Terry shrugged. "Gyong-Si told me he saw something disturbing in her future and Eun Joon got upset and ran out. I knew it was bullshit, but I needed the job. He only hired me because people would think he was having sex with me. Like I'd touch that."

"How long ago was that? When Eun Joon ran out?"

He named a date and time that chilled my blood. Eun Joon slapped Gyong-Si across the face and, an hour or so later, died at the hands of an intruder she surprised in her home.

There were no such things as coincidences. Not really. Someone *knew* Eun Joon had an appointment with Gyong-Si that day and hadn't anticipated her walking in the door. Her moment of outrage and fidelity to her husband killed her.

And I thought my love life was complicated.

CHAPTER SIX

I STOPPED at one of the twenty-four-hour *chigae* chains in the area. While their assorted tofu soup came with shrimp eyeballs and legs, their *kalbi* was incredible. I did a takeout order for two servings and a side of specialty *mandu*, deep-fried dumplings made with kim chee, pork, and tofu. The motherly woman behind the counter told me to sit down, pouring me a glass of hot green tea to sip on while I waited. A couple of *panchan* dishes joined my tea, and she urged me to nibble, probably to fatten me up for something nefarious.

Picking at the braised jalapenos dipped in red chili sauce, I dialed up Bobby.

"Hey, Princess." He picked up after a couple of rings, his husky growl hoarse from years of screaming at criminals to stop or he'd shoot. "Whatcha need?"

"Why do you think I'm calling to ask you for something?" I was, but I didn't like to be called on it. Not, at least, without first getting a hello out.

"Because it's near the end of the day when you should be heading for that pretty Korean piece who for some reason thinks you're hot enough to fuck. If you're calling me, then you need something."

"Fine, fuck you too," I muttered. "And yeah, I need you to do something for me."

I ran through Gyong-Si and his gay-for-pay fortune-telling business. I got to his exploiting his clients for sex, and Bobby whistled in disgust.

"Fucker," he spat. "Tell me you're asking me to break his legs."

"No, sorry," I replied. "What I'm hoping you can get is some info on the Lees. See if anyone's been called out to the apartment on a domestic. Everyone says her husband's a saint, but she was unhappy—about a few things. I'm wondering if he found out about her frequent trips to Gyong-Si and knew about the asshole's reputation with the ladies—his *real* reputation."

"Maybe the guy on the case is chasing down the same line," Bobby pointed out.

"If he is, then great. If not, then I'll toss it at Wong to chase down." The hot tea did nothing to wash away the sweet burn of the braised jalapenos, but it was enough to take away some of the sting. "I don't think Madame Sun has anything to do with this shit, but something's up. My gut keeps nagging at me."

"The same gut that took a couple of bullets?"

"Those hit my ribs and chest. My stomach escaped unscathed," I retorted. "I've already promised Jae I wouldn't get shot again. Anything I find, I'm throwing at Wong and then walking away."

"Just remember you said that, Princess, because if not, he's going to stomp your balls to dust," Bobby warned. "Let me make a couple of calls and see what's up. You focus on getting into your boy's pants and forget about stirring up trouble. I'll call you later."

"Don't mind me if I don't pick up." My order arrived on the table, and I slipped the waitress enough cash to pay for the meal and leave a healthy tip. "I'm going to go feed Jae and see if I can't take his mind off of work for a bit."

THE drive to Jae's studio was long enough to make me more impatient to see him. Traffic tightened around me until the Rover and I felt like a blood cell trying to squeeze down a hardened artery. From the clusterfuck at one intersection, it looked like Los Angeles ate only fried foods covered in cheese and an extra helping of bacon. I maneuvered the Rover around one of the bloated ground zeppelins the city called a transit bus, broke from the pack, and zipped down a side street.

Forced to move following an explosion that leveled his old place, Jae found a new studio a few miles from my building. With the cost of housing in Los Angeles and his refusal to move in with me, he ended up in a former auto parts store someone converted into a triplex. The store's parking lot had been large enough to build a narrow apartment building, but there was enough room behind the thick-walled triplex to park. Windows cut up high into the cinder block walls were a feeble attempt to aerate the building, but the city was not known for its cool winds. Luckily, the landlord left the industrial-grade air conditioner on the place's roof, or I'd have packed up Jae's things and tossed him into the back of my SUV.

I parked the Rover behind Jae's Explorer and locked the car up. The entrance to his place was near the street, a small gesture of privacy given by the wooden slat fence built along the sidewalk. He'd taken the long rectangular space at the back of the building, a good choice, given the two square studios in the front were nearly shoved into the butt of the apartments in front.

Faded yellow and red paint flaked off the side of the building, a reminder of its former glory providing antifreeze and oil to the masses. A scatter of ash sat near the front door, evidence of a troubled Jae using the small patio area as a smoking spot. The faint odor of cloves clung to the space, a fragrant and recent echo of my lover's infrequent bad habit.

As much as I adored Jae, he was next to impossible to get to answer the front door if he was busy. I'd had entire conversations with him sitting next to me as he processed photos on his laptop, only to have him owlishly blink at me when I asked him a direct question. While he spent most of his time at my place, the studio was his niche of independence, somewhere he could slink off to and work without my intrusion.

Well—*usually* without my intrusion.

I tested the doorknob and was surprised to find it open. Jae was a habitual locker of knobs. Even the bathroom wasn't safe from his compulsive barricading the world out, but stranger things had happened than him leaving his front door unlocked.

He'd fallen for me, after all.

I opened the door to the heady fragrance of green tea and buttered popcorn. It'd been a while since I'd been to the studio. We spent all of our time at my place—our place, really, since his cat seemed to have gained custody of the bed when we weren't in it. The front part of the cinder block studio was dedicated to Jae's photography, and a U of light boxes and low tables took up much of the area. A smaller space in the back of the rectangle was cordoned off by tall bookcases, and a pressure rod hung with glittering plastic beads served as a door between the bedroom space and Jae's working area. He rarely slept there, using a queen mattress set we'd plopped directly on the floor as someplace to take a nap while he waited for something to process.

His kitchen area was a long counter against the wall facing the alley, with a microwave, hot plate, and a double-wide industrial sink. The current owner left the concrete floor as he'd found it, sealing it with a thick urethane. The place was a dismal gray, even illuminated by the soft white lights Jae installed everywhere and the thin sunlight struggling through the high windows, but it was his, and Jae wasn't going to give it up so he could set up house with me.

I still had his cat, and my bed was more comfortable, so I figured I had enough incentive for him to come sleep with me every night. So far, it seemed to be working.

The smell of popcorn came from the microwave, and Jae stood with his back to me, shaking the popped kernels into a bowl. A red and gray striped beanie was pulled down over his head, and an oversized Oakland Raiders shirt hung from his slender shoulders, probably stolen from my dresser. I lost a lot of clothes to Jae-Min, but I liked seeing them on him.

He said it was like wearing me around him. I couldn't imagine anything that could make me happier... except maybe having him wrapped around me and screaming my name.

I came up behind him, staying as quiet as I could. Intent on the popcorn, he'd not heard me come in, and I thought I'd surprise him. I wrapped my arms around his chest, pulled him against me, and raked my teeth up the side of his neck in a biting kiss.

"Hey, Jae baby," I murmured. "I have missed you so fucking much today, it hurts. Let's go home so we can try to break another bed."

Several things happened at once, nearly too quickly for me to wrap my tiny little brain around them, but my dick sure as hell felt the fist slamming up into it, and then my ear sang from a follow-up blow.

A high-pitched screaming took up residence in my rattled hearing, and I blinked furiously, trying to wipe away the sight of Jae's face on the young woman in front of me. A popcorn bowl flew at my head, too quick for me to duck. It was a thick Fiesta ware mixing bowl Jae'd bought at a garage sale, and it thunked my forehead hard enough for me to see stars. Holding my hands up in surrender, I stepped back quickly to get away.

That apparently wasn't good enough, because what little Jae had for dishes came flying at me in a hail of vengeance.

Dodging ceramics and utensils didn't stop my brain from short-circuiting. *My* Jae wasn't actually Jae. And she had breasts, round, soft curves I'd pressed up against my arms when I'd hugged her from behind.

I was ducking away from a coffee cup when Jae came running from the back room. He let the mug fly past us both but stood in front of me to ward off anything else she decided to throw. They both stood a few feet from each other, screaming loudly in a fast Korean I had not a snowflake's chance in hell of understanding, but the one thing I did see was the color drain from Jae-Min's face when she spat at my feet.

There are times in life when a person can only stand still and let the raging rivers pour over them. This was one of those times for me. Jae would have had to be blind to miss the evidence of my rubbing up against the young woman who looked so much like him. Her neck boasted a red scrape from my teeth and the shallow scruff of my unshaven jaw. It was obscene to see an intimate visual of what I'd meant to do to my lover marbling the skin of a woman.

She was only a few inches shorter than he was, apparently not enough of a difference for me to notice in my need to put my arms around Jae. The beauty of Jae's face seemed oddly strong on a woman's features, and her black hair was razor-chopped around her face and neck, much like his.

The clothes were definitely ours. I'd peeled them off of him enough times to know them intimately, even down to the small tear under the right sleeve where my tongue fit perfectly to tease his upper arm. The sight of her breasts beneath the fabric was disconcerting, nearly as disturbing as the thought of me sliding my hands over her stomach when I leaned over to kiss who I'd thought was my lover.

"You... kissed me." Her nostrils flared, and the realization of who I'd meant to kiss finally sunk in. Her eyes widened, and she paled to an ashen gray. "*Oppa*... you meant to kiss... Jae *oppa*."

"Fuck, you're his sister." There was nothing else I could do, other than maybe find a corner to noisily throw up in. "Fucking hell. Shit, Jae, I'm sorry. I didn't know...."

I'd just outed Jae to a member of his family, and she was less than happy about the discovery.

"*Kuieo*! Faggot!" It was a hard word to hear, especially coming from a mouth so close to Jae's in shape. The sting of her words burrowed in deep, striking fears I thought I'd spackled over. "Don't come near my brother! *Oppa*, how can you... be *this*? With *him*?"

Jae's scowl tightened, and his Korean took on a pleading tone, as he gestured with his hands between us. She returned his beseeching words with a stream of words so laden with disgust I could feel my stomach turn. The look she gave me should have withered me to an ashen pile if not for Jae standing in front of me to take the brunt of it.

"*Agi*—" I touched his shoulder, and Jae flinched, pulling away from my hand.

It hurt. More than the bullets Ben ripped through me and Rick turning cold in my arms. Even more than Claudia's blood spilling from her body and leaking out from between my fingers. Jae taking that tiny step away from me opened up a chasm between us I couldn't kiss away.

My face went numb, and my limbs were stiff, unwieldy lumps of clay unwilling to budge me from my spot. They continued to fight, a maelstrom of words cutting deep down into my bones, even though I didn't understand a single thing either of them said. It didn't matter. Nothing mattered. Nothing but the devastated, broken look on Jae's face and the achingly harsh curses coming from his sister's mouth.

"Jae... baby... don't—"

"*Hyung.*" Jae turned to me, murmuring. "Please."

"*Hyung?* This *ibanin,* and you call him *hyung?*" She was off on another tear, and the gap between them closed. Her hands, small and delicate, were curled into tight fists, and she struck out with them, catching Jae across his cheek. The sound of flesh hitting skin seemed to shock her, and his sister suddenly stilled, then burst out crying.

"Tiff-ah, listen to me." My lover tentatively clasped his sister's shoulders, pulling her into a tight hug. She fought him, refusing to be comforted, and he reluctantly let her go, steering her toward the back of the studio. "Go wash up. I... we can talk more. Please, let me talk to Cole. I need to... say a few things."

It was a struggle, with warring emotions playing over her face and her taut body. After a searing few seconds, Tiffany walked away, looking over her shoulder at me. When she reached the end of the bookcase wall, Tiffany stopped and bit her lip. It was a gesture I'd seen Jae do so many times, and it ached when I thought I might not ever again be able to kiss away the dimples his teeth made.

"You did this to him," Tiffany spat. "You *made* him like this. Why? Why did you do this? How could you take him away from us?"

"He didn't take me away—" Jae protested, but I cut him off, not thinking before I spoke.

"I love him." The words slithered from me and wrapped around her before I could stop them. "I just... love him."

She visibly looked sickened and took a step toward her brother, perhaps to pull him away from me... to yank him back to the safety of their family and their beliefs. Shaking her head, Tiffany replied, "No, you can't love him. Men can't love other men. Not really. What you do is *sick.* You need to leave my brother alone."

"Let me deal with this, Tiff," Jae urged. "Go take a shower. I need to talk to Cole."

Tiffany disappeared behind the shelves, and the sound of the bathroom door slamming put a final stab wound into the corpse of my heart. Jae stood in front of me, a brittle, lithe statue of ivory, jet, and pain.

"Jae—" My fingers nearly skimmed his mouth before he stepped back.

"Don't." He shook his head. "If you touch me, I think... I will break. Don't—"

"I didn't mean to do this." I drew close enough for him to feel my heat. "I never wanted this. Not... Jae, you've got to believe me. I never wanted to do this to you. I thought she was *you*. From behind, she looks—"

"Just go, Cole." He put his hands up to push me away but didn't trust himself to make contact. "Just please, go."

"So this is it? Between us?" This time I refused to be shoved aside by his anger and pain. I wrapped my arms around him and held him as close as I could. My heart broke with every straining push he gave me to get away. "Jae, I can't lose you. Not like this. Not over something like *this*."

"You're not losing me. Maybe. I don't know. I need time to... I don't know what I need, but right now, it is *not* you." He took a small step back, putting a bit of distance between us. It was the length of a knife, and the space thrust into me, cutting at my guts and severing a burning line through my heart.

"Cole, you don't know how hard it is for me to love you," he murmured, tilting his head to the side so I couldn't see his expression. "I can't... give you everything."

"You think I don't know that?" My pain crumbled under a wave of anger. He wasn't saying anything I didn't already know. "There's always a part of you I can't touch. I thought I'd wait it out, that you'd give me enough time to touch every part of you... everything inside of you, but even when I'm inside of you, you're holding back. Don't do that now. Don't pull back from me when I can help you... when I can be with you."

"Be with me? How? When your kisses burn my skin? Have I told you that? What I'm doing is wrong, and I keep hoping inside of me that something will happen to make it feel right. I *need* this to feel right, Cole-ah." Jae turned and stared me down. "Everything you do to me is like a poison I need inside of me... something sweet that peels me apart until my bones ache from the cold air around me. Every time you touch me, when your hands are on me, I want to cry and pull away because I want it so much."

"I don't understand what you're saying, baby." I couldn't touch him. It would shatter what little hold I had on myself.

"You are an addiction I can't fall into, Cole-ah." His accent curled around his words, softening their tones but sharpening the blows to my soul. "You wanted the truth? The truth is that I cannot love you as much as you love me. I can't rip myself open for you to feed on. As much as I want to, I know that if I do, I'll be lost. I begged you to make love to me without anything between us because I thought maybe if we did, I'd finally be able to break away. The feel of you filling me might be enough for me to finally satisfy what I want from you.

"But I know, deep in my heart, that it would just make me want you more."

"Don't do this to us, Jae." Shock ran through me, sucking the marrow from my bones.

"Don't you see, *agi*?" Jae whispered. "There is no *us*. There is *you* and then there is *me*. We are so different... we want different things. Maybe it was stupid for me to dream that we could be an *us*. Where will it leave me? Like Scarlet *nuna*? Alone and unwanted when she's older? I don't want that. I don't know if I love you enough to make it worth a lonely death. You need to walk away from me now, Cole-ah. You need to walk out the door and not come back. Not for a while. Maybe not ever."

In that moment, I knew what love was. It was walking away from the man in front of me. It was turning my back on the man I'd made cry out my name and beg for more of me inside of him. I needed to turn away because he asked it of me. Whether I wanted to or not, because I loved him, I was supposed to step back into the shadows and fade from his view.

"If that's what you need, baby. I'll give you anything you need."

"I need to think, Cole. Please, give me some time. Let me talk to her. I need to figure things out." He wiggled free from my arms, putting distance between us. "Can you keep Neko? I don't think she'd be happy here—"

"I'll keep the damned cat!" He winced at the volume of my voice. I was too close to breaking. "I'm going to keep you, damn it. I'm not letting you go."

"You have to. Even if it's just for right now, *ne*?" He moved quickly to the door and opened it up to the bright sunshine that refused to chase off the cold inside me. "I will call you. I promise. I don't know when, but I will. Please, go. Before Tiffany calls my mother and makes things worse."

Brushing past him, I stole a quick kiss, lingering for a moment on his mouth before he could push me away again. "I love you, Jae. If you have to choose, please choose to let me love you. I'll wait. As long as you need me to, I'll wait."

"I don't know if you should, but I'm glad you're going to." He closed his eyes, shutting them against the anguish I'd put there. Pushing me out the door, he whispered, "*Saranghae*, Cole-ah."

Then the door shut behind me, a solid sound firm enough to shatter my heart into a thousand pieces.

CHAPTER SEVEN

I DIDN'T remember driving home. The road was a blur and the city around me a mosaic of colored squares and grayed-out faces. I blinked and found myself in the carport, the Rover's engine still running. The car lights caught on the green dumpster, and I turned them off, but bright orbs remained in my vision when I blinked. Evening had fallen, sucking all the light from the day sky.

I knew *exactly* how the sky felt.

The cat didn't greet me at the door and there was no black shadow on the stairs, but I could feel her presence in the house. From the faint whiff of tuna in the air and a mostly empty bowl on the kitchen floor, she'd eaten the offering I'd laid out for her earlier and was now probably sleeping it off in a deep food coma. That was fine with me. I had other things on my mind besides coddling Jae's damned cat.

A full bottle of Jack Daniel's sat waiting for me in the cupboard, a leftover from a party we'd thrown. I pulled it out and stumbled to the couch. The seal barely cracked when I twisted the cap, so I scraped it open until it tore. The cap flew off someplace near the apothecary chest we used as a coffee table, and I left it where it fell.

After dragging my phone from my pocket, I tossed it onto the chest's flat top and stared at the screen. There was an ache in me, a burgeoning need to hear his voice, even if he was only going to tell me to fuck off.

Anything to ease the growing empty hunger that seemed to be eating me from the inside out.

I picked up the whiskey and began my journey to the bottom of the bottle.

THE world was sideways, skewing the ceiling to the right of me. The fireplace sat cockeyed on the wall, and whoever turned the sun on was definitely a Spinal Tap fan because it was dialed up to eleven. At some point, I wasn't sure when, my stomach had crawled out of my body and rolled around in dog vomit. Loyal to a fault, it then flopped its way back. Sliding over my lips to return to where it came from, the damned thing left its foul trail on my tongue and throat. Regardless of when, I could still taste its foul journey and burped up the remains of its night out.

Strangely enough, the room was also jiggling, and something was grabbing me by the armpits.

"Come on, Princess. Let's get you in a shower."

I *knew* that voice and hated it instantly. It taunted me often enough in my daily life, usually at the expense of my legs while running or face when we were in a boxing ring. I'm sure my brain formed something intellectual and scathing, but the message got garbled on its way to my mouth, and instead of the withering, sarcastic reply I knew I could deliver, I croaked.

"Fuck you."

The trip upstairs to my bedroom was akin to following a white rabbit down a hole. Things grew larger, then smaller again with each jarring stumble against a step. My shins were singing a lament by the time we reached the landing, and my head began its own chorus, complete with pounding hammers and a full range of percussion. The last time I'd heard a bass line this deep, it'd been while working patrol in the Fashion District, where there was a free hip-hop concert with every passing car.

"Why are you here?" I'm sure that was what I said, but the confusion on Bobby's face would have been priceless if I could have seen it clearly. I tried again, enunciating carefully. It didn't make much of a difference. For all of my trying, it still sounded like I was playing the kazoo under fifty feet of water.

"Come on, dude, give me a break," Bobby pleaded with me. "Let's get you into a shower. Then we can see if I've got to take you to the hospital for alcohol poisoning."

I opened my mouth to object vehemently to the idea that I was drunk, but my belly had other ideas. Probably overfull from its midnight crawl, it began to gurgle, warning me of its impending discourse. Bobby's arms tightened around my midsection, and I suddenly found myself staring down into a bowl of bluish water, the stink of chemicals burning my nose. I didn't have much of a chance to object. Within seconds of being flung toward the toilet, my belly emptied itself of its foul mess, turning the bowl water a sickly green.

The liquid deserved to be regarded until I could find the exact phrase to describe its distinct color. This task was made difficult because my innards continued to add to its hue, diluting the crayon blue to varying shades of chartreuse and whiskey. Behind me, the shower blasted on, and I winced at the pain upon hearing the spray hitting the tiles.

My clothes were disappearing at a rapid rate, and the bathroom floor was fucking cold under my bare ass. Trying to change position didn't help because it only brought the damned tile into contact with my sac. I made a dignified noise to protest this icy assault, but Bobby only heard a whimpering moan.

If I thought the tile was cold, nothing prepared me for the shock of glacial proportions when he picked me up and threw me into the shower. With all the faucet heads turned on, I couldn't escape the frigid blasting, and the glass door refused to budge when I pushed against it. Blinking, I saw Bobby had knotted one of my ties around the handle and a nearby towel ring, effectively trapping me inside.

I gave in to the inevitable and let the shower pound the stink out of my flesh. Unfortunately, cleanliness is next to sobriety, and by the time my skin no longer smelled like Lynchburg, I remembered Jae breaking my heart.

The water felt even colder on my face, especially when my eyes were hot with tears.

"Fucking son of a bitch." It hurt. Somewhere deep inside me, the pain grew, frothing up into a geyser of anguish that choked the air from my lungs. The last time I'd felt so desolate, Mike'd been holding my hand and telling me of Rick's death.

That's how Bobby found me. Curled up into a ball and screaming for the broken pieces of my heart to quit stabbing my chest.

A COUPLE of hours later, I was sitting up in my bed, cupping my hands around my third cup of hot black coffee while Neko played *Hunt the Toes* across my bedsheets. She'd scored a few hits, nearly drawing blood from my big toe, but the taste of her kill didn't seem to satisfy her, and she continued to dance across the end of the bed, viciously attacking my feet. It felt good to have her, something tangible of Jae's to hold onto while I made sense of my crumpled life.

Bobby sat down on the bed next to me. He'd given up trying to get me to eat something, but I'd eagerly accepted the coffee. My face hurt from crying, and I was fairly certain I'd engraved tile patterns into my knees from my time in the shower. Leaning in close, he raised his hand, and I flinched, earning a reproachful look.

"Why would I hit you?" he grumbled, sliding his fingers over my scalp. The contact felt good, good enough to make me start purring, and it eased the aching tenderness in my skull.

"Maybe because every time your hand comes near my face it's got a glove on it?" I reminded him in between sips of coffee. My mood dipped again, wallowing in the shallows of my despair. "What made you come over?"

"Jae called me." I must have looked shocked, because Bobby left off his petting to kiss my cheek.

"Huh." I tried not to let jealousy cloud my judgment, but I failed miserably. "What the fuck was he doing calling you?"

"Because he loves you and he's worried about you." For a best friend, Bobby seemed to forget whose side he was supposed to be on.

"He needs some time, Cole. His sister showing up out of the blue fucked him up—"

"Didn't do me much good either," I pointed out.

"*You* didn't do him any favors kissing her."

"She was wearing *my* clothes. In *his* house. I thought it was him. From behind! She even *smelled* like him. Who the hell would think it wasn't Jae?" My voice broke and I looked away, not trusting my temper any further. Another sip of coffee and I could breathe again, the ache roiling back to a dull roar. "What am I supposed to do now? How the hell am I supposed to do shit without him?"

"Did he say you two were over? Did he tell you not to come back? Did he kill that fucked-up forever you've got going on in your head?" Bobby asked softly. "Because he told me he just asked for time. He needs to deal with his sister running away from home and finding out he's gay. That's a lot of crap on his plate right now."

"He's supposed to ask me to help eat the crap off his plate," I murmured. "Not shove me away from the table. We're in this together. He *promised* me that, Bobby. He promised me he'd stand by me in all my crap, but when it's his shit, I'm supposed to keep dancing on without him? That's fucked-up. That's not what I want."

"That's what *he* wants," he reminded me. It was a harsh reality and one I was choking on. "So, what are you going to do?"

Sobriety sucked. Nearly as much as heartache but burning my body with whiskey didn't seem like it was going to last. Sooner or later, I was going to run out of whiskey, and I could only hope Bobby didn't run out of patience before then or I'd have no one to throw me into the shower.

"Grow some balls and answer me, boy," Bobby growled. "What are you going to do?"

"Guess I have to give him time," I sighed. "I just hope he comes back to me, dude, because right now, I feel like Ben came back to finish me off."

"You survived that, kid." The bed dipped when Bobby grabbed me, his arms choking me into a tight hold. "You can survive this. No matter what happens between you, you can survive it. And I'll be with you every step of the way."

IT TOOK me a few days to get back on my feet. I wavered between leaving Jae sappy love poems on his voice mail to removing the battery from my phone so I would stop leaping for it every time it rang. After leaving a *Gone Fishin'* sign on the office door, I called Claudia's oldest to tell him whichever kid he was sacrificing to the altar of familial duty was off the hook for a few days. The volcano was set on pause, and I'd be resuming tossing virgins into the fiery pits of hell in a little bit.

Mike called a lot, and I shoved off any discussion about Jae, Ichiro, and the price of tea in China. Instead we talked about silly things and what Maddy was up to. Our younger sister'd left to go home a week ago, and she e-mailed often, claiming she missed us and wanted to live in Los Angeles. Mike and I both knew once school started, she'd be into the thick of classes and popularity contests and we'd be a far distant second to a new pair of skinny jeans.

There was even a phone call to Madame Sun, giving her a short update on what I'd been up to. I didn't get into Gyong-Si poaching on her territory or my suspicions that her rival or Eun Joon Lee's husband could have had a hand in his wife's death. Mostly, I reassured her I was looking into things and she didn't seem to be cursed.

I'd spoken to everyone I knew except the one man I loved the most. Instead of wallowing, I did the stupidest thing I'd ever done in my entire life.

I cleaned.

Like crazy cleaning. Pulling all the furniture from the walls and vacuuming kind of cleaning, then going through the fridge to toss out mustard bottles I'd never opened. By the time I was done, the place smelled like Pine-Sol and my body hurt in places I'd only gotten to ache after some intense sexual acrobatics.

There were tears. I was man enough to wait until I was in the shower and the smell of Jae's soap on me grew too much for me to handle. My body hurt from the pain bubbling up in my belly, and I bent over, letting it ride through my skin and bones until I couldn't breathe any more. It happened every time I took a shower, but I wasn't strong enough not to step into my self-imposed glass prison and smear my lover's scent over my own skin.

I slept in his sweats, washed his laundry, and put his clothes neatly away in the drawers I'd emptied for him. I ate kim chee only to have the spiciness of his after-dinner kisses on my mouth. His cat lay with me on the bed, and we both curled up on Jae's side, stealing each other's warmth.

At my darkest moment, I picked up my phone and texted *saranghae* to his phone. Just that. Nothing more. I knew what it meant. I'd known since the first time I'd heard it leave his lips, even though I didn't understand a damned word of Korean. I just needed him to know my heart was his, even as I reeked of cleaning solutions and sweat. Every fucking piece of my heart was his to hold.

I could do nothing but wait. And clean.

About a week later, after I'd showered and collapsed onto the couch, Neko crawled out of where she'd been hiding and flopped onto my lap, obviously worn out from her lengthy battle with dust bunnies. From the smell of her breath, she'd found the wet food I'd left out for her in the kitchen, and, after a few head butts against my arm, she flopped over onto her side and squeaked, demanding a belly rub.

It was about all my body could deliver, and I scritched at her fur, firing up her soft, purring rumble.

"Okay, cat. Time to do something other than take apart my house." I opened my laptop, called up Madame Sun's files, and went over the details of the case.

The last thing I wanted to do was to dig through someone else's problems. I longed to wallow in the mud I'd made from my tears and the ashes of my heart. I wanted to swear until my voice was cracked and rough, using up every cuss word I knew. But I'd already done that and nothing had changed. My phone was still bereft of Jae's silky voice, and my bed was dead cold by the time I stumbled up to it.

"The woman's nuts. The fortune-teller. You know that, right, Neek?" I spoke to the cat's twitching belly. "Why the hell would someone be killing off her clients? And why the hell do I give a shit?"

The cat, of course, had no opinion other than giving me a dirty look for pausing in midrub. Disgusted by my lack of attention, she lifted her leg up to begin another epic grooming session.

"Still, two definite victims and a guy dying of a heart attack. Did someone help him with that? A gun to the head could trigger a pretty good panic. *Someone* killed May Choi and Eun Joon Lee. Question is, was it the same person?" I murmured. "Unless you're me, getting shot doesn't happen every day, because God fucking knows I'm getting shot at like it's damned hunting season and I'm dressed like Duck Dodgers."

I couldn't put my finger on what was nagging me about the case. It was cut-and-dry. People died from violence, especially if they were in the wrong place at the right time.

Bobby hadn't gotten back to me about any domestic calls to the Lees' place, but admittedly, neither one of us had been thinking about the alleged conspiracy against Madame Sun and her clients. I'd have to wait for something more concrete before I started flinging poo at Gyong-Si, but the guy made my skin crawl. He was a part of this mess. I just needed to find out how.

"Fuck it." I closed the laptop. "Time to start poking my nose into other people's shit. Since we don't have a butler in the mix, Neek, let's start with the next best thing, the assistant."

There wasn't enough time for me to *not* think of Jae, but I needed to fill my brain with something else. If I didn't do something soon, I'd do something crazy, like go over and make love to him on the kitchen counter, or worse, finish off what Ben'd started on me.

I found Vivian Na's phone number and grabbed my abandoned cell phone from its charger. Turning it on was a mistake, one of the many I'd made over the past few years of my life. It flared to life and proceeded to scold me about my missed messages and calls. None were Jae, so I ignored them all, punching in Na's number.

She answered on the second ring with a lilting Korean-flavored voice made for selling sex. When I identified myself, her dulcet tones flattened to a chilled professionalism I admired so much I'd have hired her if I hadn't already been missing Claudia's brassy nosiness. Madame Sun had told her to expect a call from me, but I could hear the irritation in her voice. No, Ms. Na wasn't very happy to hear from me at all.

"I don't see what I can do for you, Mr. McGinnis." She clipped her words off, forming them out then snipping them closed. "I told Madame Sun we had nothing to do with the murders. They're just coincidences."

"One is a coincidence, but two is a bit sketchy. I just want your thoughts. Even if it's just to ease Madame Sun's mind." The way I was talking Sun's discomfort up with everyone I spoke to, people were going to start chasing her with a butterfly net. "Maybe we can meet up someplace. Talk over a cup of coffee, then I'll be out of your hair for good."

Her sigh was heavy enough to drag down a zeppelin if she'd been on one, but giving in, she rattled off an address. "I'll be there in half an hour. Can you make it by then? I'm supposed to meet someone for dinner, but there's a bakery nearby. We can have coffee or something."

"Yeah, I can do it in half an hour," I said, glancing at the clock. I would have to take surface streets. Thankfully, the address was in Koreatown, not downtown, because by the time I fought my way out to the 101, down the freeway, and back across Wilshire, she would have enough time to eat a seven course meal and watch an opera before I got there.

I left Neko in deep contemplation of her toes, grabbed the keys to my Rover, and headed down Rossmore toward Wilshire. Turning left onto Sixth, I was surprised to find a long line of cars waiting to be valet parked. I checked my wallet for some cash and handed control of the Rover over to a smirking kid who barely looked old enough to have been weaned, much less be responsible for my car. Sending a prayer of gratitude to my insurance company, I found the café Vivian spoke of.

It was more of a coffee and hookah café than a bakery, despite what the sign said. Situated among other Korean restaurants and clubs in an enclosed courtyard-like building, the place did a brisk business. With its outer windows on the street, the café's entrance faced the interior driveway, cutting out most of the district's traffic noise. The place's glass-encased outside seating was nearly overflowing with packs of young Asians, and I had to shoulder past a small group of frill-headed young men, their black hair cut short and shaved down the sides to form a thick brush. I wasn't certain when the Roman centurion look came back into vogue, but they were fiercely clinging to its style.

None of the men looked enough like Jae to tug at my guts, but a few were handsome enough to earn a second glance. I didn't take that second glance. My insides were too dead, and when they began to playfully chatter in Korean, it was enough to make my heart sick. I *missed* hearing the language. It was all I could do to push through the heavy doors and head inside.

It was then that I realized I had no idea what Vivian Na looked like.

Luckily, she spotted the uncomfortable, confused Sasquatch blundering about in the herd of lithe, nubile young Koreans and waved me over.

Vivian was nothing I expected. Where Madame Sun was a stereotype of a Korean grandmother, her assistant looked as if she could be strolling down the runways of Paris, swinging her bony hips to sell outrageously expensive clothing.

Sleek couldn't describe her well enough. From her prominent cheekbones to the razor-sharp bob framing her delicate face, Vivian Na oozed high maintenance and expensive trysts. Draped in what had to be designer clothes, she wore them carelessly, her body a sensual slither as she crossed the short distance between us to shake my hand.

Her fingers were cold, brushing the plump of my palm. I felt the scrape of her nails briefly on my skin, a light scoring most men would probably equate with sex and the bite of her manicure into their backs. The brief smile on her coral-painted mouth went no further than her lips, and anything she might have said to me was lost in the hail of gunfire and the windows shattering behind me. Grabbing her did no good. Her body was hot, slick with blood, and full of holes, and I was left with the remains of her face splattered all over my chest.

CHAPTER EIGHT

THE shooting was nearly over before it truly began to sink into my head. There is a long moment when the brain can't quite catch up to what's happening—the loud pounding booms nearby, the screams of people, and then the smell of blood. Nothing makes the brain freeze over more than the smell of human blood in the air.

Even if someone'd never smelled that much human blood before, the brain knows it's been spilled. The small remains of a primal lizard consciousness perks up and is ready to scatter at the scent of its species' own blood. It sticks to nostril hairs, and for a long, panicked moment, the brain wonders if the blood it's sucking in belongs to its own meat suit.

That's usually when the screaming starts. Either because the pain hits or the terror that it might. But most of all, it's because blood is all you can taste, and you drown in it, trying to find some dark corner where the chaos can't reach you.

I couldn't save Vivian Na. She was gone before I'd taken another breath. But I could drag a terrified young woman under the tables. Her friend was silent, sobbing into her own hands, and I reached through the noise and flying glass, snagging her around the waist to drag her to safety. She fought me, raking my bare arms with her long nails, slicing me open. I bled, shallow scratches of pinkish water, nothing like the ocean of red spreading out around us.

The gunshots were only whistling echoes in my eardrums, leftover burns among the continuing screams. Fear grew to horror, and the crying began, the women I'd pulled under the table included.

Keeping my head down, I scrambled to my feet and nearly stepped on a slender young Korean man clutching his leg, blood seeping slowly from his fingers.

My side argued with me, the muscles twisting around their captured nerves and scar tissue. Spasms dug their claws in deep, and I had to huff my breaths to ease away the pain. It fucking hurt, but probably not as much as the burning hole through the kid's thigh.

"Hey, it'll be okay." Any thought of going anywhere but right to his side was gone. The blood wasn't spurting, but the bleed was constant. I grabbed a few of the linen napkins from the table and gently peeled his hands back.

His jeans were soaked through, and I pressed down on the wound, staunching the flow as best I could. He blinked, and I swallowed, caught by the pain on his face. He looked *nothing* like my lover, but all I could think about was Jae. I'd done this once, pressing my cold fingers to Jae's broken skin to hold his blood in. Hopefully, I'd have the same luck with the kid as I did with Jae then. The ashen clamminess on his skin was normal, I told myself, and one of the women I'd yanked aside crawled out to touch my arm.

"Is it over?" She was shaking, shock ripping through her as brutally as the bullet tore through the young man I was pressing down upon. "Are we okay?"

"Yeah, you're fine." I nodded over to the other woman. "See how she's doing. Dial the cops if you can. We need to get some help down here."

I needn't have bothered telling her to call 911. Sirens were cutting through the air before she crawled back under the table to retrieve her phone. A few feet away, Vivian Na's body cooled, her life turning the floor sticky as people ran through her pooling blood to get to the door.

"Why did they do this? Were they trying to kill us? Is she dead?"

The *they* she was talking about was obvious. Whoever held that gun was the enemy. Her phone bobbled in her hands, and she clenched her fingers tight around the case to stop her own trembling. The boy moaned, and in another scenario, I'd have been happy to hear that tortured sound, but it wasn't Jae beneath me, and the harsh sounds weren't ones of pleasure.

"I don't know." Admitting ignorance wasn't a sign of weakness. It merely showed me what I needed to do to solve the tangled situation dumped in my lap. "But I'm going to find out."

There wasn't any going back to save Vivian Na. As I pressed down on the kid's leg, I realized I'd never even heard her speak in person, much less found out if she knew anything about the Madame Sun murders. The shooting had come through the outer windows, the café's interior lit up like a carnival sideshow. It'd been the perfect setup. Outside on the street, we'd all been sitting ducks.

Someone wanted to silence her. While others had been hit by stray bullets, the majority of the shots were meant for her, rending her apart.

"What the hell did you know, Vivian?" I turned to look at her body. "What was so fucking dangerous you had to die for it?"

"YOU sure you're not a lawyer, McGinnis?" Wong shot me an exasperated look. "'Cause you seem to show up around dead bodies more than an ambulance chaser."

"She got dead *after* I got here." I'd been accused of being macabre before but never a lawyer. I wasn't sure if I was offended or not. "Her name's Vivian Na. She's Madame Sun's assistant. I was meeting her here to ask her a few questions about Choi and Lee."

"And she happened to be the *one* fatality in the shooting?"

"I think she was the target of the shooting. Everyone else was just collateral damage."

"Got any evidence of that?

"Just a feeling," I said, shrugging.

"I can't take a feeling to court, McGinnis. How about if you talk to me about what happened when you got here?"

Wong arrived a few seconds after the blue throng, chugging through the courtyard in a Crown Vic battered enough to be in the demolition derby. Someone on the bottom of the food chain secured us both coffee, and Wong pulled me aside to grill me once it got around I'd been there to meet the victim.

Vivian Na was no longer a name. She'd become the *victim*, and depending on the detective who caught her case, she'd either remain a faceless number on a homicide report or her murderer would be an unholy grail the cop couldn't shake free.

Luckily for Vivian, she got the latter in Detective Dexter Wong.

"Not much to tell. Honestly, she never even had a chance to speak to me except for over the phone. We touched hands, and then she went down."

"And you called her because she's Madame Sun's assistant? What were you thinking she could tell you?"

"I was going to see if she knew Lee was seeing Gyong-Si or if Choi's related to him." The splash of Vivian's blood on me was drying. One of the crime scene people took pictures of the spray, and there was some talk of taking my shirt with them for evidence. "There's bad blood between him and Sun. I'm looking for something to connect the chain of events. Sun believes someone's targeting her clients."

"What do you believe?" Wong drew me out, looking up from his notes.

"Come on, tell me you can't see this is all stitched up into Madame Sun," I ventured. "First Choi, then Lee, and now Vivian Na. All of them have some connection to Sun."

"There's definitely a connection," he grunted at me and stabbed my aching side with a bony finger. "But you're going to step away from it and let me do my job. If there's something fucked-up going on, I'll find it. You agreed, remember?"

"She died right in front of me, Dex." Pursing my lips, I stared at the café's shattered windows. "Fuck, she probably died *because* of me."

"The entire world doesn't revolve around you, McGinnis," Wong retorted. "But in case it does, let's go over what she said to you on the phone."

It wasn't a lot. Our conversation had been brief and to the point. Meeting me was something she was resigned to do, not something she'd sought out. I didn't have much to give Wong other than Na's general irritation at having to start her night later than she'd expected. I knew exactly where she'd been headed after talking to me, and Wong took down what little I had to add on his tiny brown notebook.

Clicking his pen, Wong sighed at his spare scribbles. "We still on for that dinner?"

"Um, yeah, about that." I scratched at the back of my neck. "Jae and I are taking a break. Well, Jae's taking a break. I'm learning how to deal with it."

"A good break or a bad break?" He shifted closer, keeping his voice down. It seemed like an odd place to have a bonding session with a newly minted friend, but sometimes, I had to take my special moments where I could get them. "Is he just busy or did shit happen?"

"Kind of shit happening." Swallowing, I found a chunk of my pain lodged in my throat. "His sister showed up out of the blue. I kind of outed him."

"Fuck, that's a bad one." Wong whistled under his breath. "Asian families are weird, you know? When I was in high school, my mom kept throwing Chinese girls at me. Then she was happy if the girl was Asian. Now, she's just thrilled if the girl's got a pulse and I don't pay her by the hour. Pretty sure by the time I hit forty, she'll take anything with a womb, even if she's got three boobs and shaves twice a day."

"Somehow, I don't think I'm ever going to fit into that timeline there, Wong." I smirked ruefully. "Jae's family's never going to be happy he's with a guy."

"Probably not, but hang in there." He shrugged. "Don't you think they just want him to be happy?"

"They should, but I don't know if that's high on anyone's priority list but mine." Nodding my chin over toward my Rover, I frowned at the strips of yellow tape blocking off the courtyard's driveways. "Am I going to be able to get out of here?"

"Yeah, about that." Wong glanced apologetically at my trapped car. "You got enough money on you for a cab?"

I ENDED up calling that cab. The driver was a former Long Island native who regaled me with what was wrong with Los Angeles and why New York was better. When I asked him how long he'd been in LA, he told me fifteen years. Since he looked to be in his midtwenties, I wasn't going to put much stock into his opinion of the Big Apple versus Tinseltown. He wasn't old enough to have seen anything other than his grandmother's backyard and possibly a few playgrounds. During the slow drive out of Koreatown, I learned he was a vegan and was studying to be an actor.

He was about to get into the reasons method acting was the true form of his craft when we pulled up in front of my place.

I tossed him what I had in my wallet and listened to his grumbling of a small tip before he drove away. Rolling my eyes in the plumes of exhaust he'd left behind, I dug my house keys out and headed up the walk. The scent of pizza from the Italian restaurant down the street made my mouth water, and I checked the time. I could maybe be lazy enough to get them to deliver a Chicago-style pie.

As soon as I spotted the woman waiting for me on my front stoop, I debated turning around and ordering a pizza in person. Maybe even eating it on a train to New York, because the cabbie sounded pretty convincing, and I should at least check things out before making up my mind.

I would have if I wasn't damned certain she'd run me down like she was a cheetah and I was a tasty gazelle.

"Nice legs," I said, eyeing Maddy's blades. "Did you run here on those, or did you stash your car someplace because you knew I would book it as soon as I saw it?"

"I parked in the back. Since you were out, I took a run. I've got my norms with me so I can change them out." My sister-in-law studied my face. There couldn't have been much to see under the hundred-watt bulb in my porch light, but whatever she saw there made her frown. "Is that blood?"

"It's not mine." Ultimately, they'd taken my shirt, but my hands were still marbled with blood. No wonder the cab driver thought I was sketchy. Even wearing the old gym shirt I'd had in my Rover, I looked like an extra from *Sweeney Todd*. He'd definitely deserved a larger tip.

"Let me in so I can yell at you."

"Do you have to?" I unlocked the door and grabbed the soft case she used for her prosthetics. "Shit, these are heavy. How do you walk in them?"

"Good leg muscles. I can crack a walnut with my thighs. That's why I usually wait until I'm having sex with your brother before I start talking about things I want for the house. One wrong word and I can pop his weenie like a grape."

"I really didn't need that in my head." Putting the case in the living room, I said a quick hello to Neko, who peeked down from the landing to see who came in. Dissatisfied with the present humans, she ducked back into whatever black hole she'd come from. "Want something to drink? Dunno what I have."

"Whatever's cold," Maddy called out from the couch. "Did you eat yet?"

"I was going to get a pizza," I admitted, handing her a chilled bottle of home-style root beer. "Want to stay for a slice, or is this screaming at my head going to be quick?"

"Pizza would be nice." She'd gotten her blades off and was packing them up into sleeves. "And no, I probably won't be quick."

Mike'd always had a fondness for tall, pretty blondes. He'd scored when Maddy gave him the time of day. Even barefaced and slightly dewy from a light run, she was a beauty. One that could kick my ass five ways from Sunday but still gorgeous, with her strong Norwegian features and powerfully lithe body. If I'd been straight, I'd have been terrified to ask her out. She was that far out of my league. I could only admire my brother's brass ones for thinking he even had a chance with her much less begging her to marry his sorry, uptight ass.

The Italian place had a deep-dish sausage, mushroom, and garlic someone ordered but didn't pick up. Five dollars plus tip and it was mine. They'd even warm it up for me. I'd barely come back down from cleaning up when the skinny kid doing the deliveries was at my door with a slightly steaming pizza dripping with cheese and a cocky smile that earned him a ten buck tip. I'd given the cab driver less, but he didn't wiggle his ass in glee when I handed him the money Maddy fronted me.

I served Maddy on a paper plate and dug a slice out of the box to chew on. She studied the pizza, then shrugged, leaning forward to pick it up for a bite. Cheese gushed out of her mouth, and she laughed, shoving strings of it in with the back of her hand.

"This is like battle pizza," Maddy said around another bite. Nestling back into my couch, she wiggled her upper legs, stretching out her muscles. She's stripped off her legs and left her truncated knees bare, enjoying the cool air. "I don't think I can open my mouth wide enough."

"Hazards of being married to my limp-dicked brother." Her arms were too fast and long to dodge, so I resigned myself to the stinging slap she gave my arm. "Hey, I can't help it if you chose the shorter end of the stick. If you'd been a guy, I'd have been all over you."

"Well, then I dodged that bullet, didn't I?" I playfully hissed at her as if her retort stung. "You done eating? I've got head-yelling planned, remember?"

"How about if you just start the screaming, and I'll jump in to defend myself when I've got my mouth free?"

"Start with the blood. What happened?"

I gave her a quick rundown, both of the case and what happened at the café. By the time I was done, we'd polished off half of the pizza and nearly a six pack of the root beer. I didn't have enough to build a connective picture, but it was worrisome enough, especially since I couldn't figure out why people were dying or how it was all connected to Madame Sun.

"Maybe it's not through her." I mulled.

Maddy stopped putting her legs together and looked at me. "What do you mean?"

"Maybe it's not Sun they're targeting. Maybe it's Gyong-Si."

"What about the girl tonight? The one who died? How is she connected to Gyong-Si?"

"Yeah, that's a flaw, but there's something there. I think he's as tangled up in this as much as anyone else." I mulled the problem over. "Need some lotion?"

"Nah, I'm good. Got some here, thanks." She held up a yellow bottle. Slathering some on the ends of her legs, Maddy finally got to yelling at my head. "Talk to me about Jae."

"Oh, here it comes." I rolled my eyes. "What has Mike told you?"

"He said you have your head up your ass and that you can't see anything but your own hemorrhoids." She dug out a pair of white limb socks, shook them out, and smoothed out their green-woven openings. Maddy laid them on the couch and stared me down. "So why don't you tell me what's going on in that stupid head of yours and why you thought you should be out standing in the middle of a gunfight instead of asking Jae to take you back?"

"It wasn't a gunfight. It was more like a game of fish in a barrel. Whoever shot up the place *knew* Vivian Na was going to be there," I pointed out. "So they shot her."

"I noticed you avoided talking about Jae-Min."

"And I've noticed it's none of your business." I tried to look superior, but Maddy had the market cornered on that one. Years of prep school and a genetically provided aquiline nose definitely gave her an edge. I crumbled when her piercing gaze shot lasers down her razor-sharp bridge. "He said he needs time. Well, he said that right after he said *get the fuck out because you've screwed up my life*, but like Bobby said, I should cling to whatever piece of wood floats by or I'll drown."

"So that's why you went out looking for murderers?"

"I went out looking for murderers because that's what I'm getting paid for." I left off the part about not charging Madame Sun. The less

Maddy knew about the profit margin of the job, the better. "What did you expect me to do? Sit around and knit slouchy hats for alpacas while I wait for Jae to decide to throw me away? I've got to do *something*, Maddy. Work seems better than drinking. Bobby'll only pour me into bed so many times. I've already used up one get-out-of-ass-kicking card over this."

"The cops got this, right? That detective's a good guy. He'll do the job." Maddy left off tightening bolts and feet to touch my hand.

"She *died* on me, Maddy. Literally. I can't forget that. I won't forget that. I was the last person she saw in this damned life. What do you want me to do with that?"

"I want you to put it aside and think about other things," she said gently. "Like your brother, Ichiro, coming to visit. Mike invited him. He's coming in a couple of days. Mike wants you to sit down with him and talk."

"Fucking great. That's all I need right now." If I didn't already have pressure built up in my chest, I sure as fuck did now. Eyeing Maddy, I asked, "Is that why you came over? To do Mike's dirty work and tell me he's gotten me a baby brother?"

"Nope, he doesn't know I'm here." She picked up her foot piece and slid it into its slot on her leg. "He wanted to tell you after Ichiro got here. I thought you didn't need to be ambushed by your brother. The one I'm married to."

I was too tired to be angry. News of my mother's precious son descending into Los Angeles was the last straw. My life was a fucking wreck. The woman who'd taken me under her wing was lying at home nursing wounds from a madman I'd brought to my front door, and the lover I struggled to understand was playing J.D. Salinger with his sister in a cinder block hole barely big enough for one person to live in, much less two. I had a string of murders I couldn't seem to connect even though I *knew* they were, and my hands held miniscule echoes of a woman I'd never really met.

On top of that, I had an unwanted and unknown brother encroaching on my already stressed life and a furry black diva upstairs who cried in the middle of the night while she searched for the man who'd brought her here.

Yep, too fucking tired to fight anymore. It was time to just bend over and let life fuck me like it wanted to—hard and raw.

"He's going to be ticked off you told me," I sighed. It wasn't Maddy's fault I was being unreasonable. Actually, I didn't think I was being unreasonable. Mike wanted to spoon-feed me an entire ready-made brotherhood when I was still choking on my teeth after my father kicked them in.

"I can handle him." She leaned over and kissed my cheek. "Thighs that can crack a walnut, remember? Seriously, think about meeting Ichiro. What's the worst that can happen?"

"I can hate his guts because my mom dumped me with a fucking asshole father and didn't look back?" I offered. "You know, the man who said he'd rather see me dead than happy with a guy? That asshole. Remember him?"

"Don't make this about your mother or even your dad, Cole," Maddy replied. "We don't know why she did what she did or what kind of life Ichiro had with her. Find that out for yourself. Give him that chance. Yeah, you might not like him, but hate him because of who he is, not because of who he's become in your mind."

I walked Maddy to the door, making *Six Million Dollar Man* noises behind her. I earned myself another playful slap and a friendlier sister-in-law kiss good-bye. Shutting the world out, I tossed out the pizza box and turned off all the downstairs lights. Neko was waiting on the landing, meeping softly while trying to assassinate me by tangling her puffball body between my ankles.

I placed her on the bed and did all the nightly things, minting up my mouth with paste so she could sniff at my face and rub her bony cheek over mine before I fell asleep. My sheets were cold against my skin when I slid between them, and I shuffled around the pillows, trying to find a comfortable position. I was losing the scent of Jae on one of them, and I briefly pondered spritzing a bit of his cologne on it.

"Fuck, you're pathetic, McGinnis," I scolded myself. After turning off the lights, I'd just lain down when my phone chirped at me from the nightstand. The screen flashed, staying bright long enough for me to grab it.

It was a small text, nine letters sent through wires and dusty air, but they grabbed my heart and shot waves of lightning through its dead flesh. After pressing the phone to my lips, I returned Jae's text, bouncing his word back to him. The knot in my chest unraveled when I inhaled deeply, and for the first time in almost a week, unfettered air struck my lungs.

"*Saranghae* too, baby," I murmured into the air, hoping the stars would pick it up and wrap him tight until I could hold him again. Cradling my phone, I fell asleep, letting Jae's cat and pixilated affection keep my nightmares at bay.

CHAPTER NINE

I DANCED back, shuffling my feet and ducking my shoulder. It'd been too long since I'd been in the ring, and my gloves seemed heavier than I remembered. The smell of my padded helmet at least was familiar, dried sweat and rank desperation creeping past my nostril hairs. The cheek protection on my helmet made it hard to see, but Bobby insisted I buy a full mask, saying he didn't want to mess up my pretty face.

Personally, I think he was taking advantage of my diminished line of sight and blasting the side of my head with his fists. He denied it. The ringing in my ears, however, gave me all the evidence I'd ever want.

I got a jab in, one strong enough to rock Bobby's head back. It probably was a mistake. Taking the shot. Not that the shot was a fluke. I could box. I could hit hard. I knew how to put my weight against the punch and follow through. God knows, I pounded the shit out of Mike growing up and then moved on to bigger, stronger guys in high school who decided the McGinnis boys needed a beating.

No, taking a shot at Bobby's head was a mistake because it told him *all bets were off* and I was willing to go a few hard rounds.

I didn't know if my healing body could take it, but I wasn't going to have much of a choice. He narrowed his eyes and he curled his shoulders in, hunting me across the mat with a predatory stalk.

Yep, definitely a mistake.

JoJo's was normally a loud, raucous place. Men shouting and grunting as they worked through their routines of bag work or sparring.

The few women who made it past the door and into the stink were hard-eyed and lean-bodied, serious athletes who came to the boxing gym to learn the sport or to hone their muscles. Most of the men were gay and blue-collar. It wasn't a place for twinks or ass-wiggling flirtations. You walked through JoJo's doors ready and willing to get pounded on or pound the crap out of your body.

From the look in Bobby's eyes, I was seriously considering going to join the twink spinning class down the street if it would keep me safe from his gloved fists.

Oh, he hit me, but not with his hands. "So, that stupid grin on your face because of your boy, or did you finally see some sense and get a new piece of ass?"

Luckily, I could still see through the wash of red across my eyes to find Bobby's face with my fists. The smack-smack of my gloves hitting his padded head only went so far. I needed to feel him stepping back, giving way under my blows. Unfortunately, Bobby retreating back across the ring wasn't the only thing that gave way. A twinge in my shoulder burst into a larger, spreading fire, sparking a panic in my nerves. My upper arm muscle gave out first, then the ball joint, my movement scraping down to a slow crawl. Clutching my arm to my side, I didn't see Bobby's roundhouse until it was too late.

Then all I saw was the caged wire overhead lights hanging down from JoJo's camo-gray high ceiling.

Oh, and birdies. Small blue birdies. Roger Rabbit had *nothing* on me.

"Shit, kid!" Bobby's face swam into view, a wavering mash-up of eyes and a nose with a mouth slanting upward toward his right ear. "I thought you were dodging down."

"Can't," I mumbled through the birds. "Arm gave out. Fucker, you hit me blind."

"Yeah, well, we're even. You were beating the crap out of me."

"Step back, you damned gorilla," JoJo grumbled from behind Bobby, shoving him aside. His sun-wrinkled face was a blur of burnt umber and yellow teeth. He hadn't shaved that morning, so a thin mat of gray and black whiskers covered his loose jowls. "Didn't you see the boy was favoring that arm, Dawson? What's wrong with you?"

Bobby rumbled back at JoJo but cleared a space for the old man to get in. "JoJo, did you miss the part where I was the rug and he was beating the sand out of me?"

"I'm good." I tried sitting up, but the gym swirled a little bit. Bobby slid his arm under me and hoisted me to my feet.

"Let's go get you checked out. I probably gave you a damned concussion." Bobby sounded worried. It was hard to see his face because everything was skewed and a bit dark. Blinking, I tried to clear away a fuzzy line across my right eye, focusing on the black ant trails it made.

"Shit, dude." I dug my heels in. "You knocked my fucking helmet sideways. I can't see a damned thing. I'm fine. Just need to shake it off."

"Go on! Get back to what you were doing," JoJo grumbled at the boxers crowding around the gym. "Dawson, get your boy off the mat and watch his head." JoJo's palm was bright pink, his leathery skin stretched tight over his bony upright fingers. He took my helmet off, and I breathed a sigh of relief, sucking in air. "How many am I holding up, McGinnis?"

"Two," I answered. He gave me one of his patented shar-pei frowns but let Bobby hoist me under the ropes.

"Get him into the showers. If he starts tossing his cookies, you get him to the ER," JoJo muttered at Bobby's back. "Fucking asshole. Next time you don't watch where you're hitting him, I'm going to give you an ass kicking myself."

"I think you pissed him off." I was speaking to Bobby's armpit. Straightening made my head spin a bit, but it was better than before, and I was no longer whiffing my best friend's sweaty hair clumps. "Pissed me off too."

"Yeah, I thought I'd see if I could get you mad. Shake things up a bit."

As apologies went, I'd had better blow jobs from the air dryers at a bus station, and those only ruffled the hair on my crotch.

"Yeah, I don't need things shaken up," I replied sarcastically. "Least of all my fucking brains."

"Said I was sorry, Princess."

By the time we got to the showers, I was feeling better and my legs were responding on their own. I detached from Bobby's grip, stripped, and headed in to let the shower work my muscles loose. My arm stopped tingling, and, slowly, my shoulder responded. I'd strained it too much, and in a couple of hours, I was going to be purple and black from the bruising I'd given myself. Bobby joined me, taking up the next stall, eyeing me every once in a while to make sure I was steady.

"He texted me last night," I said over the pounding water. "Told me he loved me. In Korean, but fuck it, I'll take what I can get."

"Good," Bobby grunted. "You guys are good together. At least he makes sure you eat your vegetables."

"Dude, I *am* a vegetable." Laughing, I dried off and headed to my locker. Sitting down on the bench between the locker rows, my fatigue hit, and I sagged, letting my muscles begin their complaining.

"You okay?" Bobby touched my shoulder. "Really, if you're feeling it, I'm taking you in, Cole."

"No, I'm fine." Scrubbing at my face with the towel, I soaked up the water dripping from my hair. "I sent him a *saranghae* back and went to bed."

I left out the part about hugging the phone like it was my long-lost teddy bear, but there was only so much of my pride I was willing to swallow.

"Good." Bobby grabbed me by the chin and stared down into my eyes. I tried getting loose, but it was useless. I didn't know how he didn't rip his dick off when he jacked off, because his damned grip was like hardened cement. "Pupils are normal. Okay, I feel better now."

"I don't." I worked my jaw around. "Shit, that hurt."

"Poor baby," he snorted, pulling on his boxers. "Get dressed so we can get out of here. I've got some stuff to tell you about that Lee murder."

"You couldn't have started the morning off with that?" I grumbled.

"Nah." He slapped my ass, leaving it stinging. "Got to get you into shape. Once you and Jae get back together, you're gonna need your strength for all that hot rock-star sex you'll be having."

MY EARS were still ringing a little bit when I unlocked the door to my front office. I'd arranged for Martin's daughter, Sissy, to come in to answer the phones in the afternoon, promising her dad she'd do her homework while she worked while guaranteeing her she'd have access to a heavy-duty Wi-Fi. But Sissy's arrival was a few hours off, and the office was cold and lacking the smell of brewing coffee.

I took care of that first, then handed Bobby a bunch of napkins. Undoing the bacon, egg, and cheese burrito I'd gotten from a drive-thru taco shop down the street, I poured a container of tomatillo sauce over the whole mess and wrapped the tortilla back up.

"Talk to me about Lee," I said before Bobby could bite into his burrito.

He raised an eyebrow at me. "This can't wait until after I eat? Not like she can get any deader."

"Nope." I selected an extra crispy french fry from the nacho cheese soup the server ladled over my *papas* order. "I paid for the food. You sing for it."

"Okay, keep your panties on. I got some notes on my phone," Bobby grumbled. He scrolled through a few screens until he found what he was looking for. "Here we go. Got in touch a few days ago with the deet who pulled Lee's case. You were busy being emo, so I figured it could wait. It's a guy by the name of Jenkins. Stan Jenkins."

"Wait, why is that name familiar?" I playfully slapped Bobby's fingers as he made a grab for my fries. "Fuck off. You can have what I don't eat."

He made a fist and shook it under my nose. "Fuck off yourself, Princess. Or I'll tag you across the head again."

I let him have the fry.

Chewing with his mouth open so I could see his prize, he continued to read, "The name's familiar because it's Stagnant Jenkins."

"Fuck, he's still around?"

"He's only got a year left, and then he's off to a duck blind in Wyoming. Or wherever it is that people go to shoot ducks out of the sky." Bobby stole another fry, shaking the cheese off before he folded it into his mouth. "You might say he's moving even slower on this one than he does his other cases."

"Why the fuck do they still have him around?"

"Because he's old and has shit on everyone wearing a gold badge since the Pony Express," he shot back. "Now shut up and let me finish."

"Sorry, Your Highness. Please, continue."

"Anyway, Jenkins caught the case but hasn't really done much with it. Wong contacted him a couple of days ago about a possible connection to Choi, so Stan's been trying to shove Lee off on him."

"Like Dexter needs another case."

"What Chinese family names their kid Dexter?" Bobby looked up from his phone and caught my glare. "Okay, onward. Jenkins did learn a couple of things you might be interested in. Autopsy came back. Eun Joon Lee was pregnant when she was killed. About four months along."

"Fuck—" I left off picking through my fries.

"Yeah, hope the asshole who killed her gets caught in a crocodile pit. A gay crocodile pit. Very horny gay crocodiles with really big fat dicks. Barbed dicks."

"No, no." I waved my hand to cut off Bobby's protest. "Eun Joon Lee couldn't have kids. That was one of the things she and her husband fought over. The neighbor told me that."

"Maybe Eun Joon wasn't the problem." Bobby wiggled his fingers toward the ceiling. "Maybe Mr. Lee's swimmers were DOA and she went elsewhere to get her burrito filled."

"That was probably the most disgusting thing I've ever heard you say."

"Ah, kid." Bobby bit into his food with relish. "You haven't been listening to me, then. So Mrs. Lee's bundle of joy might not have been all that joyful?"

"Terry, Gyong-Si's soon-to-be-ex assistant, said his boss would have private counseling sessions." I made air quotes and winked. "Maybe that last time she went to see him, they argued about her being pregnant."

"So he sent someone to kill her?" Bobby eyeballed me warily. "Kind of quick thinking on his part. And he's got a hired killer on speed dial?"

"Hey, I'm hashing things out." Complaining only made Bobby roll his eyes at me. "It's something to look at."

"Yeah, it's something for *Wong* to look at," he shot back.

"It's Jenkins's case," I pointed out. "And you know he's not going to do shit about it. Probably the only reason they gave it to him is because there's no leads. It explains why the police report says they came in through the balcony. There's no fricking evidence of that. Jenkins just lowballed the investigation."

"Sounds like him." Bobby leaned back and patted his flat stomach. "Okay, I've got to go run this off. I don't suppose I can say something to make you drop all of this shit."

"Probably not." Shrugging, I balled up the remainder of my now-cold fries into the crumpled drive-thru bag. "Wong's up to his balls in Na's murder, and he's still got Choi's death hounding him. Lee's not going to get the time of day because she was given to an asshole who'd rather warm his chair than catch a killer. The guy's solve rate must be in the negatives."

"Fault belongs to the captain in charge as much as Jenkins." He tapped out a few letters on his screen. "Got some good pictures of the report he filed. I'll forward them to you, but it's not much. He hasn't spoken to the husband since they found the wife, not even to talk about the pregnancy. For all we know, Mr. Lee found out about the unexpected miracle and did her in."

"Dunno," I admitted. "But I'll be careful. What's the worst that can happen?"

SISSY arrived right on schedule with her slightly older brother, Mo, in tow. I'd only contracted one of Martin's children at a time, but they decided they'd both squat in my office whenever possible, if I didn't mind. To be honest, I felt better having Mo with Sissy if I were out. He was built like a slab of redwood melded to granite and wouldn't put up with anyone giving his sister shit. Sissy was no slouch, despite her petite, willowy frame. I'd seen her hold her own in a game of touch football with her brothers and cousins. Upon second thought, maybe Mo was there to stop Sissy from taking out anyone who pissed her off.

I strongly suspected every baby born into Claudia's brood endured Green Beret training before it was allowed to bear the family name.

After showing them their assistant responsibilities, I settled in to read Jenkins's report. Sissy sat down to do her homework, while Mo picked up the broom and headed out to sweep the front porch. I watched him for a moment through the screen door, and something on my face caught Sissy's attention.

"He likes sweeping." Sissy's voice was nothing like her grandmother's. Claudia dripped brash Southern hospitality and burnt molasses, where her granddaughter sounded as if she were ready to anchor the evening news. "I'll do the dishes and dust. Even trade. We don't believe housework is for women in our family, Uncle Cole."

"Oh, I know that." I reassured her with a small, tight smile. "I was just… thinking about your grandmother."

Sissy glanced out the screen door at the last place Claudia'd been before the ambulance took her. "Oh, the porch. Yeah, she's pissed off about that. Said she'd gone for some groceries down at the farmers' market that day. I think she was more mad she paid money for stuff she didn't end up using."

"She talk to you about what happened?" It was difficult not grilling a sixteen-year-old girl about her grandmother, especially since the older woman was the closest thing to a mother I was ever going to get. "I told her I'd understand if she didn't want to come back."

"Hah, good luck trying to get her to stop," she snorted, returning to her math homework. "Nothing stops Nana from doing anything she wants to do. Not a bullet. Not *anyone*. You're as much family to her as any of my uncles. She'll be climbing those steps up to work on principle alone."

"She's a good woman, you know?" I murmured, finding my spot in the report.

"Yep," Sissy agreed. "And like my dad says, everything we do is to make her proud. Guess that holds for you too, Uncle Cole."

I SHOOED them out at five. They went reluctantly. Apparently, sharing a Wi-Fi network at home meant splitting it with the rest of their siblings. Here at McGinnis Investigations, Mo and Sissy were the sole riders of my bandwidth train. It affected Mo so much he offered to move into the conference room and sleep on a cot if I needed him to.

So I assured him there wasn't any need. That's when he upped his offer to include mowing the lawn and mopping the floors. It was tempting, and as I wavered, Sissy yelled at him to get into the damned car.

Being a smart young man, he got into the damned car.

Locking up behind them, I was making plans in my head to loop around to speak to Eun Joon's husband when I spotted a battered white

Ford Explorer parked behind my recently returned Rover. I stood staring at it, waiting for it to disappear into a haze of smoke or sparkling, laughing demons when I blinked.

I blinked. Car was still there. My heart was not. It'd decided to hook little barbs into my lungs and throat to climb up to the base of my brain. It lodged there, whispering carelessly about throwing itself onto glass shards of doubt. I told it to shut the fucking hell up and headed down the walk to my house.

And found a broken angel had fallen down onto my stoop.

He looked good. I'd not seen him in over a week, and seeing Jae… *hurt*. It was more than just a pretty face and a lean body I could make sing under me. I missed the shy smiles he gave me when our eyes met while we watched television and the murmuring complaints he made when I stole a raw mushroom when he cooked. I wanted my Sunday mornings lounging in bed with our toes tangled together to protect them from the cat and the taste of his mouth when I kissed him after he'd had his first cup of tea.

My heart no longer whispered. Instead, it wept, because it damned well wanted to be stroked and reassured it still had a home in that man's hands.

I crossed the long cement mile separating us. It was over in an instant but seemed like forever. After not seeing him for *too* many days, my rapier wit and smooth charm were sharp and ready.

"Hey."

"Hi." Ah, his cunning mind served him well.

He stood up and brushed grit from his jeans. They were one of my favorite pairs, so thin in spots the denim was nearly translucent and with tears across his knees and thighs. He picked at them when he worked, playing with the strings hanging from the rips. The shirt he wore was one of mine, a vintage Dr Pepper tee I picked up someplace. The faded purple-red was nice against his pale skin, nearly the color of the bites I could make on his throat when I wasn't careful.

And, God, I was tired of being careful.

"Why didn't you go in?" I opened the front door and held the screen open for him.

"It was nice outside. Thought I would get some fresh air and wait for you."

"Your cat must be going crazy inside."

"Have you been feeding her?" Jae ducked around my arm, but his hand brushed over my belly. My stomach muscles clenched, and my dick saluted him as he went by.

"Yeah, or she'd eat me alive as I slept."

He laughed, a burbling, rough sound he also made when I hit the delicate core of his body with my cock. "Then, no, she's probably been too happy to miss me. She is pretty much a stomach with fur."

"*I've* missed you."

Yeah, it was cheesy—long, gushing cheesy romance stuff that I was never good at, but it was the truth. He turned, pausing long enough to breathe and lick his upper lip. A storm flicked up in the air between us, hot and crackling and full of a fire we'd banked between us for too many days for our bodies to count... or to care about anything but touching skin.

We made it about three steps into the house before my old Dr Pepper shirt hit the wood floor.

CHAPTER TEN

THERE are moments in life when memory fails to capture what's important. The feeling of when that first tooth is loose, what you were wearing during the first kiss that rocked your socks off, or the song playing on the stereo the first time you saw a shooting star. And then there are times when the brain kicks in and hits full record because it knows that this is the *Moment*.

My brain not only kicked in but started chiseling things down onto stone tablets to be taken up to the mount for everyone to see and follow as gospel.

If there was any doubt God loved gay men, the proof was the existence of Jae-Min's mouth.

I spent my time exploring what God gave him. Cupping his face in my hands, our bodies barely touched, and his bare chest skimmed against mine. Even through my cotton shirt, the contact peaked my nipples, rubbing them erect. Jae smelled of green tea, sunshine, and the sweet rough of male sweat. What he tasted of was pure heaven.

At some point, I'd taught him how to make cinnamon toast. He'd never had it before, and after I picked myself off the floor from shock, I proceeded to instruct my lover on the delicate balance of the pungent spice with sugar and how much fresh butter should go onto the almost-too-dark toasted bread. He was a quick study, mastering the delicate shake off and repeat maneuver I used to get the sugar soaked into the toast. It was a food he loved, munching on triangles and sipping tea, our morning kisses spiced and hot from the warmed, sweet cinnamon.

It was what he tasted of now. Of cinnamon and desire. Of love and sex. Of soft midnights and loud laughter.

The tang of him grew in my mouth until I could no longer swallow enough of it in.

I drew out the sensations, savoring the rough of his tongue against mine and the ridged smoothness of his palate when I licked at it. Lightly pressing my thumbs against his jaw, I urged Jae to open up… to let me journey deep into his taste as much as I wanted to.

He moaned and slid across my body, tilting his head back, and surrendered to my exploration.

I pulled him into the living room. I didn't care about the no-sex-on-the-table rule or even if there were still condoms left hidden someplace in the apothecary chest. I burned to be inside of him: my mouth… my fingers… my cock. Hell, if my skin could crawl off of my bones and wrap around Jae's lean body, it would have. Anything to quench the need for him.

The candles on the apothecary chest went flying. One rolled right off, along with the holder it'd been stuck into, but the other landed someplace I couldn't see. Since I didn't hear a cat yowl in protest, I figured I was in the clear. I wanted to see Jae spread out before me. The couch was too narrow, and the bed was too far away. It was going to have to be the chest.

"Not. On. The. Table," Jae gasped in between kisses. "We eat—"

"Only thing being eaten there right now is you," I growled, biting his bare throat. None of the buttons on my shirt survived, popping off with delicate pings when I tugged it from my body. "Now, shut up before I tie you down to it."

It actually sounded like a good idea. The antique chest was enormous, a square block of aged wood and ironwork with drawers running down both sides. The upper drawer handles were large rings, strong enough to hold anything I tied to them, including a writhing Korean man.

The thought of Jae stretched out and lying on the honey wood, naked and helpless against my tongue and fingers, made me hard enough to ache.

"Fuck, remind me to hide some of my old ties down here next time," I murmured into his ear. "I am so going to fuck you tied to this thing one day."

The throw pillows Maddy insisted I get were soft enough to cushion Jae's hips and head. Along with a soft cashmere afghan, it made a perfect nest to lay my lover down on. He resisted only enough to give a soft protest about the chest's dining table function, but I swallowed his complaints with a hard kiss.

"That's why they made Pine-Sol, baby." I pushed him down against the cushions and hitched his hips up so I could undo his jeans. "Trust me. I've got a fucking gallon of that shit in the kitchen."

They were my favorite pair of his jeans, but I wasn't careful. I didn't care if the rivets popped out or if I tore the buttonholes as I undid his fly. I wanted them off. Now.

His skin was nearly as white as the thinning patches on his jeans, and when I splayed open his fly, I discovered he'd left his cinder block oasis without any underwear. A line of fine down trailed from his belly button, thickening into a silken black spread above his slender cock. I left his shaft trapped beneath the stitched end of the fly, concentrating only on the slender base I'd exposed. Already aroused, Jae's cock pressed up against its restraints, plumping its base up. He moved his hands down from my shoulders and hooked them into the waistband of his jeans to pull them off, but I grabbed his wrists, pushing them to the side.

"No, not yet, *agi*." I rested my chin against the crux of his legs and stared up into his honey-brown eyes. "I want—"

I didn't finish what I was saying. Instead, I began to finish what I'd started.

Nestling my cheek against his soft, baby fine underbelly, I took a deep breath, pulling in Jae's scent until I was drunk on it. Then I licked, and the taste of him was like sipping champagne made of moonlight. It'd only been a week, maybe a little bit more, but I forced myself to be steady and take my time. Nuzzling at the straining cock base, I laved at its powdery textured skin, wrapping my tongue up and around it.

Kneading at the plump head hidden from view, I trailed my fingers down to the thick folds of stitched denim below to stroke at the sac I knew lay there. Jae's eyes were on me, a dark and wide stare following my every move. I watched his face as I licked. His teeth were a bright white splash of pain on his kiss-swollen lower lip, and he bit down hard to keep from crying out when I sucked at his base. He made a mess of the cashmere, scrunching the fine wool into mounds between his long fingers.

Twisting, Jae hooked his legs up over my shoulders, mindlessly pressing me back with each long, wet stroke of my tongue. "Cole... *jagiya...* please...."

The denim was damp under my fingers, his cock rigid and leaking. I dipped my head down, focusing my attention and mouth on the soaked-through spot coming up from Jae's crotch. It was a familiar burst of flavors, spicy and salt with a hint of cream and sex. I suckled hard, pulling on the fabric and wetting it with my tongue, drawing out as much of Jae's arousal-induced spill as I could.

It must have been too much for him, because he leaned forward to shove me away. I refused to give in, letting him push as hard as he could, then bit into the spot I'd made damp with my mouth. My teeth found purchase on the denim and the flesh beneath. Dulled through the cloth, my bite was blunted, scraping along Jae's tender head with ripples of fabric. Knowing he was bare beneath his jeans, I made sure he felt every striation of denim against his cock, hooking my teeth into the stitching and chewing at the salty mark.

When he dug his fingers into my aching shoulder, I decided he'd had enough. Especially since his nails were sharp and his scrapes stung from the sweat on my back. Jae's moans tickled my eardrums, deep, throaty purrs hooking into my balls and pulling them up into my hollow.

The apothecary chest was too hard, and I couldn't get a good enough angle to rest my knees when I climbed up Jae's body to kiss his belly. His jeans snagged on one of the iron rivets on the upper trim, and I worked it carefully free before tossing it aside to join the candles.

Rumpled, he was curved up into my chest, his hands hooked behind my neck. I supported my weight with my palms, resting them on either side of his hips, and captured his mouth, sharing the slick, musky taste I'd found in a hot kiss. I didn't let up, not until he was gasping for air, and only then did I pull away, only long enough to find the bite he'd worried into his lower lip.

I needed to bite that spot. As much as I needed to suckle the taste of him out of his jeans, I needed to sink my teeth into the depressions he'd made when I brought him to the brink of coming. Jae'd bit hard enough to bring himself to the brink of blood, and a sliver of skin had been peeled up by his teeth.

I suckled on his lip, playing with the kiss and hooking my hands under his ass before lifting him clear of the chest.

"What—?" Jae jerked, and I nearly dropped him. My shoulder felt the strain of his weight, and the scar tissue along my ribs twinged in complaint. "Cole-ah—"

"Moving you," I grunted, placing him on the couch. "Damned thing is too hard. I'm going to get ridges on my knees." Biting at the soft skin at his jaw, I mumbled. "Turn around and hold onto the back of the sofa, 'cause I'm going to fuck you through it."

Shoving the cashmere throw aside, I found the drawer we'd stashed our supplies in. I still wanted to see him tied up and spread over the chest, but it would have to wait until I got some thick padding to cover the damned thing with. There was only so much pain a guy could endure during sex, and piercing my knees with antique iron studs wasn't high on my list of kinks.

He was waiting for me when I turned around. On his knees. Bent over with his chest pressed against the rise of the couch. Legs spread and feet apart. A mile and a half of ivory skin and muscle, lean and strong with a blushed rose sac slid down to dangle in front of his parted ass. Looking over his shoulder, Jae was a blend of shadow, light and pink, pretty and cut fine with sharp bones and angles.

I slid the lube onto the couch and took my sweet time in running my hands over his shoulders, then down his back. I kissed along his spine, making a slalom run of the dip with the edge of my tongue until Jae wiggled from the contact. He tried to turn around, reaching for me and snagging the loop of my jeans. I pulled myself free, put a hand down between his shoulder blades and held him still, and used my free hand to undo my zipper.

I kicked my jeans and boxers off then flicked open the lube and scraped my fingernails against Jae's back, his muscles knotting and releasing under my touch. He rolled his shoulders back to meet my fingers, and his spine curved, splaying apart his rounded ass cheeks, and flicked me a peek of his plum-hued rosette.

He quivered when I slid my mouth down the base of his spine, his skin prickling with goose bumps under my tongue. Dipping the tip down between his cheeks, I ghosted over the apex of his crack, careful not to go any further. Not one for rimming, Jae-Min's body still had plenty of other touch points to make him sing when kissed or bitten, including the plump meat of his ass cheek.

I filled as much of my mouth as I could with his flesh and scored my teeth into his skin, twisting slightly until he tried to pull free. I repeated the marking on the other side, this time sucking hard enough to pull up a bruise. Satisfied with the welt forming against my tongue, I kept at it, forced a bit of lube onto my fingers, rubbing them together until it went slick from heat.

Then I slid two of them into Jae's entrance and caught his moaning whimper in a kiss.

He was hot and tight, twisting around my fingers and pulling them in. My cock was primed, edging up to skim along the back of his legs and leaving a silvery salt trail on the inside of his thigh. Jae reached down, ran his fingers through my leavings, and brought the damp tips to his mouth, making sure I could see every inch of his digits disappearing into his suckling kiss.

"Taste good, baby?" I murmured, finding the rise of his shoulder with my front teeth. He nodded and thrust back, spearing himself on my hand. It was difficult to get the condom on, but I kept Jae busy until I had rolled it all the way down. Jae, however, had other ideas on what busy meant.

Drawing his fingers out, he smeared his spit-and-seed damp hand over my cheek and whispered, "Feel better when you're inside of me."

Dribbling more lube over my cock, I pulled my hand away. Guiding the tip of my sex to his puckering rosette, I pushed in. Leaning my head back, I enjoyed the tight swirl of muscle closing in around me. I took my time, working deep enough to feel the spongy skin on my glans stretch to give way to his tight ass, then release with a silent sigh as I pulled back. I teased him for a few minutes, holding his hips still in my broad hands, and rocked my cock head in and then nearly out until he mewled.

"Now, *agi*." Jae's English disintegrated further, and he swore at me, a hot curse, probably imagining things my mother did with a goat or perhaps a chicken. My Korean didn't extend much further than lunch, *I love you,* and *God, that feels good*, none of which sounded like what Jae unfurled off his tongue.

In case, I didn't seem to grasp his impatience, he grabbed the back of my thighs, resting his weight against the couch to pull me in. His fingernails bit into my skin and I hissed at the sharp pain.

It hurt. Probably not as much as the raking lines on my shoulder, but enough of a sting to make me rethink being a tease. Chuckling at my lover's impatience, I plunged into his tense heat and set myself on fire.

Wildfires create their own weather. The air becomes a storm, whipping up high winds and lightning that arcs sideways, slamming into anything in its path. Sliding into Jae's body was like falling naked and drenched in gasoline into the middle of a firestorm. I knew my death would come, but the rush was pure adrenaline and it was an experience I couldn't live without.

He was home. Exotic and welcoming. A familiar mystery that drove me insane as I fought my instincts to cling too tightly when I was afraid he'd walk away or to throw my hands up in the air and run as far as I could when I didn't understand him. Nested deep into Jae, I felt my soul pour out into the furthest corners of my consciousness and fly.

Jae straightened, pulling me deeper. Resting my knees on the cushion's edge, I begin moving. Slowly at first, long, deep movements to pierce through his desire. His sweet spot clung to my cock, dragging over the ridge of my shaft. Snagging it again, I pushed down on the small of his back, closing his ass cheeks in so he could feel the burn rip through his body. Shuddering around me, Jae twisted and grabbed my hair, pulling my head forward until our mouths could touch.

We stayed that way, locked in a dual kiss of tongue and sex. I thrust harder, striking the sensitive nerves inside of him. His body went awry, unable to hold onto any semblance of restraint as I pounded the control right out of him. I felt his ass clench over my base, then a ripple under his skin telling me he was close to the edge.

I slid a hand over his hip bone, found his slender cock, brushed over its head, palming the seed it'd already leaked to rub it down his shaft. Jae hissed, startled at the too-sharp touch of his sex's yearning then curved into my grasp, fucking my palm when I tightened my fingers around him.

Neither of us had words. Not anymore. Our names became our only language, combined with whispering moans and the creaking slam of the couch against the living room floor when our efforts grew too wild for the furniture to handle. Jae's cock jumped in my hand, the first jerk of its coming, and I wrapped my arm around his chest to heave him back.

"Cole, so close," he panted. Jae dropped his head forward, and I scraped at the back of his neck, marbling the skin there with red welting lines.

Pistoning him on my cock, I drove into Jae, holding him aloft while milking him dry with my fingers. Slamming up into his heat, I continued to mark him, biting where I could reach and pulling at the flesh until I left something behind. I wanted to engrave a part of myself onto him… into him… and for the first time since he'd mentioned it, I realized I really wanted to have him without anything between us… no latex… no lies… no family pressures… nothing but the sound and feel of each other's bodies.

"*Saranghae, agi*," I whispered into his ear, nipping at the lobe. "I love you so much I never want to let you go."

He came. Violently. One second Jae was a writhing mess of passion on my lap, and the next he was filling my palm with his release. The hot spill on my hand sent me deeper into the firestorm, and I finally succumbed, letting my control become ash and my body swirl up into the fiery winds.

The world spun into a black whirlwind, and for a moment, I couldn't breathe. Choking on my own breath, I continued to plunge into him, drawing out every last gasp and mewling cry I could. Our torsos were slick with sweat, and other than the sounds of our limbs striking wet skin to wet skin, my ears were filled with my pounding heart and Jae's grunting release.

I unraveled, spilling out into my lover. The rush started up between my legs, catching my nerves unaware and twisting them about until I could no longer feel the difference between inside my body and without. Jae pressed back, his spine curved into the hollow of my belly and chest, and I sank into his curled form, bringing my arms up to hold him tight against me.

My cock continued to jerk, pumping its desire into Jae's slackening channel. No longer primed and painfully tight, he held me gently between his cheeks, undulating softly to pull me to the end. Kissing the tiny scores I'd left on his shoulders, I fell sideways into the cushions, taking him with me.

We lay there, still joined and doing nothing more than trying to catch our breaths. I made trails on Jae's belly with my fingers, using his sticky spill as it dried under my fingernails. He shifted, only enough to get comfortable, but my latex-wrapped cock slid free from him and I sighed, resigned to losing the feel of him around me.

"You know," I said when I finally could find my tongue in my mouth. "I don't think I spent enough time on your nipples." I tweaked one, and he hissed. "Huh, guess I spent enough time on them to make them tender. Give me a minute and I'll lick them better."

"I can't stay," Jae whispered. "I... didn't mean for this... to happen."

"What? *This*? *This* always happens, baby." A rush of cold air chewed up my body when Jae slid off of me. "I love *this*. I love *you*. *This* is what happens when people love each other."

"No, Cole-ah." Jae reached for his jeans, refusing to meet my eyes while he tugged them up over his slender hips. "I didn't come here to make love to you. I came here to tell you good-bye."

CHAPTER ELEVEN

I WASN'T going to have this conversation naked and with my cock wrapped in a semen-filled balloon. The condom came off with a tug. It ended up in the small trash can with all the stupid ad-cards magazines shoved in between their stapled pages. Still sticky from our joining, I peeled myself off the couch and tugged on my boxers, nearly bashing my head against the apothecary chest in my rush to get them on.

I didn't need to hurry. Jae wasn't going anywhere. In fact, he'd pulled on his jeans, then fallen back onto the couch, overlooking the fact that we'd spread most of our sex over its cushions.

Fallen back was too strong of a word. Looking down at him from the end of the sofa, his long body curled up tight in on itself, replete was a much better choice. Devastated was also a good choice, but I liked shattered best.

"I'm not going to let you say good-bye," I murmured, climbing onto the couch next to him. Lightly touching his arm with my fingertips, I ran them up over his elbow and down to his wrist. Working my fingers into his, I was shocked to find out how cold they were against the heat of my palm. "Jae, talk to me. What did you mean... *good-bye?*"

"I can't do this, *agi.*" He looked up at me, his eyes shiny with tears. They clung to his lashes, growing heavier as I watched. Then one fell, coursing down the cheek I'd kissed moments ago. Another followed, trailing down after its brother, and their combined weight formed a single drop, its heavy curve poised to fall from Jae's jaw.

"What did you mean?" I pressed, kissing away that tear before it fell onto his shoulder. I felt like I needed to keep his sorrow from falling onto his chest, away from where he kept his heart... away from where he kept his love for me. If I could do that, then I could keep him safe from whatever chased him... from whatever hurt him.

It was silly nonsense, and to spite the silent nightmares galloping through my mind, he smiled at the gentle brush of my lips across his face. He hated to be touched when emotional. He hated feeling weak and needing someone. I usually had to wait until he turned to me for comfort. In this instance, I wasn't going to wait.

Not while a blood-numbing frost spread through my chest and into my fears.

My own pussy-ass fears could wait. It was time to chase off Jae's boo-wigglies. Mine could stand by pulling on their own puds and wait their turn.

I pulled him into my arms, cradling him in my lap like I did his cat when she wanted attention. He sat there, legs pulled up under him, and let me rock him, even sighing when I stroked his hair. We stank and stuck together where our skin met, but that didn't matter. All that mattered was that our skin met, and his rigid, tense spine began to relax.

The sun set on us, lengthening the shadows in the living room. The pendant light I'd left on in the front hall gave me enough to see him, but it wouldn't have mattered if we'd been drenched in darkness. Half an hour into Jae's crumple, his threadbare control gave way, and his shoulders shook with the force of his sadness.

It hurt as much to hold him as to hear him say he'd meant to tell me good-bye. He'd held me when I'd fallen apart in the car after the worst dinner of my life. I could stand holding him through this. Even as every tear he shed burned down through me as if they were drops of molten metal on my plastic soul, he was worth the pain... worth the anguish. I told him as much, murmuring and rocking him while he cried. Jae cried ugly, shattering cascades of broken sounds and shuddering shakes in his bones.

"No matter what you're going through, Jae," I whispered into the shell of his ear. "I'm going to be here. Whatever you need, I'll make happen. It'll be okay. I promise you, baby, I'll make it okay."

The quakes subsided after an hour, but he remained in my arms, sagged over and hidden behind a veil of his black hair. I ached in places. My shoulder throbbed from my boxing bout with Bobby, and there were crawling shivers along my abused knees and thighs from the sex I'd had with Jae. A crick formed in my neck from holding Jae tightly, but I stayed still, letting him soak up whatever he needed from me.

If I died there—holding him while he cried—that would have been okay too.

"I came here to tell you good-bye... to tell you I couldn't... do this... be this anymore, but I can't. I can't do that. Not to you. Not to me."

"What happened? Was it your sister? Jae, we can work through this. You just have to trust me. Have some faith in me... in us."

"My mother called me." I barely heard him through the curtain of his hair and the occasional hiccup, but the dread his words caused in me was immediate.

A left turn in the conversation, but I followed behind him. "What did she say?"

"Uncle wants Jae-Su." He bent back, and I shifted to cradle him comfortably. Turning him slightly, I could see his face, a drawn beauty overburdened with other people's pressures. "She's lost her mind over it."

"Okay, much like playing Pictionary with you, I'm lost."

"Uncle Kim... Hyun-Shik's father... he wants to formally adopt Jae-Su. Make Su his *real* son. His *legal* son." Jae let loose another one of his shuddering exhales. "My mother isn't taking it well. She's... frantic. It's why Tiffany ran away. My mother went after her with scissors during an argument. Things up there aren't... good. It's too much, Cole-ah. My mother. My brother. Then Tiff finding out about us... it just became too much."

Okay, so his mother was crazy, but his however-many-times-removed cousin he called Uncle adopting Jae's older brother didn't make any sense. Said uncle didn't have too great of a track record. His daughter killed Hyun-Shik, his closeted gay son, and then murdered practically everyone else connected to Hyun-Shik. I'd sooner want my nuts cut off with a pair of dull, rusted toenail clippers than be part of that family.

"Back up a bit and explain that to me." I kissed the edge of his mouth when he gave me a slight frown. I was going to need a whiteboard to diagram the family's shit out. "The Jae-Su part. We'll work on the other shit later."

"Jae-Su is Uncle's son." Jae shrugged. "My mother... she was Uncle's lover. Now that Hyun-Shik is dead, he needs someone to step in as his heir, and since Grace is—"

"Wait a second." My stomach dropped, and I was almost sick from the thought. "Hyun-Shik was your... *brother*?"

"Not me." Jae rolled his eyes at me. "That's sick, even for you. Just Jae-Su. Tiff and I had the same father. I don't know who Ree's father is. I don't know if my *mother* knows who Ree's father is. Didn't I tell you this? I thought I told you this."

I'd not liked what I'd found out about his cousin while investigating Hyun-Shik's murder. He was a manipulative asshole who fucked an underage Jae, then pimped him out to a gentlemen's club to be a dancer when Jae's aunt kicked Jae out of the house for being gay. I almost would have kissed his sister Grace when I found out she'd killed him if she hadn't been trying to kill me at the time.

"No, I can honestly say this is the first time you've ever told me this." Jae's mother was kind of a whore, but that I kept to myself. Instead I focused back on the conversation. "So your aunt... Grace's mom... knows that your mom... um—"

"Had Uncle's son?" Jae sniffed. "Yeah, it's why she hates our family. Uncle is my mother's cousin, remember? They were... close when they were in Seoul, and she came to work for his family. My mother got pregnant, and when Uncle moved here, he moved her too."

Now it made sense why Jae was American-born and his brother Korean. "Is Jae-Su older than Hyun-Shik?"

"No." He bit his lip, thinking. Jae rubbed at his face. If anything, his hands seemed to spread the tired from his eyes down to his mouth and cheeks. "Younger. A year, I think. Maybe less."

"So your mom was—" It was a delicate conversation, one I didn't think I could maneuver through without damaging Jae's sensibilities. "Okay, your mom had an affair with a married guy and got knocked up. Now your uncle... third cousin... whatever... wants his grown son to step into the family business 'cause the original model is dead?"

"Yes." Jae nodded. "Uncle's sent my mother money to support Jae-Su. Now, she feels like he's being taken away from her... and she's going to lose whatever hold she has left over Uncle... and probably any money he'd been sending her. I don't know... it's *complicated*. How do I tell her I love men? Now? When it looks like I'm the only son she has left?"

Fucking hell. Jae's mother already had a tenuous hold on reality. Losing a meal ticket would send her over the edge. Losing Jae, however, would kill me.

"So you came here to break it off with me." Made sense in Jae's mind. My guts weren't too fond of the plan, but I had to admit to his logic. "Going to be honest with you, I'm kinda glad you couldn't go through with it. What changed your mind?"

"I want to be happy, Cole-ah." Resting his cheek on my arm, he stared up into my face. The old-fashioned lights along the walk were on, pouring a soft yellow glow through the living room windows. It softened the agony lines on his face, although not as much as the smile he gave me when he touched my face with his fingertips. "I want to be happy with you. I *want*... you've made me want things I can't have, and now, when I feel like I'm losing everything... that I *have* to lose everything, you're still here. Holding me. Loving me. And that hurts me, Cole-ah. As much as I love having you, it breaks me inside."

It was time to be brave. Even if it broke me. I had to be... a man.

"Do you want me to let you go?"

Jae's guileless brown gaze raked over my face, searching for something I didn't know if he'd find. If he wanted me to let him go, I would. I was tired too. But if he needed me to be, I'd be strong enough to walk away. Or at least walk until he couldn't see me. Then, I'd be able to stumble into the broken glass he'd left behind for me to fall on.

"No, *agi*." Jae twisted in my lap, straddling my thighs. Placing his palms on my cheek, he kissed me.

After months of having him in my life, his kisses could still take my breath away.

When he was done, I decided breathing was really highly overrated.

"So, no, then?" I cocked my head, staring up at the pretty-faced, feral man who could only tell me he loved me in Korean. "Because I'm telling you, once you say *No, Cole, don't let me go*, that's a done deal. You're never going to be able to get rid of me."

He brought his lips close to mine so I could feel his mouth moving against mine and said, "No, Cole-ah, don't *ever* let me go."

This time, it was my kiss that stole the air from our lungs, and Jae somehow ended up underneath me and pinned to the couch. His hands were in my hair, twisting about and pulling me closer, refusing to let me up. Our tongues fought their own battle, ignorant of the explosive sex we'd already shared. My cock stirred, telling me it was ready for round two. I ignored it.

Sometimes, it was all about the kissing and cuddles. Especially when a certain feral Korean needed to be held.

"I need to be this man with you, Cole-ah. A man who loves men, and it scares me. It scares me so deep inside, I am cold from the fear of it, but," he whispered in the deepening darkness, "I want to come home to you. When we're here, I feel... *safe*. I feel wanted. You make me doubt when I'm happy because I feel like I can't hold it inside of me. Being with you is like... my soul coming with happiness. Does that make any sense?"

"It makes total sense." I bit his chin, getting him to laugh. "If it makes you feel any better, you make my soul come too."

"Good to know I am not the only one, then." He laughed again, a sharp sound but freer than I'd heard in a long time. "What am I going to do? My mother... this would kill her. I know it. Even if I'm not... Jae-Su, she depends on me."

Mostly, I thought she used him for money, but that was my take on their relationship. "Is Tiffany going to stay with you?"

"No." Jae shook his head. "She has to go back. She has school. But my mother, she's not well."

"If she wanted to stay... she can stay here with me... with us," I offered, and even in the shadows, Jae's glance drizzled hot sarcasm over my sincerity. "I'm serious. Hell, there's enough room for both of your sisters. If you think your mom can't be trusted with them anymore, we'll move them in. Whatever you need."

"And if I need to move someplace large enough for my sisters but not here, you'd be okay with that too?"

"No." Making a face, I gave myself points for honesty. I wasn't going to let myself feel elation. It burbled up from some fragment of hope I couldn't seem to kill over the past week. Damned hope didn't spring eternal. It grew like fucking kudzu in places I couldn't reach. "But if that's what you need, then yeah, okay. I'll do that with you too."

Jae would need time. He was always cautious, warily easing into something new after viewing it from all angles. The only time he lost himself was behind a camera... and when we were making love. As passions went, they were limited, but he threw everything he had into those moments. Seeing him lose control... and knowing I'd brought him there... fed my ego like nothing else did.

"You make me feel like being nothing to my family is worth it. I have to get used to that. I have to... learn how that feels." He sniffed at himself and made a face. "Can... you make me some tea? Or should I shower first? I smell."

"How about if you hop into the shower and I'll bring you up your tea?" Leering at him, I waggled my eyebrows. "Or maybe we can just go have hot piggy-bunny sex in the shower, and then I can make you tea?"

"Piggy-bunnies do not have hot sex," Jae grumbled, sliding off of me. I missed his warmth, but he was right. We were odiferous.

"If anything should have hot sex, it should be piggy-bunnies." I stood, hugging him from behind and biting the velvety skin of his nape. "Bacon and rabbits. Both very conducive to the smexy. Come on. I'll even show you where they got the word porking from."

JAE left me with kisses and a promise to call me. He took my heart with him too, but that I didn't mind. The Dr Pepper shirt I was beginning to miss, but he'd claimed it as his. He also left me the cat. The morning dawned, and other than my muscles aching from being stretched over Jae's body, I was feeling pretty good.

"Don't give me that look," I told Neko when she came down to investigate my boots. "Your daddy came by. Fed you *again*, like you needed it. You're going to sleep off that fat belly. You're not even going to know I'm gone."

She miaowed a complaint at me. It could have been about anything from the price of salmon to the state of my socks. With Neko, one never knew.

Bobby opened the door without knocking. He had a key and wasn't too shy to use it. Leaning over to scritch the cat, he looked up the length of my legs, raking his gaze up my body until he got to my face, then smirked. "You had a booty call."

"*You* have booty calls," I grumbled, sitting down on the hallway bench to pull on my boots. "I make love. Especially where Jae's concerned."

"Did you call him?" The foyer light caught on the few silver strands in Bobby's close-shorn hair. "Or did he call you?"

"Neither," I admitted. "He was waiting for me on the front porch."

"So, he pretty much knew it was a sure thing, then?" Bobby buffed his nails on his chest, posturing against the banister. His bulk blocked out most of the light I needed to see my shoelaces. I pinched him in the ass. I couldn't get much meat through his jeans, but it was enough of a squeeze to get him to move. He shifted, but only to block more of my light.

"Dick."

"Asshole," Bobby countered. "You guys good, then? Kissed up and made it all better?"

"No, not… better." I cocked my head to look at him. "Different. We're in a different place now. He's struggling still, but at least now he knows I'm there with him. It feels… stronger. More solid. My insides don't have tentacles in them anymore."

"Just don't get hurt, kid. Jae's too pretty for me to kick his teeth in. I'd feel bad." Bobby's rough, handsome face softened, and he smiled crookedly at me. "But could you hurry it up, Princess? We've got a woman to interrogate."

"We're not interrogating her," I reminded Bobby. "I just want to ask Madame Sun a few questions and give her my condolences about Vivian. I tried calling her, but it goes straight to a messaging service. They told me she'll be in but isn't seeing anyone. She's probably taking it pretty hard."

Koreatown was becoming my second home. If my cases kept circling back to the Wilshire area, I was going to have to give a zip code discount. During the day, the area was a bit more businesslike, stashing away its glitter. Approaching early evening, the district was beginning to loosen up with small crowds of people walking to bars and restaurants.

We'd just passed by a twenty-four-hour dumpling soup place when Bobby hit me up for some information.

"Why am I coming with you, again? Other than you probably can't drive because your dick's been peeled off and it hurts to pee."

"I wanted to see if you could ask anyone who works around Sun's place if they'd seen anything funky," I explained. "Kill two birds with one stone. I need to see if she knew about Eun Joon's pregnancy or if Gyong-Si is connected to May Choi somehow but mostly to extend my condolences about Vivian. She's probably not in the mood to talk much, if she's there at all."

"If she's not, then you owe me some lunch." Bobby steered around a lumbering MTS bus.

"If she is, I'll still buy you lunch."

"Nothing Asian. I want something with meat in it."

"Dude, Korean food is practically all meat. They even put meat in the damned pancakes." My stomach rumbled at the thought of a steaming *kimchijeon*. "You have to *ask* for stuff without meat."

Bobby stretched his mouth out to a satisfied half smile. "Excellent. Then Korean's fine."

"I should have gotten some flowers." Fuck, it was the one rule Jae hammered into my head. Actually, it was pretty much a universal rule. Someone dies, you bring flowers. Or a casserole. When Rick died, I had enough frostbitten casseroles in my freezer to make pucks for an entire hockey league. "Do you give the boss flowers? Or do you ask for the family's information?"

"I'd go with the family," Bobby suggested. "Good way to find out if Vivian was seeing anyone too. She might have been dating someone connected to this. For all we know, she's hooked up with someone who's using Sun's clients for easy marks."

It was a good plan. A very good plan. Except for one little hiccup. By the time we got to Madame Sun's salon, the cops had beaten us there, and someone from the coroner's office was wheeling a dead body out of the building on a squeaky gurney.

CHAPTER TWELVE

"OKAY, Princess," Bobby sneered playfully as he parked. "Looks like you killed another one."

"Fuck you," I muttered, getting out of his truck.

Unlike Gyong-Si's crayon-bright spa bungalow, Madame Sun saw her clients in a professional building off of Irolo and Wilshire. It was one of those tall blue glass buildings that made people nervous during an earthquake, casting a long enough shadow onto the street that the cheap fast-food restaurants living under its skirt never saw the light of day. The smell of garbage and fried potatoes greeted us when we hit the sidewalk, and I'd gone about four steps before one of Los Angeles's finest stopped me.

She was a pert-bodied woman, a California blond with a tan and her hair pulled back in a ponytail under the uncomfortable hat some asshole bean counter thought would look sharp with the equally uncomfortable ill-fitting uniform. I could literally smell the new coming off of her, a blood-in-the-water scent most veteran cops sneered at, forgetting a time when they'd not worn the creases out of their street blues.

As I expected, Bobby's sneer grew wider, especially when she squared off her shoulders and approached us, her hand on the butt of her weapon.

"You remember being that young?" he asked, jerking his chin at her.

"Remember? Fuck, I still am." I met his smirk with one of my own. "You're the old man. Not me."

"Sir… I'm going to have to ask you—" She'd got that much out of her mouth when a familiar face broke away from the pack of cops milling around the building's entrance and hailed Bobby.

"Dawson!"

The last time I'd seen Detective Dell O'Byrne, she'd busted my chops about one of Grace Kim's victims. A tanned, lean woman with strong Latino features and dark, sharp eyes, she was a cop's cop: no-nonsense and blunt. A cop either pulled their own weight or got out of her way. She was the kind of woman one expected to be wearing a bat cowl or wielding a golden lasso. If she were a man, Bobby would have been in love. As it was, she made me seriously consider switching teams.

If only she didn't dislike me so much.

Her long legs crossed the sea of concrete separating us. "Stand aside, Martin. He's one of ours."

"Yes, sir," the blonde mumbled, stepping back.

"You can shoot the other one, though." O'Byrne gave me the eye, a smile tugging at her mouth. "Dawson, don't I have enough trash around my crime scene, you gotta drag in some more?"

"Princess, you remember Dell, don't you?" Bobby gave the detective a quick, manly hug, the tight shoulder to shoulder pat he'd give any of his fellow cops. "Good to see you, kid."

"Yeah, we know each other." She looked down her nose, assessing me for misdeeds. "I almost arrested him for murder once."

"Didn't do it." I grinned, holding up my hands.

Bobby glanced around, taking in the swarm of blues. "Aren't you a bit out of your district, O'Byrne?"

"Nope, got transferred in last night." The detective shrugged and jerked her thumb toward the building. "Jenkins dropped dead at his desk yesterday, and the brass decided to expedite my request to transfer up. It's closer to home, so I won't have to fight the 405 every day."

"Jenkins's dead?" Bobby whistled under his breath. "Shit, that's a shock. He was so close to retirement too."

"How is it a shock?" I stared at Bobby like he was insane. From what I'd remembered of the man, Jenkins's hands were yellow from smoking, and he didn't eat anything that wasn't deep-fried or covered in mayonnaise. "The man was a walrus. He rolled his chair into the bathroom and peed into the urinal from it, then wheeled back."

"Respect for the fallen, McGinnis. Even the walruses," O'Byrne chastised me but gave me a wink to soften the blow. "I caught a 217 here. The intended vic's son was in the bathroom when his mother was attacked. He grabbed one of those brass urns people put on their lobby tables and beat the shit out of the guy's head. Couple of bashes and our assault and burglary suspect becomes a 419. EMTs pronounced him DOA as soon as they hit the floor. Coroner just got here."

"Shit, that's rough. Is the mother okay?" Bobby glanced at the gurney being loaded up into the death-mobile. "I can see that guy's not."

"She's a bit shaken up." Tapping lightly at my arm with her notebook, Dell asked, "My question is, what are you two doing here? Can't be for the fabulous cuisine, unless there's something about that Burger King I don't know about."

"Nah, Princess here's got a client in the building." He grunted when I nudged him in the ribs with my elbow.

"Let me guess. Your client's Park Hyuna Sun?" Dell blew out her cheeks when I nodded. "Why did I know that?"

"Because the universe hates you?" I suggested, and she very unprofessionally flipped me off. "Are you guys done with her? I'd like to see her. Her assistant was murdered yesterday."

"Yeah." Dell consulted her notes. "Vivian Na. Drive-by through a street-facing window in a café. Wong caught that one."

"So did I." I made a face back at her when she grimaced dramatically. "I was meeting her to talk about Madame Sun's case. Next thing I know, she's bled out and there's other vics on the ground. I'd like to see her if I could. I was the last one to see her assistant alive. I'd like her to know it was quick."

"Let me see what I can do." O'Byrne became all cop, curtly nodding. "Follow me. We've got her and the son in a conference room on the third floor. Let me clear it with her, and *maybe* you can talk to her."

We cooled our heels for only a few minutes. In that time, Bobby got a proposition from a tranny dressed in a low-neckline aqua sequin dress, and I'd been given a plastic daisy and a mini rubber duck by an old woman waiting for the bus. The tranny had a five o'clock shadow thick enough to grate cheese on, and his dress was so short, his dirty mud-gray BVDs flashed every time he took a step.

All in all, I scored with the daisy and the duck.

"McGinnis!" Dell poked her head out of the building's side entrance. "Come on. You've got five minutes!"

I hurried. For all I knew, she had an Amazonian spear she could chuck from where she was standing and pin me down into the cement. I wouldn't put it past her.

Bobby stayed behind to talk shop. Any plan for him to wander the halls and hit up the other businesses for information was blown. O'Byrne had a uniform lead me to a glass-enclosed conference room on the second floor. It was one of those rent-to-impress places a building had for its tenants to use.

From the looks of the faded carpet, there wasn't much impressing to be had.

At some point in its life, the place had been a spotless, gleaming edifice of glass, polish, and swank. Now, it sagged, a tired old woman whose breasts brushed the tops of her knees. Still, someone had tried to keep her spirits up, layering a spackle of thick, bright white paint to hide her wrinkles, but her age was carved too deep into her skin.

The conference room held three occupants, a grim-faced uniform cop, the middle-aged Korean man I'd seen waiting for Madame Sun, and the grand dame herself. From the grief pouring from every inch of skin on her face, I suddenly wished I'd bought out a flower shop, if only to give her a little joy.

Joy was going to be a long time coming to the droop-shouldered old woman I saw curled up in a conference chair at the far end of the room.

Madame Sun had aged at least twenty years since I'd last seen her. Her skin was a pasty gray, caved in with deep lines around her eyes and mouth. Crinkled cracks formed in her thick makeup, the edges flaking off onto the dark table, and her clothes were slightly askew, as if she'd been tugging at her sleeves or hem. Sun's helmet hair sat unevenly on her head, the right side a bit higher than the left, and she sat nearly still except for the frenetic play of her fingers twisting her rings and bracelets.

Her son didn't seem to be in much better shape.

He stood when I approached, automatically reaching for my hand when I held it out for a shake. His fingers were cold against my palm, and they shook slightly when he came in for the grip. His eyes were as red as his mother's, his long lashes spiked with drying salt.

I'm sorry seemed like such a small thing to say, a single spit of water being dropped into a portal to hell. I said it anyway, and he thinned his lips, forcing his emotions back down his throat.

"Thank you for coming, Mr. McGinnis," he murmured. "I'm James Bahn."

"Madame Sun's son," I acknowledged. "You picked her up at my office."

"Yes." His nod was curt, his eyes drifting over to his mother's crumpled form. "The detective said you wanted to speak to us... and my mother... Vivian."

"I'm sorry for your loss." I'd hated hearing that at the small memorial service we'd had for Rick after I got out of the hospital. Even two months after the shooting, his death gutted me. Loss was the stupidest fucking word to describe the emptiness inside of me, and here I was, parroting out an ingrained clichéd phrase like I was whoring for a cracker. Clearing my throat, I tried for a more personal touch. "Did you know Vivian long?"

"Long?" James's expression churned together his grief with immense confusion. "I've known her all her life. She was my... sister."

JAMES and the uniform left me alone with Madame Sun. The older woman murmured a need for tea and privacy, and her son immediately jumped to action. Before taking the cop with him, James put his fingers over his mother's and kissed her temple, reassuring her that he would take care of her. From the slight cuts on his hands from the urn he'd smashed over the intruder's head, I'd say he had a good start.

Sliding out one of the leather conference room chairs, I sat down next to Madame Sun, angling my seat to face her. The cushion squeaked as I lowered myself into it, nearly rocking back before it adjusted to take my weight. Amid the creaks and squalling, I searched for someplace to start. There were so many things going through my mind, I couldn't find the one thread leading to the core of the Gordian knot James had tossed into my lap.

I didn't have to search for long. Madame Sun not only found the end but began knitting me a mental sweater to wear with the tangled threads of her past few weeks. First, she had to ask the one question that bubbled up every time someone died unexpectedly. I know. It was the first one I'd asked when I found out Rick truly was gone.

"Did she suffer?" If anything, Sun's hands were colder than her son's, and they clutched mine with a frenzied strength. "You were the last one to see her. Did she know? Was it...."

"She never knew," I murmured, patting her shaking hands. "It was very sudden. I'm sorry I didn't come sooner. I should have come to you that morning. I'm sorry."

"No, no. It is okay." Her hair bobbed when she shook her head, throwing the carefully sculpted curls further out of place. "You didn't know. No one... really knew. She was... always troubled about being my daughter. Even now, her dying has left behind problems. I loved her, but... my daughter was hard to like. Nothing was good enough. She always needed the best. I gave her a job because she needed to work, but... she never liked doing it. She wanted to do other things."

"I wanted to ask you a few questions." I tested the waters. Now that I knew Vivian Na was Madame Sun's daughter, her death was even more intimately connected to the other murders in my head. If Wong didn't see it, then he wasn't as smart as I thought he was. "If you don't mind."

"No, please, ask," Sun sniffed, wiping at the tears cutting deeper through her makeup. "The police... they don't have any idea who killed her. And today... that man... he looked like someone who would know Vivian's boyfriend. She had many, and none of them were good. This last one... Park Hong Chul... he is the worst of them. I thought maybe that man upstairs belonged to Hong Chul's gang. They are... *beom joe ja...* criminals."

"He's Korean, then? The man who attacked you?" I scribbled Park Hong Chul in my notes, drawing a line from his name to Vivian's.

"Yes, but I don't know him. Vivian might have. I wonder if he was the one who—" She swallowed, her throat wobbling. "If he was the one who shot her, then I am glad Jin-Woo... James... killed him. I am sorry my son has blood on his hands, but... he is a good son. That man would have killed me... like he probably killed my daughter. It is too much of a coincidence, yes?"

It was. There were too many bodies piling up with matching bullet wounds. Theoretically. Wong hadn't come back with any news about ballistics or eyewitnesses claiming a one-armed man fled the scene, but it seemed like it wasn't only my gut saying things were connected.

"Yeah, it's too much of a coincidence, Madame Sun." Probing further, I asked, "Do you know who Vivian was going to meet up with the night she died?"

"Maybe James? Sometimes she would have dinner with her girlfriends and James would go along."

"Could she have been going to go see her boyfriend?"

"No, she broke it off with Hong Chul. Do you think he might have killed her because she left him?"

From what I remembered of Vivian Na, she'd been dressed to kill, not be killed. A woman didn't dress up like that to have a cup of coffee with a detective. She was definitely out on the prowl. Either to catch herself another guy or perhaps to coax the one she'd tossed aside to come to heel. Or I could have been totally off-base and that was what she always wore to a family dinner.

"I don't know," I admitted slowly. "Was Hong Chul violent to her?"

"He is a *criminal*," she spat, rage edging away her sorrow for a brief moment. "She would never talk about him to me. Everything was… *it's none of your business* and *you don't need to know*, but there were times when I would see bruises on her arm. She would say she hurt herself, but I *know* he had something to do with it."

"I have to ask you, Madame Sun. Why didn't you tell me Vivian was your daughter?" I needed to get her to focus without trampling all over her grief.

"She… wasn't my husband's." As shame went, Sun's went deep. She crumbled in on herself, nearly folding in half. Her voice cracked under the weight of her pain, and I reached over to place my arm across her shoulders.

"You don't have to—"

"No, no," she sniffled. "She was… a mistake. *I* made a mistake, but she paid for it."

"I'm sure you did your best." I hated to admit it, but crying women could pretty much write a check and cash in my soul. Sun's tears stung me.

"I did *nothing*," she insisted. "My husband… James's father left me, and I couldn't raise two children. My sister took Vivian as her own. Vivian found out I was her mother five years ago. That was when she came here. I asked her to give me a chance to be her mother. She wanted to be *here* but not with me. I was just… convenient, but I tried. I would give anything to have her back with me. Even if she hated me, she was still my daughter."

"How did James get along with her?"

"James?" Sun looked confused. "Fine. He liked her. She was good with men. Even her brother… she was nice to him." Sun went back to twisting her rings. "They grew up thinking they were cousins.

They were never close, but when she came over to live here, he was good to her. A true brother. He's a good son."

"He defended you today." Holding her wrist to stop her nervous wringing, I stroked her papery skin to calm her. "That's the sign of a good son... a good man. You should be proud of who you raised. Do you know how Vivian met Hong Chul? Maybe at a bar? Someplace where he hangs out? It might be a good place to start looking for him."

"Oh no, she met him here." Her mouth twisted into a sour wrinkle. "He brought his grandfather for a reading. I told you about him. He was Bhak Bong Chol, the man who died in his office... from a heart attack."

Shit, the Gordian knot just retangled itself. Park Hong Chul would have motive to kill Vivian Na if he was upset over their breakup, and there definitely could have been family dynamics to lead to his grandfather's death, but everything was too nebulous. Plus, there was nothing to indicate his grandfather's death had been anything *but* natural.

I also had nothing to connect Choi and Lee. Since Choi and Gyong-Si shared the same last name, there could have been something there, and my instincts told me Lee wasn't carrying her husband's bundle of joy. She'd probably fallen for Gyong-Si's manipulations and found herself *enceinte*.

I was stuck with two suspects, Gyong-Si and Hong Chul, and with only the slimmest of motives when I had them. Now wasn't the time to press Madame Sun on Gyong-Si. I'd have to wait until she'd had time to deal with her daughter's murder.

"That man... the one James hit... he was going to kill me. I know it. James stopped him." She met my gaze, her eyes drowning in her tears. "Do you think it's over? The deaths? Was Vivian the last one? Do you think?"

"I don't know that either," I confessed. "If the man who attacked you today is connected to Vivian's, the cops will find that out."

"The police... they don't agree this is all together... all connected. How can they not see this?" The tears began again, turning the pancake chasms on her face to rivers. "You have to find out who killed her, Cole-sshi. Someone *killed* her. How could they just… *take* her from me? Before I had a chance to make… it all better? I didn't have a chance to get her to love me. Isn't that what all mothers want? For their children to love them?"

I left Madame Sun in her son's hands. James had nothing to add. Finding out Vivian was his sister had been a surprise, but he'd accepted her into his life because it made his mother happy. A good son, his mother'd said. The perfect Korean son.

It made me wonder what secrets he was hiding.

I SPENT the rest of the next day chasing down dead-end leads and paying bills. Wong wasn't answering any of my calls about the case, and I was hitting a dead end on Gyong-Si. There was nothing on the Internet about why he left Korea, or if there was, it wasn't in any language I could read. By midafternoon, Martin's kids hit the office for a couple of hours, bringing with them a blueberry pie their grandmother, Claudia, baked for me. I thanked them profusely, and I got a patented Claudia smirk in return.

"Are you kidding? It's all Nana's doing," Sissy snorted at me. "If she doesn't go back to work soon, we're all going to be rolling around like Violet Beauregarde."

"That was my favorite book as a kid…." I trailed off when I caught the looks of confusion the teens threw me.

"There's a book?" Mo cocked his head. "I liked the first movie. The remake was kind of weird, but hey, a river full of chocolate. Nothing wrong with that."

"Yeah, um… okay." I waved them off, feeling old. "I'm going to take my pie and go home now."

People were starting to flow back into the neighborhood, coming home from their day jobs or from carting their children to soccer. The granola chick coffee shop across the street from my office was having a brisk business, the early tide of bearded hipsters and their fuzzy-armpitted girlfriends taking up most of the café's outdoor seating. A particularly enterprising beanpole of a man had set up his guitar in the hopes of filling his case with tips. From the screeching twang coming from his instrument, he'd be there a long time before he made enough to get a single cup of joe.

Juggling the pie, I hopscotched over my front lawn, taking note of where the newly laid sod wasn't catching. One of the bushes blown to ribbons by Grace Kim seemed to be thriving, sending out green shoots from its stubby branches. I patted it as I went by. The landscapers wanted to yank it up by its roots, but I'd wanted to give it a chance. We were both survivors, although from the looks of things, the bush was doing better than I was. My side ached a bit from sitting in traffic, and I promised my tense back and legs a run once I fed the cat and put away my pie.

That all went to shit when a car door slammed behind me and I turned my shoulders to see who it was, still tuned up to violence so soon after the shooting that took Claudia down. The sedan parked by my curb had the look of a rental car, a nondescript beige two-door chunk of metal no one with any personality would buy for themselves.

The car quickly faded from my attention. No, what held me firmly to the ground, clutching a plastic-film-wrapped pie as if it were my long-lost teddy bear, was the young man coming around the trunk side of the vehicle. The face he wore was a bit like mine but, more importantly, nearly an exact echo of Mike's.

Lankier than Mike, he probably stood a few inches taller as well. Dressed in Doc Martens, jet-black jeans, and a gray T-shirt with the words *L'Arc-en-Ciel* on it, he would have blended in with the hipsters across the street, except that his jaw-length red-streaked ebony hair was clean and his chin was bare of any scruff. I couldn't see a patch of his milky skinned arms through the tattoos running up from his wrists and disappearing under his short sleeves. They were bright, blending seamlessly from one image to the next, and in some cases, they shimmered together until I couldn't tell what exactly I was looking at.

He drew closer, close enough to see we had the same mouth, and I fought the urge to throw the pie in his face. It was a good pie. No one could bake like Claudia, but right in that moment, it would have been worth it. I wasn't ready for him. Not after the week I'd just had... the evening I'd had the night before and the day I'd spent wading through blood and other people's dirty laundry.

"Hello, Kenjiro." He slowed his approach, drawing up in front of me. It was impossible to read his face, but a hint of friendliness ghosted through his eyes. "I'm—"

"Yeah, I know who you are. I just wasn't… expecting you." That was the understatement of the year, but as Bobby would say, time to pull up my big-boy panties and man up. Jerking my head toward the front door of my house, I said, "Well, since you're here, Ichiro, might as well come in for some pie, and you can tell me why you came over."

CHAPTER THIRTEEN

HE WASN'T what I expected. Actually, he was *nothing* like I expected. The tattoos, the silver rings on his fingers, and the bad boy cut of his scarlet-sooty hair was... odd and so not a part of the image I'd had in my mind for my mother's youngest son. I wasn't sure what to say as he watched me cut into the pie Claudia baked for me, pursing his mouth at its bright blue color. It was too odd to see parts of me and Mike on someone else.

"I don't think I've ever had fresh blueberries before." His English was nearly flawless but with an odd cant to it, different than Jae's. It wasn't hard to understand him. Just different. I wondered if our mother sounded like him. If I would have grown up listening to the peculiar cadence and somehow mimicked it in my own speech. "Not in a pie. It smells good."

"Claudia, my... she's kind of like an aunt... made it," I replied. The whole scene was too domestic to be real. I plated a couple of slices, put them on one of the dining trays Jae liked to use, and pulled two cups of coffee from the brewing pot. I tossed a handful of the sugar packets and creamer cups I'd stolen from the front office onto the tray and jerked my head toward the living room. "Head over that way."

Neko decided to join us. I'd say it was my stellar company, but the truth was, she liked sucking up creamer from the cups. I opened one for her, set it on the chest, and stroked her fur while Ichiro mixed up his coffee. He chucked her under the chin when she went over to investigate his coffee and smiled when the damned cat declined his advances, returning to her own creamer.

I flipped on the sound system, keeping the volume low. I skipped over the playlists until I found one of Jae's and felt the tension slip down my shoulders and away from my back at the now-familiar burble of Korean playing through the house. Letting G-Dragon howl about getting his cray on, I settled back down, moving Neko's tail out of my pie.

"I like that you named her Neko." He leaned back, cradling his cup and studying the pie.

"She came that way." I probably sounded like an asshole, and I still wasn't sure where the whole *come on in and let me give you pie* courtesy came from. I blamed Jae. God knows, I've never been the crinoline skirts and pearls type. 'Course I'd never say that about him... out loud. "We're working on our relationship. I expect her to be a pet. She expects me to be her slave. We're trying to find a common ground."

"I wish you luck with that, brother." Ichiro saluted me with his coffee cup.

"Yeah, about that brother thing—" The pie didn't hold my interest, which was a shame because I had a weakness for blueberries. Okay, a weakness for pie in general, but blueberries were up there. "How long are we supposed to have polite conversation before you tell me why you showed up here?"

"Depends." He pursed his mouth, thinking a moment. "Are we going by American or Japanese standards?"

"How long would this shit take Japanese style?"

"We'd probably be here until one of us is a grandfather if we do this Japanese style. I say let's go American... how long is that?" Ichiro grinned, and damned if he didn't look like me right at that moment.

"Pretty much you thank me for the pie and then we get on with it."

"Thank you, *oniisan,* for the pie. It is delicious." He saluted me with a forkful of blueberries. Chewing around the mouthful, he continued, "So where do we start?"

"You know I don't want you here... didn't want you here." I exhaled, confused and unable to unravel the emotions inside of me. Pushing my plate away, I leaned back and rubbed my face. I went for blunt honesty. It pissed me off that he was a nice guy. I wanted him to be an uptight fucking asshole, but the whole genial tattooed guy thing was throwing me off. I *wanted* to be pissed off. "I don't know what to... do with you. I'm sorry. I'm just not ready for this. For you."

"Mikio told me you were direct. Actually, he said you were a blunt ass." He cocked his head, catching my rueful smirk. "Ah, you probably don't even think of him by that name. Mike, then. It's hard to think of him with that name. I don't think of you as Cole. All my life, you've been Kenjiro."

"So you... knew about us, then?"

I wasn't sure how I felt about our mother talking us up to someone else, much less to a brother she'd had with another man. She couldn't have known anything about me. As far as I knew, she and my father had no contact. She'd literally packed her shit up and walked out of the door without looking back. The last time she saw me, I'd probably been spitting up formula and couldn't see anything but blurry shapes.

"I knew." Ichiro nodded. "She talked about you sometimes. Even if she had to leave you behind, she thought about you. So, I thought about you."

"I'm... sorry she passed." That was a truth. No matter who Ryoko McGinnis-Tokugawa was to me, she'd been *his* mother.

"It was hard," Ichiro admitted softly. "She was never really strong. And when the cancer came, I think she just gave in to it. In a lot of ways, she was more a child to me than I was to her. Delicate—that's the word for her. My father is very traditional. I think that made life easier for her. I, on the other hand, am the opposite. He's probably trying to figure out where I came from and how the hell he can return me there."

A woman like that wouldn't have survived my father. My stepmother, Barbara, could at least hold her own with the dick. She even matched him punch for punch in the asshole department. Ryoko wouldn't have stood a chance.

"Is that why she left us? Left my father? It was too hard over here?" It was the most pounding question in my head. I couldn't fathom a woman abandoning her sons. It was what I'd struggled with ever since I'd answered Ichiro's phone call a few weeks ago. The *why* of it bothered me, nestled into my brain, and grew burrs to hook into my thoughts.

"Living wasn't easy for her." He reached for his cup and cradled it, looking more like he needed to do something with his hands rather than needing a drink. "When a couple divorces… where I am from… one parent assumes custody of the children. Usually, the other parent doesn't have contact with the children again. Or rarely. You are… registered… with a family's lineage. The absent parent doesn't have any say over you anymore."

"They just walk out of their kids' lives?"

"Yes, because they no longer are connected… bound to the children. It's very ritualistic in ways. Mother would have followed that." Ichiro picked a blueberry from his dish and chewed on it, sipping his coffee afterward. "Even if she didn't want to, she would have left you to your father because that's what we do. She was very Japanese. That's all I can guess."

"Did my father do something? Or did she just fall out of love with him?"

"I don't know. She never spoke about your father or why she left him. But knowing my mother—our mother—she wouldn't be able to survive outside of her own place." Ichiro shook his head. "She wasn't strong, Kenjiro… Cole. Physically. Emotionally. She always needed someone. In many ways, she was like a little girl. Your father's career would have been hard on her. I can't imagine her surviving here, but she carried you with her. So much so that I knew you."

He slicked back the sleeve of his T-shirt, exposing more of his right arm for me to see. The pale of his skin was banished beneath vivid colors and deep, shadowy blacks. Covered from shoulder to wrist, his arm was a collage of three animals and natural elements.

An Asian stylized rat sat on his upper arm, its fur dotted with bright pink cherry blossom petals. Farther down, a battle-armored horse ran strong past his elbow, its tail flowing down to tangle around the ends of a brilliant-hued rooster. Interspersed between the animals were more flowers, strange, wide-frilled petals of blues and yellows.

"This is our mother's birth year. I had this done for her. My art, but my teacher did the ink." Pointing to the rat, he smiled again, softer and more wistful than before. "She was very young when she went away with your father. Not quite eighteen and, really, not very ratlike. Most Rat Year people adapt easily to new environments. Our mother... didn't. She couldn't stand to be away from her home. I think it's why she finally left."

He spoke of a woman I never knew existed. As far as I knew, Ryoko McGinnis died on my birth day or soon after that. To my knowledge, she'd never held me... never spoke my name out loud. Now here was a man with my mouth and Mike's eyes telling me she thought of me... thought of my brother... even after abandoning us to our father.

"The horse—that is Mikio. From what I can tell, he's truly a Horse. Very energetic. Very cunning. I like him. He seems strong."

"You haven't met him?" More than a bit confused, I looked at a brother I'd never imagined having. "I thought you were staying with him."

"I came a day early," Ichiro admitted softly. "I wanted to see you. To talk with my brother who seems to hurt inside. Just the two of us. Without Mikio stepping between us to shove us together. He seems to like maneuvering things. Very much the Horse, no?"

"I don't know. Neither Mike or I are very Japanese. Hell, up until I met my... Jae, ramen and takeout sushi was the most Asian thing I was around." I picked at the pie again, spearing a berry from its guts. "Jae... a friend of mine said something about birth animals once, but I wasn't paying a lot of attention."

Mostly because I'd been stripping his jeans off of him at the time and sucking at the dip in his belly.

Ichiro touched at the spot where the horse's long tail curved into the rooster's bright red tail feathers. "This is you, Kenjiro. The rooster. Of the two of you, she was more worried about you. That your father would move too much. Roosters are social creatures. They need people around them, long-time friends. She worried you would only have Mikio for company."

"He's not bad company," I confessed. "Once you can get him to stop bossing you around."

Ichiro grinned at me. "I've had him pushing at me. He's hard to resist."

"A swift kick in the nuts worked when we were kids. Can't do that now. He's got a wife. Too much damage there and they won't be able to have kids." Staring at the art covering his arm, I was at a loss about what to say first. "Why did you ink that on you?"

"Your birth signs?" Ichiro pursed his mouth when I grunted a yes. "Because I didn't know you... didn't have you. I needed you with me... needed *umma*... our mother with me. It was how I kept you close to me. You are my brothers. My family. Even if I didn't know you, I carried you with me. Does that make sense to you?"

"Yeah, it makes sense."

My shame soured the sweetness of the blueberries in my mouth. The colors of his ink blurred, and swallowing didn't seem to get the chunk of emotion clear from my throat. I had to look away, focusing on a loose button on one of the pillows. Neko slammed her head into my arm, nudging me from my thoughts, and I looked up to find Ichiro staring at me, his face a calm mask. His hand was still on his tattoo, stroking at the images he'd laid down under his skin. Lacking our faces, he'd given himself as much of us as he could reach, mythical creatures drawn from our births and our places in his life.

Would it be so horrible to have another brother? Would it be so bad to have someone else to turn to when life got too tight around me? There was only one way to find out. The ultimate test of family, a few spoken words whispered over the space between us and I'd know if Ichiro was someone I could have in my life.

"Did Mike... Mikio... tell you I'm gay?" My breath was caught between my throat and my lungs. A trail of fears burnt down through my stomach. I took my gaze off of the pillow and met my brother's gaze full on, watching him process what I'd said.

He ran his hands through his hair, another one of my own habits, oddly familiar but strangely freaky to see someone else's hands... hands too much like my own. Everything about him was too much of me, too much of Mike. I was having difficulties sifting through the similarities to find the Ichiro bits amid the chaff.

"How much do you know about Japan, *oniisan*?" Ichiro slid forward until he was at the edge of the sofa cushion and reached out to touch my knee. I jumped at the contact, startled by his fingers on my leg.

"I know that not all sushi is raw and rice shouldn't be instant," I said, shrugging. "Other than history, a total pissed-off fucking hell feeling about atomic bombs being used, and what seems to be a weird obsession with a big-headed cat with a bow on its head, not much."

Ichiro laughed, a husky sound rolled with mirth. "Sanrio owns Japan's soul. I'm sure of it."

"That's who makes the cat?" I snorted when he nodded. "Thing gives me the creeps. All of them. Their heads are fricking huge."

"I think it's an acquired taste, or maybe you have to be a little insane. Japanese women love her," he agreed. Ichiro's laughter soon dissipated from his mouth, leaving his face somber. Skimming his hands over his arms, he said. "What I've done to myself... how I wear my life on my skin... isn't welcome in Japan. Too many people associate tattoos with violence... with criminals. I cannot go into a public bath, and if I ride the subway with my arms exposed, people recoil from me. Even as tightly packed as the trains are, they skirt around me and avoid touching me. To them, I wear violence on my skin, and most Japanese are very troubled by that. I *disturb* their lives by having my art on my skin."

"That's insane." I bit my lip, suddenly hearing my words from Jae's point of view. "Sorry, I'm too... American sometimes. It's hard to take a step back sometimes. What about your family there? They know you're not like that, right?"

"My own father is…." He paused, taking a breath. "My family is very traditional. They pride themselves on being traditional. From my great-grandfather on down, they all believe the bloodline should be pure Japanese, clean of any influence or heritage that is not Japanese. To them, I'm an abomination… an aberration of culture. Who I am… what I have on my skin… what I choose to do with my life… distances me from them. Their doors are closed to me. I am barely tolerated in my father's house, and if he is able to have another son with his new wife, I'm certain he would turn his back on me as soon as the cord is cut. So I understand how you feel about being shoved out for being who you are… what you need to be."

"But you *chose* this," I pointed out, gesturing toward the tattoos. "You didn't have to do that to yourself."

"Life is not always a choice. Your loving men isn't a choice, not inside of you," he replied softly. "Could you have lived a life without men in your bed? Yes. You could have buried your want of men deep inside of you and sought out women. Would you have been happy? Probably not. Your true self would eat you up from inside, poisoning your blood with self-hatred until you could no longer breathe through the stink of your rotting soul."

I nodded, lost in his words. "So, you feel like you didn't have a choice. You couldn't be anything but… this… you."

"No, I couldn't be… won't be anyone else but me." He softened the bitterness of our conversation with an engaging smile. "Tokugawa Ichiro, inker of tattoos and reviled son of his family."

It was confusing. He'd purposely stepped outside of what'd been expected of him… of who he was supposed to be. There'd been a small part of me that still wished I'd been born straight, a part of me that denied the normality of my homosexuality. It'd been a malevolence inside of me, a cancerous longing bred up from society pressuring me… from my parents' rejecting me… and an innate need to just be… *normal*. Because being gay… even loving as deeply as I'd been loved and have loved… still wasn't *normal* yet. I hated feeling that way…

hated having that whispering need to be like everyone else slicing up my happiness. Life would have been easier if I'd just been... straight.

But then I wouldn't be me.

I wouldn't trade the touch of Jae's mouth on my skin for the world, and my heart thrummed with the thought of touching him again. The normal I'd been judged against had never been mine. Never would be mine. It was as much of a *normal* as anything else, and fuck anyone who couldn't see that, couldn't embrace that as a truth.

Maybe Ichiro really didn't have as much of a choice as I'd thought.

"Why did you do it, then? Why did you choose... this?" It seemed such a trivial thing. Tattoos were common here, meant next to nothing, and in some places like the hipster-hippie coffee shop across the street, I'd expect the barista to have them, almost as if to validate who they were. In essence, Ichiro'd chosen to be his own kind of gay, pushing himself out of his family. "If you knew they were going to be assholes about it, why did you do it?"

"I chose to ink myself... to ink others, because it speaks to me. I crave bringing a piece of another person up out to their skin with my art. To me, tattooing means I touch someone's heart and find who they are, leaving it behind after I am done." His shrug was elegant, a bird sweeping through the air toward the horizon. "So in this, *oniisan*, you and I are the same. You love men and I love ink. We made the choice to live as we are... not as others want us to be. So the question is, Cole Kenjiro, can you accept me as I am while I learn to accept you as you are?"

WE BOTH agreed we'd need time to get to know each other. First thing we'd work on was what to call one another. He went by Ichi, and I'd never been Kenjiro. Mike was on his own. He'd be Mikio the Horse until the end of time if he didn't speak up. I'd asked if a jackass counted as a horse. Ichi said he'd look into it but didn't think it would fly. At least not for Mike.

He was so similar to me in so many ways, but in others, so different. Mike was going to have a hell of a time bossing Ichi around like he did me. Maddy was going to love him. Walking him out to his rental car, I gave him better directions to the double Ms' house than his GPS did. Avoiding the 405 during its reconstruction was key. No mapping program ever took into account the asshattery of Los Angeles's roadwork.

Bobby was driving up just as Ichi was getting into his rental car. My supposed best friend eyed my younger brother's ass as he climbed into the sedan. His eyes sparkled with sexual awareness at Ichi's long legs, and he even bent forward to catch a last glimpse of my brother's face.

"Nice." He whistled under his breath as Ichi drove away. "Decided to toss aside your—"

"Shut the fuck up. That's my brother." I elbowed him and pushed him up the walk. "And no, Jae's not going anywhere, you fucking asshole."

"Just saying, damn." Another whistle and he strolled up the walk toward my front door, his meaty fists in his jeans pockets. "Your mother grew some pretty boys."

"Thought you weren't into Asians."

"I can make exceptions." Bobby winked and smirked. "I did for you."

I'd already put away the rest of the pie and wasn't planning on offering any to Bobby, especially after he ogled Ichi. More concerned about finding a cold beer in my fridge, he shoved aside Claudia's pastry for a couple of Guinness Black Lagers. After popping one open, he took a sip and swished the brew in his mouth.

"Kind of… coffee-ish," he declared, passing me the other. "I like it."

"Thanks. I'll sleep better tonight knowing you like my beer." I cracked open the Guinness, padded back to the living room, and took back my place on the couch. "What'd you drop by for?"

"To check up on you." He slumped down on the other end of the larger sofa, dislodging Neko from her bath. She gave him a foul look and stomped down the cushions to knead at my lap. "See where you are on this stupid case you're determined to break your fucking head on. Unless you want to talk about your hot brother—"

"No, not talking about Ichi." I shut Bobby down. "He's not gay. Or even if he is, quit being a perv."

"Never know till he tries," He took a sip of beer and nearly choked on it when I shot him a foul look. "Okay, Princess. I'll back off. Just joking."

"Shit's turned around in my head right now, dude," I explained softly. "I don't need more crap to deal with, okay?"

"Yeah, I know." Bobby's voice softened, and he leaned forward and pulled me into a one-armed hug. It felt good to be touched. Even as rough as he usually was, Bobby gave good hugs. I didn't know I needed one until his arm was around my shoulder. He took my beer and placed it on the chest with his, then tugged me nearly into his lap so he could get a better grip on me. "There's been a lot of shit on your plate, kid. You sure you want to take on this thing with the fortune-teller?"

Lying against Bobby's chest, I could feel his heartbeat through my shoulder blades, and the sound throbbed through to my chest. Hooking a leg up over the arm of the sofa, I contemplated dropping the investigation.

"Heh, I can see that look on your face." His chuckle rumbled into my spine. "You can't walk away from this, can you?"

"No, not really," I admitted. "It's not just that I am pissed off someone killed that girl in front of me… because I am… really fucking angry that she died. Someone took her away from her mother. And for what? Nobody knows. This is all fucked-up to hell, Bobby. I can't just let it go. It's not fair to Vivian or to Madame Sun."

"So what now?" He grabbed his beer and handed me mine, trailing drops of cold condensation down my face. I wiped at it and glared. All that got me was a patented cocky Bobby grin.

"I don't know. This thing is so screwed up. Everyone's tied into each other. Eun Joon Lee and May Choi were Madame Sun's clients but also have a connection to Gyong-Si. Lee was his client, and Choi's last name is the same as Gyong-Si's. I didn't like how he looked nervous when I poked him about her. Vivian Na is Madame Sun's daughter but not her husband's, so there's shit between them there. Vivian'd been seeing a guy named Park Hong Chul, who's the grandson of Madame Sun's other dead client, Bhak Bong Chol."

"But that guy wasn't murdered," Bobby pointed out.

"No, but who the hell knows what really happened. They might have just called it cardiac arrest and not looked for anything on tox. I was going to ping Wong to see if he could ask about the autopsy, but, well, shit happened." The lager was cool and potent, especially when I realized I hadn't really eaten anything that day, other than a few bites of Claudia's pie.

"I can see what Dell's got on the dead guy from today. If he's connected to Gyong-Si or that Park guy, it'll help you out a bit."

"Thanks. I need to connect the dots here, Bobby. There's too many stray lines. We know Lee was pregnant but don't know if it was her husband's. Gyong-Si's known for screwing his clients, saying that it's therapy, so the baby could have been his. But the biggest question in this fucking mess is… why? Why are all these people dying? That's what really doesn't make sense."

"Money or sex, isn't that the first place to look?" He cocked his head, staring down at me from an angle. "Only part of this with sex is that fake gay guy, Gyong-Si. Suppose Choi wasn't his niece but someone he fucked too? Maybe even Vivian?"

"That's kind of sick," I countered. "Okay, mostly because her dying is just too… close to me, you know? But why would they die because they're sleeping with Gyong-Si? Someone who wants him all to themselves? I've seen the guy. He's not someone to kill for."

"Not everyone wants the same thing, kid. You like Korean boys…."

"One… one Korean boy," I corrected. "I can't find a money angle in this. No one seems to gain anything from the deaths. Not like Gyong-Si or Madame Sun took out million-dollar life insurance policies on these people. That would have popped up on the cops' radar. No, this hasn't anything to do with money."

"Or at least not that you can see. Does Gyong-Si really need to snipe Sun's clients? It sounds like they've been in a death match for years."

"Yeah, they trained with the same master fortune-teller guy back in Korea." I sat up, nearly hitting Bobby's chin with the back of my head. "Fuck, Madame Sun said Vivian wasn't her husband's. Suppose she was Gyong-Si's? Maybe someone's trying to get Gyong-Si's relatives out of the way for some reason. What do you think?"

"Not what I think," Bobby murmured. "It's what you think, kiddo. You're the one chasing the smoke monster."

"I've got too much to chase down. That's what I think." My stomach rumbled, reminding me that blueberries and lager did not make for a good dinner. "Come on. Let's go grab something to eat. Then I'll get rid of you and see what my Korean boy's up to tonight. Push comes to shove, I'll take phone sex over your company any day of the week."

CHAPTER FOURTEEN

I DIDN'T get my phone sex. Tiff and Jae were having a deep discussion, and he'd snapped off a quick text to me when she ducked out to go to the bathroom. A short promise of a future dinner and a *saranghae* was all I got. It was enough. I was more than primed to go upstairs and jack off in the shower using Jae's soap.

I would have done it in bed, but the cat watches me, and that would have been too weird. She already had a toe fetish when I moved my foot. I wasn't going to give her any chance at my dick.

Still, despite the lengthy time imagining my hand was Jae's mouth stretched over my cock, I woke up feeling like my skin was on too tight, and I badly needed to be buried deep inside of his body before the week was out. Or at least get another kiss. I'd have killed for the smallest of kisses right after brushing my teeth.

By the time I unlocked the office and made coffee, my itch for Jae'd become a disgruntled annoyance I could live with for a few hours. After my first cup of ink-black java, I was almost ready to take on the day. Tuning up the enormous laptop Jae'd convinced me to buy, I tapped into the office network to stare at the flowchart I'd made of Madame Sun's case.

To tell the truth, it looked like the Flying Spaghetti Monster having a three-way with a couple of krakens. I got myself more coffee, even making an extra espresso shot to boost up the power, and settled myself in to a long morning of picking through the threads of a seriously fucked-up cat's cradle of a case.

Or at least I was until Detective Dexter Wong walked in, ready to kick my ass nine ways from Sunday.

"What the fuck were you doing at the Sun scene with O'Byrne?"

It wasn't the most pleasant of greetings. In fact, by anyone's standards, mine or Ichi's, it was pretty fricking rude.

"Hey, Dex." I held up my coffee cup. "Glad you could drop by. Want some, or are you happy with chewing on your own bile?"

"Don't fuck with me, McGinnis. She chewed my ass through like it was a couple of *char siu bao* at a Sunday breakfast," he grumbled at me but stomped over to the coffeepot. "O'Byrne wants to know what the hell you're doing in the middle of our cases and why I haven't shot you in the knee or something."

"Because the LAPD frowns on shooting innocent citizens?" I offered, smirking when he glared at me over his shoulder. "I was there because I was giving my condolences to Sun. I didn't know Vivian was her daughter until yesterday. Looks like you or O'Byrne didn't either."

"I don't care what you did. You pissed her off. She wasn't really getting a damned thing out of Sun until you waltzed in, and suddenly, there's a Korean gang and maybe some sort of serial killer. Her open-and-shut self-defense case was blown to bits. O'Byrne doesn't like messy, and you, my friend, are one hot mess looking for a place to happen. She thinks you're a menace."

"Look, she's just pissed off because I got info she didn't have. Na being Madame Sun's daughter complicates things, but you've got to admit, it's looking like she's not crazy and someone's really trying to kill off people around her."

"If it'd been anyone but O'Byrne, I wouldn't have gotten chewed out," Dex said, sitting down in Claudia's chair. He squeaked it back and forth while he sipped at his coffee. "She's a good cop but a fucking hardass. Captain's got his boxers in a happy twist 'cause she's assigned to us now. She's got a solve rate that's through the roof."

"Dude, *anyone* after Jenkins would drive your solve rate up." Pointing out the obvious only seemed to make Dex cross his eyes at me.

"In the immortal words of Sun Tzu, fuck you."

"Don't think Sun Tzu's ever been quoted as saying fuck you."

"I paraphrased," Dex sneered at me. "Pretty much everything he said boiled down to fuck you or fuck them. It's all in the translation."

"So you came all the way down here to tell me Sun Tzu pretty much told the world to fuck off?" I'd been making a list of things I wanted Mo and Sissy to take care of when they came in because I'd made plans to hunt down Vivian Na's boyfriend, but that wasn't anything I'd planned on sharing with Wong. He'd just make some noise about how I was interfering, and I'd have to pointedly ignore his pleas to get out of his business.

"Mostly, I came over to tell you to stay out of the case, especially since O'Byrne has a hard-on for you. But since you're going to ignore me and sneak around behind my back, I came to shake down any info you might have that I don't. Some of Jenkins's cases rolled over to my desk, including one Eun Joon Lee, so, tell me everything you've got, since it's probably a damned sight better than what Jenkins ever wrote down."

I went over everything I had, including my suspicions. Dex added nothing to the conversation, merely grunting at certain points like he was an acting coach and I was delivering a poor rendition of Hamlet's monologue. When I got to the part of Gyong-Si impregnating multiple women, he almost choked on his coffee.

"He's on my list of people to talk to. I got him on the phone, and he felt… off. Like he's *too* gay. Everything's neon bright and flashing," Wong mused. "So he's faking it? Putting on a show? That's what you think?"

"I know guys who are more femme, for lack of a better word. It's a part of who they are. Nothing wrong with it. Some guys just *are*." I cocked my head. "Gyong-Si? He's a plastic cutout. I think he picked out things that would make him look gay and camps it up."

"But why would he do that?" Wong asked, stabbing at the desk with his finger. "Koreans hate the gay, right? Why would he act that way if he knows it would kick him in the balls?"

"We don't know how he acted back home." Pointing out the obvious to Wong didn't seem to gain me any points. "Look at it this way. He was trained by this famous fortune-teller over there. Wouldn't that give him a golden ticket to the candy factory? So why toss that aside to come here where he's got shit for reputation and would have to build things back up? He must have run from something. I just don't know what or who to ask."

"Why'd Sun come here, then?" Dex asked. "That makes as much sense as Gyong-Si coming over if she's going to take a hit to her rep."

"Her son's here. Gyong-Si, as far as I know, doesn't have any family connection to anyone," I said. "He's hiding something… and I think it's his supposed sexual therapy. I'm betting he got into trouble over in Seoul and it came back to bite him in the ass. Coming over here, he's got a huge Korean population to pull his clients from, and by pretending he's gay, he's got his bases covered while he tiptoes through the tulips, as it were. Husbands are assured their wives are safe, and any women who fall for his bullshit about the healing properties of his gay peen aren't going to tell their spouses they fucked their fortune-teller. Maybe it goes under getting a massage or pedicure."

"Shaky, but it's a maybe." Wong pursed his mouth. "Where'd you get the idea Gyong-Si was faking it?"

"Info came from the man's very pretty and gay assistant." I smiled despite myself. "Seriously, the guy's assistant is hot. *You'd* hit on him. But Gyong-Si doesn't."

"So hot you forgot about Jae-Min?"

"Dude, I'm… I might have Jae, but—" I'd almost said I was taken. It was on the tip of my tongue, and I swallowed it whole, wondering if Jae'd considered me really his. Leaving off the lack of interest from my cock where Terry was concerned, I smiled. "I'm not dead. I'm still going to look."

"I don't know, McGinnis. Your theories are kind of weak."

"I've been meaning to circle round on Gyong-Si to see if he conned any other women, but shit's been going on. I was hoping to see if I could find some of the man's other clients and verify the assistant's story. But there's Lee's husband too. I was planning on seeing if he had something to share."

"Let me do that," Wong interjected. "I can shake that down from my angle. I've got to hit up the woman's husband and see if he knew she was pregnant. If he did—and knew it wasn't his—I've got a motive there."

"You going to share what you learn?"

"Are you?" he countered. "Because I know you, Cole. Even after everyone tells you to back the fuck up, you keep going. Didn't we already have this conversation once before? Actually more than once?"

"Yeah," I conceded. "But I promise, anything I dig up is yours."

"And when it comes to taking someone down?"

"Your name is on my speed dial. I will take nothing down but license plate numbers and addresses." Crossing my heart, I tried to look as sincere as possible. Truth was, I didn't want to get shot again. It fucking hurt. "Now share what you know."

"Actually, it's not much." Wong made Claudia's chair squeak again. "You know Vivian Na was seeing a Korean thug named Park Hong Chul. His street name is C-Dog. Minor stuff. For all the talk about gang activity, he's pretty clean on that front. No arrests. No domestics or violent crimes. No affiliation but does have a group of like-minded, stalwart friends he hangs out with. A group that used to include one Darren Shim, but Mr. Shim had the unfortunate luck to encounter a very heavy urn yesterday, and now C-Dog's pack is down one mutt."

"Did you get to talk to Park?"

"C-Dog. You know he worked hard to earn that nickname. It's very original," Wong chastised me. "And no, he's on O'Byrne's list of people to hassle. McGinnis, you've got to remember that the only place these are all connected is in that tiny little lizard brain of yours. The rest of us are chasing this down like actual police cases. I've got Lee and Choi now, and since there *is* a connection through the fortune-tellers, I can go harass *those* people without the captain going apeshit about me stepping on toes."

"Just go easy on Sun," I murmured, finishing off my coffee. "She just lost her daughter."

"Everyone on my list's lost people, McGinnis," he said mournfully. "I just gotta make sure I can find out which bastard did it before we lose any more."

I NEEDED an in. Actually, I needed a Korean, preferably one who slunk around the underbelly of certain places and possibly had some contact with the area's underground element. Luckily, I knew one. I wasn't happy when he went stalking around in the dark, but I'd given up trying to get him to stay safe a long time ago. Now, Jae's penchant for crawling through the gutter... both figuratively and literally... was going to come in handy.

If only I could convince him to help me.

"Hello?" He answered on the second ring. A positive sign for me. The grumpy in his voice was a negative, but I could get around that.

"Hey, what are you doing?"

"Why?" His sigh was epic, a tidal wave of sound against my ear. "What do you want?"

"You," I murmured.

"Cole-ah...." Another sigh, but this one was different, laden with promises and seduction. "Sometimes I don't know what to do with you."

"Really? 'Cause there's this guy named Vātsyāyana that's got a manual that might help," I suggested, rocking back in my chair. "We might have to fake it for a couple of pages, but I think we can work it out. You're pretty bendy."

"My sister is here," he reminded me, but the sultry rasp in his voice remained lurking behind the scold. "What do you *really* want?"

"Honestly, I do need your social skills, what you have of them, anyway." Teasing Jae was always fun. He made little disgusted kitten noises, and I wasn't disappointed when a few echoed through the phone line.

He cut straight to the chase. "Cole-ah, stop teasing."

"No, really, I do need you." I gave him a quick rundown of the situation, ending with my need to find one Park Hong Chul, better known as C-Dog.

"And you think I somehow have an *in* with criminals now?"

"He's not really a criminal. Who hasn't done some stupid stuff when they were kids? Wong pretty much said Park keeps his nose clean. And it's more like, you talk to a lot of people in Koreatown," I explained. "Maybe someone who knows someone? He's not really on the cops' radar, so there's not really some place he hangs out. Especially if one of his boys probably gunned Vivian Na down before getting his head bashed in. If he wants to distance himself from that kind of shit, he might be reluctant to talk."

"That would make me… reluctant to talk," Jae agreed. "What do you think I can do?"

"Lend me some cred?" I caught myself doodling on my notes, mostly trying to write Jae's name in *hangul*. I sucked at it, but eventually I'd get it right. "I've got an address, but it's his mom's. I don't want to show up at his mother's house to shake some info out of him without someone who can speak Korean. We might end up talking to his parents, and I want to stack the deck in my favor as much as I can. Now, I *can* take Bobby—"

"God no, the two of you together means a trip down to the police station to bail you out," he grumbled. "I'd come with you, but I've got Tiff here. I don't want to leave her alone."

"What about the friends she went out with the other day?"

"She's never seeing those people again." The growl in Jae's voice perked my slumbering dick up a bit, and I reminded it that it would have to wait until later. "She came back smelling of pot and beer. I'm going to find them and kill them. She says she didn't do anything, but I don't believe her. God, I'm getting old. I don't want her doing those things."

"She's your sister. You can be old where she's concerned. Tell you what, bring her over here," I suggested. "She can maybe connect with Mo and Sissy. They're good kids. At the very least, I've got a fridge full of soda and game systems she can mess with."

"I don't know," Jae stalled. "I don't want to just dump her at your office—"

From somewhere close to Jae, I heard his sister yell, "Does he have a real Internet?"

"Shit, that's right. Your stone box isn't a hot spot." Jae's curse was almost lost when I laughed. "Just that one dedicated line to your computer."

"It was enough for me," he grumbled. "I only use it for work. Apparently, splitting the connection, it isn't good enough to download episodes of *Sungkyunkwan Scandal*. It works fine for batch uploads. I just let it go overnight."

"Dude, just bring her over," I coaxed. "She'll be fine. Hell, the conference room's got a big flat screen. She can watch her—whatever that is—on that."

"She's already packing up her bag." From the increased sounds of traffic, I'd guessed he'd stepped outside of his gopher hole. The rasp of a lighter and then he exhaled, hard. He'd be smelling of cloves when he got to me. "I don't know what good I can do with Park Hong Chul."

"He doesn't have any priors for violence," I explained. "He might feel better talking to someone... Korean. Besides, you know the area. If we've got to run for it, you'll know all the escape hatches."

"You're not making me feel better about this, Cole-ah."

"Hey, personally, I'm hoping we can duck into someplace dark and hidden. If it's small enough, we might have to get close, you know, to conserve space."

"And let me guess, you're going to bring some lube in case it's too tight?"

"Jae, love," I whispered, hot and bothered. "You are always the right kind of tight for me."

PUTTING three teenagers in a room is kind of like playing with a bottle of shaken up Diet Coke and a fistful of Mentos. Tiff and Sissy mentally circled each other while Mo was torn between sticking by his sister or chatting up a hot Korean girl. Hormones won over familial ties, and he was the first one to cross the invisible line, offering to get her an iced latte or something from across the street.

Tiffany Kim looked a lot less like Jae once seen from the front and with her hair pulled back. A little bit shorter than her brother, she had his body type, lean legs she showed off to her best advantage in a pair of denim shorts. The tank top definitely wasn't her brother's. Its bright pink fabric was studded with rhinestones in the shape of that large-headed, mouthless cat I couldn't seem to avoid.

"That thing creeps me out," I whispered in Jae's ear. He smelled good, and I wanted to kiss his cheek or his neck. Tasting his skin on my tongue was one of my life's pleasures, and it'd been too long since I'd had the silk of him on my mouth.

"What? What thing?" He looked around, confused.

"That cat thing she's wearing. Looks like it farms fava beans to go with its dinner."

The girls made their initial contact, establishing home territories and interests, and then Sissy's face blossomed with a wide smile. Tiffany's stiff demeanor shifted, and she dropped her arms from their crossed stance over her chest. From what I could make out, Sissy had a deep love of a show Tiffany was following. Everything out of their mouths became a mishmash of Korean and English with a heavy dose of squees and giggles.

Within a few minutes, the girls bonded over Korean dramas and streaming services' bad translations. Before Jae and I could give them a few ground rules to follow while we were gone, they were setting up Tiff's laptop and plotting out the afternoon's entertainment.

"I'll watch the door." Mo edged in past the screen door, juggling a carrier full of iced coffees. I held it open for him, and he grunted a thank you. "Sissy's usually only got Hyunae to watch those things with."

"Hyunae?" Jae dropped his voice down to a whisper. "Marcel's girlfriend, right? We met her at the hospital."

"Yep." I nearly hooked my arm around Jae's waist, stopping midstep before Tiff saw me. "You guys have our numbers. If something happens, call. We should be back in a couple of hours."

Tiff rolled her eyes, a very not-like-Jae gesture. For a seventeen-year-old girl, she seemed to drip more sarcasm and bitters than rainbows and ponies. Jae didn't seem too worried about it. Putting his hand on her shoulder, he spoke briefly to her in Korean. He could have been saying anything from behave to don't worry, he's not going to be sticking his dick up my ass. I wasn't going to ask. Some things are meant to be private.

Whatever he said didn't seem to lighten her mood. Her eyes did another circuit around in their sockets.

The girls disappeared into the conference room before we'd even said our good-byes. Mo shrugged and saluted us with his coffee. "Have a good time, Uncle Cole. I'll hold down the fort."

"If the giggling gets too loud, close the door," I cautioned him.

"Close it? Shiiii…." He cut himself off before he swore in front of me. "I'm a'gonna nail it shut."

CHAPTER FIFTEEN

I CAUGHT Jae's face in my hands before he could get into the Rover. Pressing him up against the car's steel door, I dipped my head down and captured his mouth with mine.

Like I'd imagined, he *did* taste of cloves, sweet and spiced from fragrant smoke, but there was something else there, something so uniquely Jae I couldn't put a name on it. I would imagine moonlight would taste of Jae, a heady slice of silver and darkness. Moonlight poured through a cup of espresso, because there was an echo of the sip he'd stolen from Tiff's latte.

I wanted to say fuck it all about the case and drag him into my— our bedroom. Nothing sounded better than stripping him bare and laying him out on the mattress, then taking my time making him mewl.

Jae moved slightly under my touch, turning his face so his lips ran over my palms. The tip of his tongue sought out the lines on my hand, following the creases up until he found the V between my fingers. Licking at the web between my index and middle finger, he suckled me until I grew hard with the thought of that mouth… those sweet lips… curled around my cock and my hands wrapped tight with strands of his black hair.

"The kids can probably see us. Okay, maybe just Mo." Those were not the seductive words I wanted whispered into the wet cup of my palm. My dick took notice of the chilling effect and promptly went back to pretending it was a dead octopus tentacle.

"I just went from hard to soft like I got dropped in a snowbank. Thanks for that." I gave him one final kiss and pulled back. His own jeans were tight around his crotch, and I brushed the back of my fingers against the bulge, giving him a conspiratorial wink. "Hold onto that thought. Maybe I can take care of that later."

"Pervert," he grumbled at my back but got into the Rover after I opened the door for him.

"Guilty as charged," I admitted, shutting the door. "But only for you, Jae. Only for you."

KOREATOWN had slippery boundaries. Tendrils of it wove through outer neighborhoods, mingling with a meandering Hispanic population. Many people placed the edge of K-town at Vermont and Wilshire but spots of it sprung up farther beyond, an Asian thrum underscoring the area's more Latino beat.

Hong Chul's house sat in one of these areas, a single story bungalow with a flat roof lined with earthenware ginger jars. It wasn't the only home with an odd arrangement of kitchenware along the roofline. Squeezed in tight on small plots, nearly all of the older structures sported covered pots of some kind, either battered enameled steel or ceramic hulks. The only reason I knew they were for fermenting kim chee was because Jae told me. Even knowing that, the neighborhood looked like it was gearing up to dump hot oil on any invaders or scammers selling fake magazine subscriptions.

Color seemed to reign supreme, not nearly as bright as Gyong-Si's place but blindingly close. The Park home was green, a lime hue not found on any citrus tree. The front porch was almost hidden by a wall of plants, but the steps were clear, a sparkling white wooden stairway up to a dark red door. A pond of slippers pooled out on the left side of the threshold. A pair of vivid pink floral flip-flops stood out, tiny rubber footprints floating on top of the darker sea.

I got out of the car and nodded to the porch, probably pointing out the obvious to Jae. "There's a kid living here. Little sister, maybe?"

"Maybe. How much do you know about Hong Chul?"

"Not much," I admitted. "But Madame Sun wasn't that impressed with him. She might be biased, but Wong says he's been a good boy for a while now. I think Sun's a bit... old in the head. Hell, she probably thinks I'm sketchy."

"You are."

My palm itched to touch him, but we were out in the open and in a Korean neighborhood. I couldn't reach over and cross the space between us. I clenched my fist, digging my fingernails into my palm, hoping the pain would take away some of the desire to run my hand over his skin until I'd turned it pink with arousal.

"Well, if he is sketchy and he shoots at us, you better hope he kills me, because I'm going to kick your ass," Jae teased under his breath.

"Honey, if he shoots at us, I'll jump in front of the bullet," I promised. "Because I won't be able to live without you."

As soon as the words left my mouth, I thought of Rick and a night I wished I could go back in time to change. Jae must have seen something in my face, because he took a step toward me, a long enough step to brush his fingers against the back of my neck. I'd barely lived through losing Rick. I couldn't go through that again with Jae. I just... couldn't.

"It'll be fine, Cole-ah." He'd known me long enough ...well enough... to know where my mind wandered off to, and Jae's touch was calming, dragging me back to the present. "It will all be fine."

The driveway was two lines of cracked cement leading behind the house, and from the loud clanking sounds coming from the back, I thought I'd try there first instead of knocking on the front door. Jae followed me up the drive, a long-legged duckling stepping over the trimmed down grass lines pushing up through the breaks in the concrete. His sneakers made squicking noises, and I couldn't help but smile when I caught sight of Jae's jumping shadow as he played an odd hopscotch behind me.

Someone in the house definitely had a green thumb. An overhead lattice near the house covered about six feet of the driveway. Clusters of long green squashes stretched down from the top, and I had to duck to avoid hitting them. The sash windows on the side of the house were open, and something spicy was simmering inside. It reminded me of coming home when Jae was in a cooking mood. I missed the spicy aroma of his dinners.

I did not, however, miss picking shrimp heads out of my stew.

The banging turned out to be coming from a weathered single car garage. At some point in its life, the structure had lost its rolling door, and plywood covered most of the gap left by a missing side window. In the cramped garage, a young Korean man with a tight crew cut hammered at a length of steel. Behind him, a swirl of metal shapes rose up from a wooden base, their burnt edges beaten and folded in. The sculpture looked a bit like a mutated lotus flower on crack, lopsided and obviously still being worked on.

The guy probably came up to my shoulders. His hands were encased in welding gloves, and one held what looked like huge tongs, their ends pinched tight around one side of the flame-shaped metal. The other wielded a soft mallet, and the steel belled with each strike. His features were coarse, with blunted cheekbones and thick black eyebrows above a crooked nose. Shirtless, his short torso rippled with muscle, and his arms bunched with power every time he swung down.

He had tattoos—so different from Ichiro's elegant, flowing art— and they covered his arms and back with uneven blue-black jigsaws. *Hangul* and English battled for space on his shoulders. His arms were a mess of crosses, odd symbols, and more *hangul*. There didn't seem to be rhyme or reason to the ink other than to scrawl pieces and parts of whatever he'd been thinking about that day. From what I *could* read, he was C-Dog from K-town and he really liked his area code, scrawling both pieces of information across his belly in patchy gothic letters.

He turned to pick up something behind him, and what was on his back simply took my breath away.

The tiger was nearly twenty inches long and about half a foot wide in places. Done in shades of black, it wrapped up from his lower back, its head bowing down toward his hip and its tail curling up over his right shoulder blade. Its front claws pierced a banner scrawled with a July date, and its jaws dripped with saliva into marshy grasses near its feet. It was beautiful and totally at odds with everything else on his body.

Nothing on him matched the artistry of the tiger. It was as if his needs changed with that piece. It was something different. Something he *truly* wanted to wear.

"Park Hong Chul?" I called out loudly enough to be heard over the pong-pong of his hammer strokes.

"Yeah? What do you want?" He'd stopped hammering, glaring at us over the bent steel. Jutting his jaw out, he tilted his chin up defiantly. Looking me and Jae over, he growled, "I already talked to the cops. What the hell do you want?"

"I'm not a cop," I replied. "Cole McGinnis of McGinnis Investigations. Madame Sun hired me to look into a couple of things."

If Hong Chul had been suspicious before, he was steeped in it now. He put down the mallet, slowly worked the gloves from his hands, and tossed them onto a workbench against the wall. Having nothing more substantial than a business card, I still held one out. Despite having the gloves on, he'd gotten dirty at some point, and his fingers were smudged with black soot, smearing it over the engraved paper.

He glanced at Jae, then his eyes snapped back for a second look. Jerking his chin toward my lover, he grunted, "Hey, I know you. You're that photography dude. You had some stuff at the Korean Festival a couple months ago."

First I'd heard of Jae showing his photos, and I turned in time to see him duck his head.

"Just a few things." He had the good grace to give me an apologetic look. "*Nuna* is a good friend with one of the organizers. They just wanted more stuff for their art show. It wasn't a big deal."

"It was nice. You do some raw stuff." Hong Chul dismissed Jae's humility with a derisive snort. "Only black and white?"

"For those shots," Jae mumbled. I could see we were going to have a discussion about keeping me informed about his showings. "I do color sometimes. Depends on what I want to show."

"It was cool. I didn't get anything done in time for it, but maybe next year."

Bringing Jae was a good idea. Hong Chul's shoulders relaxed, and I didn't get the feeling he was ready to rip our heads off. He might have been shorter than me by a head, but he looked like he could double for Stretch Armstrong. Pounding steel with a mallet seemed like a great workout program. I'd have to mention it to Bobby. His attention wandered back over to me. "If you're not a cop, why are you here? I didn't have anything to do with what happened over at Sun's place. Shit, I haven't even talked to Darren in months."

"Actually, I didn't want to talk to you about Darren Shim," I said. "I really wanted to talk to you about a woman you were dating, Vivian Na."

The tough on his face melted, and Hong Chul inhaled sharply. The beat in his throat skipped twice, and he blinked furiously, but that didn't stop his eyes from pinking with tears. Then, for the second time in a week, I heard something that made my head reel.

"I never dated Viv," he confessed. "We were close, yeah, but that's 'cause she was my sister."

A TINY knot of a Korean grandmother served us hot coffee on a back porch barely wide enough to fit four plastic lawn chairs. Jae and Hong Chul spoke in reverent tones to the stooped-over old woman as she ferried cups back and forth from the kitchen, standing to take things from her as soon as she came outside. I didn't understand a word of the chatter, but my smile must have been good enough because she patted me on the chest every time she tottered by.

They grew them small in the Park household, because when we'd all been given cups large enough to float our bladders, I spotted a little girl peeking out from around the back doorframe. Not much more than a toddler, her wispy black hair was pulled up into a single spout on top of her head and tied off with a bleeding-eye pink hair clip. Smiling shyly, she edged out onto the porch, stepping carefully onto the painted planks, then bolted across to hide behind Hong Chul.

If any place on that porch was safe, it would be by him. He flexed his arms and growled playfully at her, scooping the little girl up into his arms. The grandmother clapped softly and motioned the girl to go back inside, but Hong Chul waved her off.

"It's okay, *halmeoni*, I'll watch her." Hong Chul planted the girl on his lap and blew a raspberry on her belly. She giggled, kicking up her feet and wiggling toes with nails painted nearly the same shade of pink as her clip. Pulling at the hem of the toddler's green plaid shorts, then tugging on her purple floral blouse, he laughed, "Did you dress yourself today, baby girl?"

His grandmother said something to Jae that brought a blush to his cheeks, and she cackled before stroking his hair down. After checking on the girl one last time, she headed back inside, leaving the back door open behind her.

"She likes you," I whispered over to Jae.

"Mostly, she wants to know what I see in you," he shot back in a hot whisper. "She said you're too big to be a good guest. You'd break everything in the house when you turned around."

"Liar," I teased, but I still sat back with a niggling worry in my brain. If Hong Chul's grandmother parsed that Jae and I were lovers, I had to be more careful when I was around him. "Does she really think—?"

"Don't worry about it. She also said she's got a couple of granddaughters she can marry us off to," Jae replied. "I told her you were half Japanese, and she said it didn't matter. They're getting old. She'll take anyone she can get."

"Nice. I'll toss Ichiro at them." I paused, realizing I didn't know if my brother was single.

The little girl appeared to have overcome her initial shyness and edged closer to me, her eyes wide with curiosity. My experience with kids was pretty much limited to tossing out full-sized candy bars on

Halloween, so I wasn't exactly sure what to do when she began to climb into my lap. Shocked, I panicked and made helpless noises at Hong Chul, but he'd begun to stir sugar into his coffee.

"Just let her sit with you," Jae suggested. "She'll get bored in a few minutes and climb down."

Hong Chul finally looked up from his coffee and spotted her on my lap. Patting his thigh, he called her over. "*Aish*, Abby, don't bother him. Come here, *halmeoni* brought you some juice and cookies."

Drawn by the bribe, she dismounted my lap with all the aplomb of an Olympic gymnast and pranced across the boards to her cookies. Hong Chul pulled her onto the empty chair beside him and handed her a kid's cup to sip from. She drank noisily, burbling bubbles back into her juice through the plastic straw.

"She's cute." I didn't know what else to say. The last little girl I'd been in contact with got me arrested while wearing a dog strapped to my belly. She'd been cute too, and all she got me was a night in jail and a pissed off Jae-Min.

"Yeah, she's kind of why I'm trying to get my shit together. Her mom and I hooked up a couple of years ago. Karen didn't want a kid, but I couldn't... I didn't want her to get rid of it. So, I got Abby, and Karen went back to partying," Hong Chul replied. "Viv liked her... Abby. She didn't like Karen much."

"How did you—" There wasn't an easy way to bring this up in a conversation so I plowed ahead. "How did you find out you and Vivian were siblings?"

"My grandfather. Well, from some stuff he left behind. I was going through his office and found what he wrote. Viv and I were friends before that, but it kind of made things... real, you know?" Hong Chul picked up his coffee cup, nudging his chair into an angle to prevent Abby access to the stairs if she went wandering again. Jae and I both murmured some words about being sorry for his loss, and Hong Chul ducked his head in a quick thanks.

"Did he know Vivian? From Madame Sun's?" I asked.

"Yeah, Grandpa liked her but didn't want us dating. I told him it wasn't like that between us. It wasn't. She had a hard time over here.

Viv's family back in Korea treated her like crap, and when she found out Madame Sun was her mother, she wanted to come over here because maybe it would be better." He shook his head, obviously troubled by something. "She was too used to Korea, you know? Things are different here. Guys here are more... sexual. She was... kind of conservative. Not how she dressed, but inside. You wouldn't know it by looking at her, but she was. Holding hands was a big deal for her."

"Can I ask how you two are related?" I kind of already knew, but I wanted to hear it directly from Hong Chul. Abby had dislodged herself from her chair, and for a moment I was scared she'd head my way again, but she seemed more interested in Jae's sneakers.

Hong Chul glanced at the open door. "Abby, go find *halmeoni* and ask her to watch cartoons with you, okay?"

Jae helped her down, and she gave us all enthusiastic waves before snatching up the last of her cookies. She stretched up as far as she could reach, grabbed the doorknob and, with a very serious look on her face, pulled it closed behind her.

"She's like an echo. I probably am going to catch crap for saying shit in front of her. She'll bust that out during dinner." Hong Chul chuckled, then sobered. "Gangjun Gyong-Si seduced my mom back in Seoul. He was my grandmother's fortune-teller, and my *umma* would come with her to his place."

"Your grandmother here?" Jae motioned to the house.

"Yeah, *halmeoni* was upset, but my mom was a kid, you know? Maybe not even sixteen." He stared down into his coffee as if he could see the past in its creamy depths. "My grandparents arranged for her to marry my dad, and then they all came over here. *Harabeoji*... my grandfather... didn't want me to know that my dad wasn't my real father. I haven't told them I know. I'm not going to. My dad's been there for me through everything, and he loves Abby to death. They did their best to raise me right. Not their fault I fucked it up."

"Couldn't have fucked it up too much if you've got Abby," I pointed out. "Some guys would have just walked away."

"Nah, I don't want to be like that." He shrugged it off. "She's my kid... my family... you've got to take care of family. It's just what you do."

I didn't want to correct him on that. I'd had plenty of experience with family walking away.

"How did your grandfather know Vivian was your sister?" Jae asked softly.

"I guess Madame Sun told him. I didn't read everything he wrote. Most of it was about people I didn't know, and not a lot of it made sense. I saw Viv's name and read from there. She and I are about the same age. There might be a couple of others. It's been... shitty since *harabeoji* died, and now Viv—" His voice broke, and he coughed to cover it. "We didn't know we were brother and sister. Not until after Grandpa died, but it was like... suddenly everything made sense. Why we felt like we were close even... why she loved Abby."

"Do you still have those papers?" I inched forward on the chair's seat. "It might help clarify a few things."

The suspicion was back in his face. "What kind of things?"

"I'm trying to find out who killed Vivian. I was there at the coffee shop when she died. I was supposed to meet with her about Madame Sun's clients when the shots came through the window." I leaned forward, keeping my voice down. "It was fast, Hong Chul. I'll tell you what I told her mother; it was very quick. She never knew."

"And you think it's got something to do with Gyong-Si?" He cocked his head and stared me down. Hong Chul might have stepped back into line, but it wasn't hard to see him as an intimidating piece of gangbanger.

"It looks that way. So far, everyone who's died is connected to him in some way."

"The cops are saying Darren's probably the one who shot Viv, but they don't know why. I wish James Bahn hadn't killed him. I'd want to fuck him up something fierce." The power in his voice left me with no illusions of what he'd do to the person who'd targeted his sister. "If someone else's responsible for this shit, then I want a piece of them. She was my sister too. Fuck, she was my sister before I even knew we were related. I owe her. She was there for me when Abby got sick a while back. I've got to be there for her now, you know?"

"Darren *might* have killed her. I don't know," I admitted. "But there's got to be a reason. Maybe someone hired him?"

"Maybe. Yeah, he didn't really even know her." Hong Chul's eyes grew distant. "I think they might have met like once or twice, but that's it."

"If it wasn't him, then it was someone else we don't know about. So far, everything I've got connecting comes through Gyong-Si," I said. "If you've got something that can point me toward someone else, I'd like to take a look at it. Before someone else gets hurt. Or worse, killed."

"You find out who did this, you tell me." His eyes burned with a nearly religious fervor. "Because I want to be there when they drag him in. I want to make sure that fucking bastard pays for what he did to me... what he did to my family. 'Cause if the cops don't do it, then I'll find someone who will."

CHAPTER SIXTEEN

"SO WHAT do you think?" I turned down the main thoroughfare toward my place. "Think he's telling the truth?"

"What? Hong Chul?" The look Jae gave me could have been called incredulous if not scathing. He'd been thumbing through the papers Hong Chul gave us, briefly murmuring over some of the man's comments. "What would he lie about?"

"Him and Vivian Na being lovers." I had to stop the Rover as a bunch of bearded slackers ambled across the street toward the granola girls' coffee shop.

"No." Jae's disgust was palatable. "People *can* just be friends. You and Bobby are just friends, no? You've never…." He trailed off, going someplace in his mind that he probably didn't want to go. I opened my mouth to respond, but he leaned over and pushed my jaw shut with the back of his hand. "No, I don't want to know. No matter which way it was, I don't want to know."

"You sure? Could be interesting." I smirked at his derisive snort. "Bobby's done some fucked-up shit."

"I worked in a host club. Pretty sure I've seen things Bobby hasn't even thought of."

The hipsters were stalled in the middle of the road, seemingly having a long discourse on the price of wool jumpers and totally oblivious to the Rover. I honked my horn, startling them into action. There was not a single apology from the duckling pack. Instead, I got outraged glares through the Rover's windshield, and one of them had the nerve to flip me off.

I would have stepped out of the Rover to discuss his gesture, but one of the hairy-pitted women who owned the café hustled out and grimaced an apology at me, ushering her ill-mannered customers in. She and Bobby'd had words before, mostly Bobby having words and her wincing at the volume. A few weeks ago, one of her regulars decided spitting on Bobby's truck was a good idea while he'd waited for them to cross the street and, once again, they'd stopped to talk midroad. He honked and spittle flew.

Things escalated from there. Lessons learned that day: never spit on an ex-cop's car, especially when you're heading over to a coffee shop with a *special* garden growing in the back alley.

"They're very... rude." Jae watched the herd pick up their pace and shuffle to the sidewalk.

"You, love of my heart and loins, are a master of the understatement. What they are, are assholes." I drove the Rover up onto my driveway and parked it in the carport. Jae'd parked his Explorer on the cement pad next to the driveway, and I checked the windows and tires automatically when we walked by. "But if I start screaming at them to get off my lawn, put me in a nursing home, okay?"

The office was quiet when we came through the screen door. Mo was behind his grandmother's desk, buried deep in what looked like a calculus book thick enough to kill a dinosaur. The conference room door was open wide enough, and a murmur of loud sound effects and steamy Korean seeped out. I couldn't follow a lick of it, but it sounded sensual. I shot a look over at Jae, but he seemed unconcerned.

After calling the girls out, I then dealt the first salvo in a battle I had no hope of winning. Still, handing Tiffany a sheaf of hundreds from petty cash so she could go get some clothes that didn't belong to me or Jae seemed like a good idea at the time.

Her brother didn't seem to think so.

Mo did what Mo did best. He analyzed the situation, then herded the girls outside amid confused, querulous objections and closed the screen door behind him. I made a mental note to give him a bonus.

Maybe a car. Hell, an aircraft carrier wasn't out of order. Next thing we heard was the Mo and Sissy mobile firing up and pulling away from the curb.

Jae was going to argue with me. I could see it before he even drew in a full breath. "Cole-ah—"

"Hear me out." I put the cashbox back and locked it up. "She brought nothing with her, right? Dude, she's wearing *my* clothes. How fucked-up is that for a teenaged girl? I'll give her a few hundred dollars, and she can get some of her own stuff. We can order some pizza and go over the papers Hong Chul gave us."

"Cole—" He wasn't weakening. Not by a long shot, but I had a trump card up my sleeve he couldn't fight.

"You promised we'd do this kind of shit together." I was stretching the words that'd come out of his mouth, but if I could get him to give on this, it would lay a groundwork for larger things. I needed something to budge between us. At some point, Jae was going to have to acknowledge I was standing beside him. "Trust me. Money is pretty small shit in the scheme of things."

"I don't want her to... depend on your money." He exhaled hard, leaning against my desk. I stepped closer, letting the warmth of my body wash over his skin. "It's not—"

"We're together in this, remember, babe?" I softened my voice to a whisper. "*That* means everything. Whatever you need to get done, we can do it together. And as for my money... dude, it's there. And there's enough of it that all it does is make more money. I don't spend a lot. This place was the biggest purchase I've made. Hell, I was still driving my old Rover until Grace decided she needed to blow it up."

"I hate that I can't give her things like... this." He finally broke, and his pride crumbled. The stoic façade he wore to argue with was gone, swept away by frustration and something fragile I couldn't quite name until it dawned on me he was ashamed, hurt by the inability to hand his sister a few hundred dollars to go shopping.

Reaching for him was easy. Holding him close was even easier. Jae folded into me, curving his body against my chest and wrapping his arms around my waist. It felt good to have him tuck his head under my chin, and the tickle of his hair in my nose was a sublime pleasure. It was like having a full-body orgasm encasing me in its tight grip.

"I don't have money," Jae murmured. "We've never had it. Anything my mother got from Uncle was for Jae-Su. He didn't send enough to support all of us. I can't... wrap my head around the money you have."

"Hey, you think I'm good with it?" I kissed the top of his head and stroked at the small of his back until he nearly purred under my touch. "You know why I've got it?"

"'Cause of Ben... because he shot you."

Besides me, the only other people who knew exactly why the department shoveled boatloads of cash at me to keep me quiet were Mike and Maddy. It was probably time to talk to Jae about the whole mess.

"Kind of." I hesitated. "See, Ben'd gone to the department shrink after one of our cases. He was losing it. Really losing it. Drinking too much and not talking enough. The captain thought he needed some talking *to*. The doctor... I don't know what Ben said to him. No one really does, but the doc told the department Ben should be given a leave of absence. That he needed some time to work through some issues. The department disagreed."

"How long—" Jae couldn't finish his sentence. His words choked somewhere in his throat. "Before he—"

"Two days," I answered. "Two days later, Ben shot the doctor when he was leaving his office. Man lived, but... Ben caught him in the spine and the neck. It went up through his head. He's lucky to be alive, but the dude's not all there anymore, you know? No one knew Ben was the one who shot the guy until later."

We'd begun to lean on one another. I was no longer the one pouring strength into him. His heart picked up the beat in my chest, and we breathed in together, joined as close as we could be without scandalizing the spider sitting up in the corner of the ceiling.

"When did they figure it out?"

"It wasn't until after Ben shot us... killed Rick... did the department make the connection. Ballistics and all that crap. By then, it was too late to do anything but cry." It was hard to talk about it. Even after three years, it still hurt to find my world suddenly missing not only Rick but Ben, the man I'd counted as much of a brother as I did Mike. "That's why there's money. It's got blood on it. Mine… Rick's… the doctor's. Hell, even Ben's, because they could have stopped him from blowing his own brains out. But they didn't."

"I wish they'd stopped him. Even if it meant… Rick." Jae swore into my chest. I knew what he was trying to say. It was impossible to express with words without sounding like an asshole, but he tried anyway. "Even if it meant you and I… someone should have stopped Ben. They should have fucking listened."

"Yeah, they should have listened, but since they didn't, they dumped a bunch of money at me and told me to get the fuck out of the department. So, giving Tiff some money to go shopping for clothes is nothing in the long run. What's important is that she feels comfortable and is happy. Life's too short not to try to be happy. Fucking let me tell you, if anyone knows that, it's me."

"Okay." His voice was barely a whisper, but the hug he gave me was tight enough to nearly bring me to my knees. "Thank you."

"Now come on, let's go home." Reluctantly, I let him go and pushed him toward the door. "Your cat probably misses you, and I could really use a beer."

NEKO greeted us at the door, then abandoned ship once I'd popped a can of smelly crap into her porcelain dish. I took a couple of beers from the fridge, padded into the living room, and stepped over Jae's discarded sneakers.

Jae had thrown himself onto the couch, having tossed the journals and papers we'd gotten from Hong Chul onto the apothecary chest. Sitting on the chest in front of him, I tucked his knees between my legs and put my hands on them. I bent forward until our foreheads touched and kissed his nose.

"You want something to eat first or just start tearing apart the papers?"

"Papers?" Jae's sloe eyes were nearly black when he glanced at me. "But... we don't have a lot of time... alone, no? Just a few hours until Tiffany comes back...."

I liked how my boyfriend thought.

Even better, I *loved* how he felt against me. Preferably naked.

"Well, you know, there's a spare bedroom. Hell, even two if you count the Murphy bed in that den I don't use," I murmured back. "You two could spend the night. Can't be very comfortable over at that place of yours. I've napped on that bed of yours. Couldn't walk for a week afterward."

"You never let go of things, huh?" He broke contact with me, shaking his head in disbelief. "You're not going to be happy until we've moved in."

"Hey, if I've got to suffer your cat's farts under the blankets in the middle of the night, you should too," I countered. "We'll give Tiffany a pass. There's only so much angst a teenager should have to suffer through."

"I don't know if I'm ready to sleep with you... while my sister's in the house," Jae admitted. "That's a lot to ask her to handle, Cole-ah."

"Okay." It was hard to say. Even harder to swallow. "Agreed."

I had to give him that. We'd have to take baby steps where Tiffany was concerned, and if she was going to stick around, she'd have to be folded into our lives as carefully as we could. Frustrating, especially since my dick missed having Jae to nudge up against in the wee morning hours, but it was going to have to suck it up.

Didn't mean I didn't want to let her pick out colors for the spare bedroom so she could set up camp there, but like Claudia always told me, hold my fucking horses. Things happen when they happen.

That being said, it was time for certain things to happen. Especially since we had only a few hours to get to them.

"So, you wanna go upstairs and um... how did Mo put it?" I crouched forward, nipping at Jae's neck with my teeth.

"I am not your something-something," Jae hissed, but he tilted his head back anyway, carding his fingers into my hair to draw me closer.

"Baby, you're my *everything*." The words were out before I could hear them in my head. "Fuck, that's cheesy."

"Smoked Gouda cheesy. Maybe even a triple cream Brie," Jae agreed, hooking his arms around my neck. "But it's okay. I like cheese. Just not too… much of it. Lactose intolerant."

"Jae, honey, I've got a lot better things to feed you than cheese."

WE MADE it upstairs, but our clothes didn't quite get past the steps. Well, my jeans did. Jae's shirt was left someplace in the living room, and his pants were mostly off by the time I pushed him back onto the bed. My hands going down the front of his undone fly did the rest of the job, peeling the denim off his long legs in one fluid push.

Strange how a few hours didn't seem enough time to spend worshipping Jae's body. I needed—wanted—a few days. A week if possible, but I'd take what I could get. Especially where he was concerned.

Climbing up onto the bed, I sat on my knees, and stared down at him, taking in the sight of his lean, pale body against the dark chocolate sheets. Tracing the cut of his hip muscles with my thumbs, I dropped down and kissed the dip of Jae's belly button, scraping at the ridge with my teeth.

Erotically boneless, Jae curled up over me and cupped my side, stroking at the shiny blotch of scarring along my ribs. Shifting under me, Jae edged his knee up between my legs and guided me to the side.

"Lie down." His voice was thick with need, painted with splashes of seductive, round Korean. "Let me do something… this time. Please."

I didn't know what he was asking. His words were too lost in the desire coming up from inside of him, but I understood him enough. I slid over onto the mattress and lay back onto the pillows. The sheets were already warm from our bodies, a light hint of lavender coming up from the fine cotton where we'd been.

Jae took his time unzipping me, the snick of metal teeth a loud, slow tease in between my heavy breathing. He slid the jeans down my hips and over my thighs, pausing every few inches to suckle at me. My skin was glowing pink by the time he was done, a rush of blood pouring into each press of his teeth and lips on me.

"Jae—"

Reaching for him was useless. He only pushed my hands back down to my sides and shook his head, the fall of his black hair ghosting over my hard cock. I could already feel my dick leaking. A trail of moisture glistened on my flat belly, and Jae's tongue found the edge of it, lapping at the salty liquid in long strokes. His mouth was soft on my skin, a glide of rough satin smoothly taking in the smear of my seed.

"God, you are so fucking gorgeous," I whispered.

He was. There was no denying how beautiful he looked with his pinked mouth curving down over my abdomen, then the obscene intimacy of seeing it wrap over the head of my cock. I found his hair with my fingers, tangling them up into the strands before I stroked down the length of his neck. I had to strain to reach him. He was too far away, barely allowing me the pleasure of running my palms over his shoulders before I gave up and brought my fingers back up to curve over his cheekbones.

His eyes were hooded, his gaze on me as he sucked and pulled on me. I felt the sharp edge of his teeth catch me on my glans, and I hissed, aroused by the slight pain. Jae dropped one of his hands off of my thighs, burrowing it between my legs. A hitched breath later, my balls were cupped in his long, elegant fingers, rolling about on his palm as he squeezed them lightly, enough to tug my mind off of his mouth's erotic journey and onto the sharp pull of my sac.

The sheets no longer smelled only of lavender. They'd taken on the sweet-salt musk of our sweat, a glorified masculine odor I'd treasure once Jae left me for the evening. Even better, the linens would catch the sticky joining of our bodies, and I'd end up sleeping amid the wet until it stained my flesh with its flakes

"Come up here." I wasn't too proud to keep the edge from my voice when I begged.

"No, you always get what you want, Cole-ah. It's my turn now," Jae whispered. "Every time I have you in my mouth, I want more. I think of the taste of you when I'm alone, and sometimes when you look at me, I want to drop to my knees and wrap my mouth around you. Having you in me... the scent of you in my mouth... takes away any doubts I have... any pain I might feel. I've missed that. I *want* that, *agi*."

"Jae, I'm not going anywhere. You won't ever get rid of me." I arched my back when his fingers found the length of my cock. Twisting his grip around my base, Jae huffed a breath over my shaft's head, the tight skin along my sex roiling beneath his hand. "Forever, hon, remember? I promise."

"I remember. I love doing this to you." He climbed up my body, stretching out over my chest until our mouths could touch. Sliding his lips over mine, he shared the taste of us from the mingle on his tongue. "I like making you shake. It makes me feel... powerful. Because you let me do this to you. Let me do more."

Jae lifted away, leaving me behind, a gasping, writhing mess. Trailing his mouth down to my chest, he first kissed at the scars across my shoulders and down my sides, lingering long enough to make me twist at being tickled. Jae's clever fingers took up a journey of their own, twisting at one of my nipples until it was a plump, taut pink nub.

"You're mine, Cole-ah." Jae grasped my dick and fondled its velvety head. "This is mine too."

He returned to suck at my mouth, driving his tongue in past my lips. I took as much from him as he would give, licking at the roof of his mouth until he could no longer stand the feathering against his palate. Grinding his hips down into mine, Jae began a slow, circular roll on my crotch, pulling up every nerve he'd stoked with a fiery passion. His legs were sleek against my thighs, a soft, silken touch against the fine hairs growing there. His cock caught on my skin, leaving behind a thicker moist trail.

"I... want to do this while I suck on you, Cole-ah," he murmured, pushing a digit up against my entrance. His fingers found my taint, caressing the soft skin there while the heel of his hand pressed in and out against my sac. His touch fluttered, circling at the tightness he found there. "Can you stay still?"

I wasn't even sure how to say shit fucking no around the lump of shock in my throat. The best I could come up with was, "Um, sure?"

He swallowed me down to the base of my cock, short-circuiting my brain. My stomach and muscles trembled with the strain of keeping myself from spilling into his mouth. Pulling back, he dragged a shallow bite along my shaft, leaving behind a light red scoring. I'd probably feel it for a couple of days.

Personally, I couldn't wait.

Fuck, I wanted his cock in me. Hell, I'd be happy with his fingers, but his cock would be better. I liked the heft of it, its length, and how it curved slightly to the left. I'd had it down my throat, tasting its spicy sweetness. There'd been times when I'd thought about being around him, but the thought of it had been distant.

"Can you grab the lube?" he murmured around the base of my dick. His cheek lying against the hair spread around my groin was obscenely erotic. "I don't want this to hurt. I just want to touch inside of you while I have you in my mouth."

There were condoms and lube on the nightstand, left over from the last time we'd been together, and I stretched out, snagging what we needed. A snick of the bottle opening and the scent of almonds were the only warnings I got. His fingers moved in, spreading me apart, and I gasped, lifting my hips up from the bed.

I moaned when the lube hit my crack. Resting my head on the pillow, I groaned when his fingers scooped up the twisting trail and pressed into my entrance. It'd been years since I'd been penetrated, and my shoulders tensed up involuntarily at the intrusion. Jae's touch was gentle, but I hadn't felt the hissing pain of flesh breaching past my inner ring for a long time.

And when his long fingers found the core of my nerves, I jerked from the intensity of the sigh escaping my lungs.

Then burned from the touch of his rough skin against the slick flesh inside of me.

The smell of almonds battled with the lavender scent coming up from the pillow beneath me. Jae's fingers withdrew for a moment, returning with a fresh spill of oil. This time, he slid in easier, breaching me completely with his knuckles, spreading my ass cheeks when he dug in.

Jae spent more than five minutes laving my cock. He leisurely spread butterfly kisses along my hip bones, then retraced his path with his teeth. The tip of his tongue traced out the wrinkled skin on my sac, tickling my flesh into a wave of goose bumps. I hadn't moved all of the pillows out of the way when I'd splayed out on the bed, and I'd trapped a bolster against the dip of my torso. It jutted my hips a bit, thrusting my crotch up toward Jae's full mouth. He took advantage of my lifted hips, his tongue meandering down the sides of my cock.

He was driving me crazy. And he knew it.

Running his fingertips up the inside of my legs, Jae murmured appreciatively when I tilted my hips and tightened the cleft of my ass around his hand. His mouth continued its journey downward, teasing at the pucker of my ass until I squirmed under his tongue. I wasn't going to last long. He'd primed me to nearly spilling just with his mouth on my skin. I wasn't going to make it to the end if he actually slid his tongue into me.

But damn it, I wanted him to take his sweet time.

"Jae, baby...." I groaned when his fingers flexed into my ass cheeks. "I'm going to blow if you keep that up."

He pinched my right cheek, twisting the bit of skin to get my attention. "Don't move, then. I'll be right back. I'll get you a condom. Maybe I'll even roll it down with my mouth."

I didn't have to pull at my cock to keep it interested. It leapt back to attention, leaking down around its head. Reaching down, I stretched my hand out until I could feel Jae stroking up and down into me. He bent forward, kissing my neck as his thumb played with my fingers, hooking me along for the ride. I felt the first shimmer of my release tightening in my belly, and I pulled away, breaking away from Jae's hand.

"I'll get the damned condom, because if you have those fingers on me again, I'm going to lose myself all over that pretty face of yours." I yanked Jae down to the mattress. Giving him a fierce kiss, I growled into his mouth. "And I don't know if I have enough time to do you twice before your sister gets home."

CHAPTER SEVENTEEN

HIS mouth tasted of promise and stars. If I could, I would have crawled inside of him and stayed there. I should have been used to the feel of Jae on my body or the taste of him, but with every sip… every touch… I found myself wanting more. Wanting him was going to be the death of me, but having him would be worth every agonizing moment we'd spent apart.

The squirts of lube on my palm warmed up under my fingers, but I didn't touch Jae yet. I couldn't trust myself. He'd left the scent of his body on mine, and every time I moved forward, my senses were filled with him. Sprawled on his back over the rumpled sheets, Jae's honey-kissed gaze never left my face. I took a moment—a very long moment—to drink him in.

His pale body glowed against the rich brown linens, his dark plum-pink nipples luring my eye to his muscled chest. Jae's long legs and supple torso rippled with a coiled strength normally hidden beneath loose-fitting clothes. Stripped bare, he was a feast of planes and shadows, a beautiful contrast of masculine power compared to his almost androgynous face.

I'd never asked God to send me someone after Rick. I'd already consigned myself to the doldrums of a loveless life, and finding Jae-Min behind a murderer's door seemed like an oddly delivered divine gift. If God wanted to strip the wings off of one of his own and deliver him to me, who was I to argue with fate.

But damn if Jae didn't make me work for every scrap of his heart.

His knees parted when my weight dipped the bed near his hip. I bent over him, needing to have his mouth on mine when I ran my fingers along the split of his ass. His muscles tightened involuntarily, responding to the shiver of cold left in the lube, but he forced his thighs apart, urging me forward.

Hooking my palm up into his cleft, I circled his entrance, playing at the tightness I found there until it relaxed under the slight push of my fingertip. I pulled the air from his mouth, sealing us together while I spread him open. His body fought me, repelling my intrusion until he sighed and surrendered, letting me in.

I slid in carefully, spreading as much of the oil around his core as I could. His muscled ring sucked on my index finger, pulling me in further than I'd wanted to go, but when the tip brushed against his nerves, Jae hissed with pleasure, and the sheets twisted into spirals from his clenched fists digging in.

His cock pearled, spooling out a glistening drop for me to suck on. I lapped at the velvety head, trapping it against his belly. He curled up, hugging my shoulders to his chest. His arms were strong, muscled and sinewy. He held me as much as I held his cock, carefully stroking down my backbone and over my shoulder blades with his long fingers. His pubic hair tickled my chin, a soft, wiry kiss on my skin. Enclosed in the shadow of his embrace, I suckled at his length while working my fingers deep into his recesses, preparing him for my entry.

We could have stayed there—wrapped about one other—all day. With Jae's arms around me, I could have died and been in heaven. There was something sublime about his touch. Bowed over me, sighing soft Korean words into my ear, he was exposed and vulnerable. Open and raw, he was finally free of everything... of everyone pressuring him to be something... someone other than who he truly was.

I loved seeing him... feeling him stripped free of the shroud he wore around his soul. When we were alone, I could see the angel wings the world clipped short so he couldn't fly. In those moments, I felt him soar... and finally reach out to touch the sky. With his body around mine and my mouth on his shaft, I felt like I was drinking heaven dry.

He mewled, twisting in my mouth. Jae was close… too close for me to continue. I let his cock go, letting it slip free from my lips, but kept pushing up into him. The taste of my lover on my tongue slithered down my throat, a tinge of musk curling down into my belly. I hit the spot of nerves deep inside of him, and Jae groaned, begging for more.

"*Jagiya… saranghae*, Cole-ah…."

One day, I would hear that in English, but for now, whispered between our sweaty bodies, I would take his love any way he wanted to give it to me.

In the movies, lovers came together in a graceful tangle of legs and kisses. He and I were never that fluid. We had no ballet of bodies forming to become one. Instead, I slid my hands under him and coaxed him up over my lap. His knee hit my shoulder, striking me in its most tender part, but the throb between my legs took precedence.

So did the look of desire flushing Jae's beautiful face.

I pulled him up so he could put his back on my chest, his legs straddling my lap. My sex burned to be in him, a deep-seated heat working up from my balls and into the raging tip of my cock's head. He clenched my thighs, and Jae thrust himself up, pressing his shoulder blades back against my chest. With his back arched into me, he reached underneath until he grasped my shaft in his hand. The feel of his fingers tightening over my erection was almost my undoing.

Huffing in short breaths, I tried to steady my raging hard-on until I felt the tip of my cock touch the oiled ring of his body. At the first give of his muscled entrance, Jae gasped and dropped his head back, curving his neck over my shoulder. In the afternoon light, his hair bled blue shadows across my skin, exposing his throat and face to the sun. I bent my head sideways and kissed the corner of his mouth, urging him to turn his face toward me.

Our lips touched when I slid into him, and Jae gasped, his mouth rasping open against mine. His teeth snagged my lower lip, and I tasted a spot of my own blood when I breached him. The heat of his body closing over my cock seared away any thought of taking things slow. Gripping his hips, I dug my fingers along his bones and drove up into him, struggling for control as his teeth scored my lip. Letting my mouth go, Jae's ravenous appetite spurred him on to find another target. He chose anything within reach, satisfied only when he had a good grip on a chunk of my flesh.

His nails raked at my thighs, his soft, husky murmurs urging me onward. My spit thickened with the effort of pacing my plunges up into him. A sudden squeeze of his ass around me and I ground my hips into his ass, pushing him down hard onto my cock. Jae took me, lifting himself up onto his knees before meeting me in a wet slap of skin.

The sound of our thighs striking was nearly lost under the burble of Korean coming from Jae's panting mouth. I found his nipple with one hand and plucked at the nub with nerveless fingers. My mind was numbing beneath the growing spiral of pleasure wrapping my cock, and I needed to bring Jae over with me.

My own release was nothing without his. I needed more than two hands, and, not for the first time, I wished I could bend over to suckle him off while I was inside of him. Instead, I let the hand on his chest drop, and I clasped his tight, hard cock. A few strokes were enough for Jae to peel back away from my hand, but I refused to let him go.

"I want to ride you, Cole-ah." His husky whisper became a needy mewl when I passed my rough palm over his cock head. "Too... soon...."

"Baby, we've got forever," I promised, biting his earlobe. "Let go, Jae. Let me hold you. Let me feel you in my hand."

Smearing the come gathering along his slit, I worked the viscous fluid down, smoothing my journey along his shaft. His movements were nearly too hard for my cock to take. The skin of my shaft was growing tender and raw. My balls were tucking up against my thighs, as if they too wanted to crawl up inside of my lover and join the party.

Thrashing on my shaft, Jae's shoulder blades and spine rubbed against my nipples, searing them with friction. The pulse in his shaft skipped, and I held on tighter, working my hips as hard as I could. He shivered every time my dick hit his pressure point, and I knew my strokes were getting to him when he began to tremble and shake.

We were no longer in a rhythm. Instead, we'd fallen into a frantic push-you-pull-me dance I never wanted to end. The outside world was gone to me. The sunlight through the window only touched us, filling the room with light solely so I could see Jae's tense form working me into a frenzy. Stretched out over my body, he was a spectacular length of sinew and pale skin, his muscles curving and pulling with every contortion of his hips and arms.

Sweat pooling on his brow ran down his cheek, falling onto one of his shoulders. A drop curled down the rise of his collarbone, leaving behind a smear of wet on my lover's ivory skin. I strained forward and licked the spot, tasting him in my mouth. The fragrance of his essence lay in that drop, the faint hint of his come lingering in the salty aftermath of his skin.

The touch of my mouth was enough for him. His nails gouged my skin open, and the cold air stung my scored flesh. Straining, his body went rigid, and I saw a flash of white when he bit his own lip to keep from shouting out loud. A moment later, his cock let loose, splattering my hand with his hot seed.

With the scent of Jae's spill in the air, I lost my mind. Gripping him tightly, I pulled at his base, jerking him onward while taking one last plunge into his searing depths. His climax ripped through both of us, his ass muscles clamping down on my sensitive sex. The pull was too much. I couldn't keep up the beat of our bodies, and I gave in to the rise of seed demanding to be released.

Wrapping my arms around Jae's waist, I fell forward, pinning him to the bed. Trapped by my weight, he writhed for a moment, then thrust his ass up into me, taking me in deep. Covering his body with mine, I hugged him to me as tightly as I could, hammering down into his passage.

The first wave of release made my face tingle, and my mind ran cold from the sensations crowding it. Jae's hands closed over my wrists, and he worked his fingers between mine. Curling his shoulders down, he kept me plastered against his back. We slid together, our wet skin and stray splatters of the lube slicking our flesh.

I took a breath, and Jae said my name, a sweet drop of sound filled with so much emotion, it filled me.

"I love you." It was all I could get out before my climax hit me. Shuddering already from its initial wave, I was still ill-prepared for the shattering strike of my release's intensity. I lost touch with everything. I could only feel Jae's ass cheeks and legs on my crotch and thighs and the press of his fingers against my palms. The taste of his skin and sweat was on my tongue, and a butterfly wing of a kiss came from his mouth when he twisted slightly to find my lips.

I poured everything I had into him. My trust. My love. Everything I could give him short of stripping my skin off and wrapping it around his heart to keep him safe and warm. If I'd had a knife right then, I would have made the first cut and begged him to take what he needed.

In that moment, I wasn't sure everything I had would be enough when, in the middle of my gasping breaths, I heard him whisper, "*Saranghae*, Cole-ah."

As quickly as it had hit me, the sensations were gone, and I was left limp and boneless. I carefully slid free of Jae's clench, pulled the condom off, tied its end, depositing it in the small waste can by the nightstand. He lay where I'd left him, panting and worn out. Kissing his shoulder, I snuggled up behind him, letting him rest back against me. Still out of breath, I made small puffs into Jae's sweat-damp hair.

Between the lubricant and Jae's release, we would be a sticky mess if we stayed there much longer, but I was loath to move away from him. Running my hand over his belly, I rimmed his navel with my fingernail, chuckling when he jerked away from the tickle.

"We're going to be cemented together, you know." I kissed the blade bone rising up on his back.

"Mmmm… probably," he murmured in agreement. "What time is it?"

Peeking at the clock, I rested my chin on his shoulder. "Less than an hour since I dragged you upstairs to have my way with you."

"How long does it take a girl to spend a few hundred dollars?" His eyelids were dragging down, more sleepy than aroused. The shadows under his lashes were deep and blue, a hint he'd skipped more than a few nights in bed since he'd left the house.

"A couple of hours. Maybe they'll go see a movie or have some dinner before they get back." I'd handed Tiffany much more than a couple hundred dollars, but Jae didn't need to know that. "I don't know how long that would take. You and I seem to be able to either get the movie *or* the dinner part done before we have to crawl into each other."

"That's not a bad thing," Jae whispered. "Think we can just rest here for a while? A little while?"

"Sure, babe." I nodded, yawning. "I'll set the alarm on my phone."

And that was the last thing I remember saying until I smelled the perfume of cooking ginger filling the house.

I'VE never been a spring-out-of-bed person. It took me at least half an hour from crawling out of bed in the morning before I could focus long enough on a mirror to brush my teeth. Me waking up at dusk after a nap wasn't much better.

The smell of food cooking pulled me out of bed, and I stumbled to the shower, half wondering why Jae hadn't woken me up sooner but mostly silently thanking him for letting me sleep. From the pungent fragrances coming up from the kitchen, it seemed like he'd changed his mind about the deep-dish pizza, so I took my time showering, scraping off the flaky scum of our afternoon from my skin.

Scrubbing at my hair with a towel, I grabbed my jeans and underwear off the floor, intending to sit down on the edge of the mattress to pull them on, when I noticed something odd about the bed.

Jae was still in bed. Asleep.

His hips were swaddled in the billowy duvet I'd bought to keep the chill off, but he'd taken advantage of me crawling off to the bathroom and flung his body diagonally across the bed. Stretched out over the pillows, his arms nearly touched either side of the king-sized mattress, his dark hair a splash of black on the brown linens.

The smell of ginger was joined by the sizzle of browning garlic, and Neko popped her head up over Jae's legs, her ears flicking in interest at the promise of food.

"Fuck, who the hell is downstairs cooking, then? Shit!" I left my jeans unbuttoned. For a second, I debated breaking out my Glock, but sanity eventually wormed its way back into my lizard brain.

No one breaks into someone else's house to cook them dinner unless that someone else actually *is* dinner. Since I personally didn't know anyone with cannibalistic leanings, the Glock wasn't necessary.

The wooden stairs were cold, and I skidded on the runner spread over the landing. Taking the steps two at a time, I rounded the corner of the front hall, almost hitting the archway when the kitchen tile grabbed at my bare feet. The sweet fragrance was much stronger in the kitchen, a pile of grated ginger crackling in a frying pan on the stove. A handful of cracked garlic cloves sat on one of the larger chopping boards, their skins peeled off and swept off to the side.

I guessed dinner and a movie hadn't wormed their way into the kids' plans. Not a problem. I could handle a teenage girl. I even had one as a sister. Of course, I'd never walked in on my baby sister when she was holding a large kitchen knife and possibly murderous.

Tiffany grabbed one of the intact cloves and placed it on the board. She put the flat of the blade against its plump curve and brought her hand down against the steel plane, slightly crushing the clove and popping its meaty flesh free of its skin.

She gave me a look over her shoulder, one of confusion with a dash of sneering disgust at my bare chest. Nodding to the laundry room, she said softly, "I washed the shirts I got from Jae-Min. Probably one of them is yours, if you want."

"Ah, thanks." Stunning her with my witty retort, I dug out an old rugby Jae'd stolen months ago and tugged it on. Returning to the kitchen meant talking with Tiffany, but short of moving into the wash room, I didn't see any other option. After making sure my fly was closed, I headed back into the kitchen and, as casually as I could, grabbed a beer from the fridge and held it out to her. "Want one?"

If I thought Jae's derisive looks were withering, they had nothing on his sister, who put the full weight of her snark in her gaze. "Um, I'm seventeen."

"Shit, forgot that," I said sheepishly. Looking back into the icebox, I dug out a few soda bottles. "We've got Diet Coke, Dr Pepper, and Sprite. Want any of those? Or there's some of your brother's iced green tea, but it's plain. You'll have to add some sugar to it."

She took a Diet Coke, popped off the plastic bottle top, and let it sit open on the counter. I joined the soda, taking up residence above the dishwasher. Her eyes bugged out a bit, and I sipped at my beer, grunting slightly when I swallowed. The air was thick with unspoken feelings and tight words. I went for casual, hoping to charm more than brittle politeness out of her.

"Yeah, your brother gets pissed when I do this too." I shrugged. "We've come to a compromise. I sit over here, and he doesn't cook anyplace near where my ass has been. How'd you get in?"

"You left the front door unlocked." She sniffed, and the corner of her mouth curled up in disgust. "Guess you forgot about it when you dragged my brother upstairs. I guess you didn't wait that long after we left before you sickos started fucking."

"Sweetheart, let's get one thing straight," I cut her off, gesturing at her with my beer. "What goes on between your brother and I is something very special to me. You can fucking hate my guts all you want because you're a kid and your world's still kind of black and white. I get that. But don't you ever say anything bad about how much I love your brother or what he means to me. Everything else is on the table. Just not that."

She put the knife down, probably not trusting herself with it. I was within stabbing range, and while I might have outweighed her by about a hundred pounds, Tiffany must have known she was safe from any attack on my end. Not only was she a teenaged girl, I was sleeping with her brother. She could come at me with a Sherman tank and I'd have to lie down on the ground and take it.

"We understand one another?" I pressed.

She rolled her lips in, and for a moment I worried that I'd made her cry, but instead, Tiffany nodded once and went back to chopping up garlic.

I wasn't good with kids. Hell, my own sisters scared me. The only teenagers I'd ever been around for an extended period of time were Claudia's grandchildren, and they were freaks of nature: well-behaved and polite. The only time one of them got out of line was in the hospital right after she'd been shot, and the family jerked on his chain pretty fast, reeling the young man in before he could tear into me. I wasn't sure how to handle a bundle of hormonal nerves... much less female hormonal nerves.

One thing I learned was God and Nature hated a vacuum. That same rule usually applied to people, especially teenagers. Leave something empty or silent long enough, someone would come along to fill it up. Tiffany was no exception. She lasted about two cloves before she cracked.

"Do you... how can you love him?" The knife stilled, delaying the great garlic massacre. "You're both... guys."

This was *not* a conversation I wanted to have with Jae's little sister. Especially not with him still sleeping upstairs. I could have opted to take the coward's way out, telling her to wait until Jae woke up, but something told me she would have an easier time talking to the big bad Gay Man sitting on the counter than her brother. I was... safe. Someone distant she could throw poop at like an enraged baby baboon when she felt cornered. Tiffany wouldn't be able to do that with Jae.

Well, she could, but she would end up breaking his heart, and for all of her teenaged angsty drama, she loved her older brother. Her world was fucked up because she found out Jae loved men, but she was struggling to come to grips with it.

I only wished I had some answers for her.

So I gave it my best shot.

"I don't know." Problem sometimes with being honest was admitting I didn't have all the answers, but it was all I had. "I can tell you it's something inside of me. I can't speak for Jae, but when I'm with him, I feel... good. Better than good. Like between the two of us, we can do anything. And when he's hurting, I want to make everything okay for him. I can't put it better than that. Not really. That's pretty much what it is. Something inside of me becomes… greater… when I'm with him. He *makes* me more human… more than what I am just by being with me."

"And that's the same thing as… a guy and a girl?"

"Dunno," I said with a grin. "I've never ever liked a girl like that."

Suspicion must have been handed out by the bucketful at the Kim house, because they used it liberally. Tiff's sidelong glance at me was dripping with it. "Really? Did you try?"

"Try?" I snorted. "I can't count how many times I've wished I liked women. Hell, high school sucked ass. Do you know how hard it was to hide my… um… you know… behind a towel in PE class? Showering with a bunch of guys when men turn you on is not the best way to spend puberty."

"Didn't you see a doctor?" She turned to face me, thankfully leaving the knife on the counter. "To try to fix it?"

There was so much *youth* on her. Her fresh face was drenched with the arrogance of teen knowledge and a deep-seated belief that she had all the answers in the world if only someone would just *listen* to her. It made me wonder how in the hell so many of us survived to actual adulthood, considering our delusional pubescent state.

"Doesn't work that way, sweetie." I was gentle in my reproach. "If anything, trying to change who you love just fucks you up more. It's better to change who you are inside so someone can love you."

"But—" She was conflicted. No one handed out manuals on how to *feel* about things. I floundered with trying to make sense of my thoughts when I was her age. I'd fought against what the people who should have loved me unconditionally were telling me. In the end, they'd done more damage than good, laying minefields of insecurity and doubt.

"Who Jae loves… isn't what's important. What matters is that the person loving him treats him right and treasures him for who he is. Isn't that what you'd want for him? For your brother?" I asked softly. "I've got a brother... hell, I've got two now, and I can tell you this, I wouldn't care whether or not they loved someone with inside or outside parts. I'd want them to be loved by someone who gave a shit about them. Because that's what love is. That person... that one person that makes you feel like you can do any damned thing you want to do really giving a shit about you deep down inside of their soul. *That's* love."

CHAPTER EIGHTEEN

A COUPLE of hours and a very embarrassed Jae later, I was packing up the rest of Claudia's blueberry pie and urging the Kims to take the king-sized inflatable mattress I'd bought for a camping trip. I left Tiff one of my suitcases to pack her things in when she was done with a video game Bobby'd left behind, then joined Jae on the front porch when he stepped outside for a smoke.

Staring at the cement slab that served as my stoop, I sat down on one of the steps and nestled up against my lover. Nudging him with my shoulder, I grinned at Jae when he narrowed his gaze at me.

"I can't believe you talked to her about... us. About me being gay." That sensual mouth I'd seen wrapped around my dick closed over the end of his Djarum Black, sucking out a bit of smoke. "What the hell... I can't—"

"To be fair, we also talked about the fact she's felt bad about telling you she's allergic to cats when she's not." It was a weak defense, but I went for it anyway. "She only said that because she thought Neko was mine and it would keep you away from me."

"Did you tell her *you're* allergic and tough it out for me?"

"Hey, one little white pill with my coffee every morning is a small price to pay to have you in my life." I caught a whisper of a smile at the corner of his mouth, and I leaned forward to catch it with my lips before it slipped away.

He looked behind us, furtively peeking at the picture windows in case Tiffany was in view. I could see her in the living room, playing a dancing game he'd bought a few months ago, her eyes frequently drifting to where we were. Chuckling under his breath, Jae returned my kiss with a small, casual peck, staying long enough to swipe the tip of his tongue over my lips.

"She's going to see you," I warned, but I savored the taste of Jae's clove-spiced kiss.

"I don't think I care." There was too much caught up in his exhale. Smoke and tension bled out of his body in a swirling plume. A tinge of guilt flushed through his eyes, and he ducked his head, his laughter turning on a nervous thread. "Okay, maybe a little bit. It's... hard to suddenly... have everything out in the open. I'm not sure... I feel like... I'm laid out for the world to see me and I'm naked. It's... hitting me a little bit hard."

"Do you feel overwhelmed?" It was a safe question to ask. If I needed to pull back from Jae physically, I would. I needed him to tell me how much was too much. How we were... how we acted... was totally up to him. "Whatever you need, babe. I'll make it happen."

"This one... I think I have to do on my own," Jae murmured, nodding to where his sister halfheartedly did the Dougie. She stumbled, and we lost sight of her head as she took a gainer to the floor.

"Your sister... not so graceful on the dance moves there, babe." I elbowed him, turning away to watch a plane's tiny blinking wing lights disappear into the clouds.

"That chest is hard to dance around. She should have moved it. It has those coaster things under it. It just needs a good push." The tip of his *kretek* flared red. "I'm going to go back to the studio and have a talk with her about... us. Do you mind?"

"No, I'll be okay... you'll be okay. That was a shitty book, by the way." Smirking, I jerked my chin toward the car parking on the street near my driveway. "Besides, I think I've got company."

Ichi's ambling stride was deceptively swift, and he was up the walk quickly. Despite the slight chill in the air, he wore another black short-sleeved T-shirt advertising a tattoo shop in Takeshita Dori— wherever that was—and jeans with more holes than fabric. Jae studied

Ichi as he approached, noting my brother's ink and a smirk that looked like it'd crawled off of my face and found a new home on his.

"He looks like you," Jae finally said.

"Really? I thought he looked more like Mike." Looking down at the frayed remains of his pants, I muttered. "But he dresses like you."

"Hey." Ichi smiled at Jae and held his hand out for a shake. I could hear the slight differences between Jae's tones and my brother's. Ichi's words had a staccato beat, sliding in and down as he spoke. I was more used to Jae's rolling tones, rounded off at each of his sentences, dropping before rising up again. "I'm Ichiro, Cole's... brother."

"I'm Kim Jae-Min." He took Ichiro's hand but gave a small bob over their clasped fingers. "I'm... Cole's boyfriend."

I'd honestly never believed the shock of hearing something spoken out loud could render someone speechless.

Boyfriend was not a word I'd ever heard come out of his mouth. I'd heard other words to describe me, and not all of them were complimentary. I called him my lover or boyfriend when speaking to other people, but he'd never really ever... outed... that word when referring to me before.

For the next few minutes, all I heard was a high-pitched buzz punctuated by my brain repeatedly muttering *what the fuck did Jae just say* someplace near my forehead. They continued to talk. I could see their mouths moving and, further behind us, Tiffany flailing away at some dance move that had her flinging her arms out like a demented starfish, but beyond that, I was gone.

"Cole-ah, did you hear me?" Jae's worried voice punched through my daze. "Ichiro can help you translate the papers. He reads *hangul.*"

"If you want the help." My brother looked at me like I'd grown a second head. "Since Jae is leaving—"

"You read Korean?" I must have sounded like I'd been dropped on my head, because both of them stared at me.

"I learned Korean a long time ago. A lot of my customers come up from South Korea. We were *just* speaking it." Ichi cocked his head and studied me carefully. "Maybe you weren't listening... perhaps?"

"Because Korean is so difficult to recognize when it's spoken," Jae scoffed at me. "It's like birdsong or maybe the sound of cars passing?"

"My brain was just elsewhere," I muttered, lightly cuffing Jae on the shoulder. "Did you eat, Ichi? I think there might be leftover pizza, but I don't know if it's edible. And some of whatever Tiff made, I think."

"If you didn't eat it for breakfast, then chances are it's not edible." My lover sidestepped another cuff.

"Sure you can't stay?" I asked. While the conversation Tiff and I had in the kitchen went a long way in lessening the tension between us, it'd spiked back up to prickly once Jae'd woken up and slunk downstairs. He and I both agreed she probably needed a little more time before we asked her to help pick out our china pattern.

"No, we had a couple of good hours between all of us." Leaning into me, Jae slid his hand over my ribs, a casual, intimate touch I'd have considered bold for him a few months ago. "I'm going to take her back to the studio before she gets grumpy."

"Grumpy?" Ichi glanced through the window at Tiffany. "She looks sweet."

"Oh, little brother, how little you know the mind of a teenaged girl," I said mournfully. "Let me help you pack up the car, Jae. Ichi, if the pizza's shit, I've can make you a sandwich or something."

Loading up Jae's car earned me a brief kiss on the lips when I leaned through the driver's side window to say good-bye. The kiss got me a disgusted hiss and an eye roll from Tiffany, who, in turn, earned herself a sharp look from her tight-lipped older brother. After promising to call me later, Jae backed the Explorer down the driveway and drove off.

"Have you guys been together long?" Ichi had snuck up on me when I wasn't looking, and I jerked in surprise. Laughing, he put his hands on my shoulders to steady me.

"I don't know," I said sheepishly. "Not too sure when to start counting. I'll have to ask him, but how the fuck do I work *that* into a conversation?"

I ended up making Ichiro a sandwich that would have done Dagwood proud. I then had to explain who Dagwood was, but his mouth was full of meat, bread, and cheese, so I don't think it mattered whether or not he understood me. I sat down on the couch and began to flip through one of the books Hong Chul gave us.

"I probably should have called first," Ichi said between bites. "You could have been busy."

"Nah, I figured Mike was driving you nuts and Maddy was out saving the world, so you couldn't hide behind her." He laughed, and I knew I'd guessed right. My brother... our brother... liked to pry and poke. A few hours in his company and a guy would begin to wonder if he'd somehow stumbled into an odd CIA interrogation. "Coming over is good. We can do that get-to-know-one-another shit we'd promised to do."

The folio I'd chosen was an address book. While the addresses were in English, the names themselves were in Korean. A few of the places were familiar, and I recognized Gyong-Si's immediately. Hong Chul's grandfather, Bhak Bong Chol, had been meticulous and kind of a stalker. Under Gyong-Si's address, he'd listed who appeared to be the fortune-teller's assistants, both past and present. The last name was the only one not scratched out.

"Terry Yi. And once again, why so many of the same last name? Too many Koreans are named Yi and Lee. It's nearly as bad as Kim." Ichiro gave me a look that damned me for being ethnocentric. "Look, I just have a hard time keeping track of who the hell is related to whom sometimes. My brain doesn't work that way. Why did Bhak write that name in English instead of *hangul*?"

"Terry's English? The word, anyway," Ichi said around a mouthful of potato chips. "Kind of hard to write that in Korean." He wiped his hands on a napkin and dug into one of the folders. "What exactly are you looking for?"

"Don't know," I admitted. "Bhak seemed to keep track of this fortune-teller from Seoul. Guy tries to pass himself as gay over here, but our English-named Terry told me Gyong-Si is about as gay as sugar is sour."

"Maybe he's bi?" My younger brother shrugged. "Or at least curious about guys. I am. Well, have been. About some guys."

The chip I'd stolen from his plate caught somewhere in my throat and I choked, spitting up oily crumbs over Bhak's papers. The sip of beer I'd sloshed into my mouth did little to clear it away, but the liquid washed away enough of it to let me speak.

"Wait, what?" Coughing, I glared at Ichi. "You're what?"

"Curious... kind of." He shrugged it off and went back to looking through the papers. "I've been with a couple of guys. Nothing too much, but it was okay. They weren't anyone I was in love with or anything, so I think that would make a difference."

"Jesus, does Mike know?" I finished coughing and rubbed at my chest. The spasm jerked my scar tissue into a twist, and a tingle of pain rolled through me.

"Don't know why he would. It didn't really come up." Ichi frowned at something he was reading.

Whistling under my breath, I went back to reading through Bhak's address book. "Dude, you are... a bundle of surprises."

"My father puts it a different way," Ichiro laughed. "But then he doesn't know about the boys either. If he did, I think he'd drown me."

We spent more time drinking beer and trying to read Bhak's handwriting than matching up names to my flowchart. About an hour into the *hangul* and English ping-pong game, I stared down at the pieces of paper I'd taped together and tried to make sense of the lines and boxes we'd mapped out.

"Shit, he's had... maybe... ten kids? Maybe? And no one's tapped him for this?"

"This guy... Gyong-Si... he's kind of a whore." Ichi traced one of the lines. "Take a look here."

My flowchart looked like I'd taken a pot of macaroni and thrown it down on the paper. I'd switched colors at some point to differentiate where he'd impregnated his clients. He had a red kraken leading out of his spot to the women he'd gotten to in Korea and a black octopus to his clients in California. One box had both a red and black line.

"Eun Joon Lee." I whistled softly. "Fuck."

"Considering he got paid by most of these women, pretty much… yeah. Wasn't she one of the murdered women?" Ichi asked.

"I think that's the only question I've got an answer to," I replied. "Yeah, she was, but Bhak didn't know she was pregnant. *I* filled in that black line. But he *knew* she'd gotten pregnant before. He might have been in touch with her here in Los Angeles. He's got her address in his book."

"So what happened to the baby?" Ichiro stacked up his notes and ran through them quickly. "Bhak doesn't say anything about it. Just that she had a baby by him when they were both in Seoul. She must have been a kid. Maybe she lost it or something?"

"Gave it up for adoption? Like Madame Sun did?" I suggested. "But then why would she go back to him and get pregnant again? That doesn't make sense."

"*None* of this makes sense." My brother rubbed at his full belly and belched, laughing when I chuckled. He grinned back at me. Nothing said brotherly bonding like shared gas. "So Gyong-Si's got a lot of kids. Why would anyone care?"

"Jealousy?" I guessed. "Or maybe he's got money someplace and someone's trying to take out the competition? I don't know, but it's the only straw I've got to grasp. Nothing else makes sense."

Ichiro's phone sang out "Love Addict," and he grimaced, pulling it out of his pocket. "Hold on. It's our brother."

"Yeah, I make that face *all* the time when he calls." I gathered up the two empty bottles and paper plates. Stepping over Ichi's legs, I nearly stumbled when he nudged my calf. Grumbling halfheartedly at him, I dumped the trash into the recycle container and came back into the living room, where he was packing up his stuff. "Heading out?"

"Yeah, he wants to go over a few contracts I had drawn up. I'm thinking of starting a shop over here. What do you think about that?" He looked like a little boy asking for a cookie. "Mind having your little brother around the city a few months out of the year?"

"Nah, it'll be cool," I replied. It would be. We got along well enough, and it seemed like we'd formed a half-assed alliance against our control freak older brother. "At least I'll have someone else to read Korean for me. Pretty sure Jae's figured out I'm only using him for his brain and not his hot body."

"I'll mention that to him the next time I see him," Ichi teased, slinging his backpack over his shoulder.

"Thanks, 'cause I don't want to ever have sex again." I walked him to the door and stopped short when he pulled me into a fierce hug. It took me a moment before I thought to wrap my arms around him, but it didn't seem like Ichiro noticed.

Pulling back, he slapped me on the shoulder. "It was good doing this with you. Gave me an idea about what you do. Next time, we go out and get you some ink from one of the guys I'm thinking about hiring. You can live in my world for a few hours."

"No fucking way. I'd sooner get blown off through a glory hole at an orthodontic trade show." I shuddered at the thought. "Dude, the only person I'd trust to put a bunch of needles on me would be you."

That little bit of sharing got me another hug, a fiercer lung-squeezing than before. Stepping back, my younger brother nodded manfully and patted my arms.

"Thanks," he mumbled. "That's the nicest thing someone's ever said to me. Glad it came from you."

"I meant it. You're okay." It was getting a bit too teary-eyed in the foyer for me. We weren't totally comfortable enough with one another for me to break out the whiskey and get I-Love-You-Man drunk, but it was getting close. "I can't kick the shit out of some stranger who fucks up my skin, but since you're technically my younger brother, I can beat you and write it off as sibling love. You're the bottom of the food chain now, Ichi. All part of learning how it is to be one of the boys."

"And Maddy?" He crooked an eyebrow up. "She one of the boys too?"

"Fuck no. First, you don't hit a girl," I snorted. "Secondly, she can run you down like a cheetah and pound you into the ground with her purse. Don't fuck with that woman. She carries cinder blocks around just in case she has to build a wall or something."

I closed the door behind my laughing brother and headed back into the living room to soak in more of the Pastafarian Ouija board I'd created. The notes Bhak wrote down were sketchy. I had no idea when Eun Joon'd first gotten pregnant or even when she'd come over from South Korea.

"Let's see, Eun Joon, you were... what, forty-one? Forty?" I didn't know a lot about women, but it sounded kind of late to be having a baby. "Maybe you were pregnant before but lost the first baby, and getting a kid from your husband wasn't happening. Did you go back to the guy who knocked you up before and then try to pass the baby off as Lee's? Or can Lee even *have* kids? Then he found out about Gyong-Si and killed you."

I really needed Wong to get back to me about Lee. The rut I was stuck in seemed only to get deeper and deeper the more I ran around, and I couldn't see a way out. If I kept it up, I was pretty certain I was going to be buried under a pile of maybes with no clear answer.

My phone rang while I was staring at those damned red and black lines leading to Eun Joon's name. Thinking it was Mike calling to yell at me for not coming with Ichiro, I let it ring a few times before picking up.

It wouldn't do if Mike thought I lunged to answer the phone each time he called. That kind of thing led to a swelled ego, and his head was big enough without my help.

Except it wasn't my bossy, overbearing older brother. Instead, the male voice on the other end of the phone had a harder edge to it, something cut from violence and tightly held back emotions. I couldn't understand what he was saying. Then it kicked in that he was speaking a fast, guttural Korean I had no chance in hell of comprehending, even with my limited understanding of the language. To make matters worse, it sounded like whoever was calling was in the middle of an arcade.

"Whoa, hold up," I cut him off. "First, English. Sorry, but my Korean's only good for ordering off a menu. Who's this?"

"Fuck, hold on. I… shit, hold on. I've got to get out of this room."
The chatter and beeping in the background faded, and all I could make
out was the guy's breathing. "Is this the guy who came to see me?
Um… Cole McGinnis?"

"Hong Chul?" I hadn't been around him long enough to recognize
his voice, but he sounded rougher than I'd remembered. "What's up?
Got through a lot of your grandfather's—"

"I didn't call you about the damned papers, man," he spat into the
phone. "I called you because someone knifed my daughter this
afternoon. What I want is for you to tell me who the hell is doing this
shit so I can go return the favor. Swear to God, man. Abby dies and I'm
going to fucking kill anyone who ever had anything to do with Gyong-
Si. And then, I'm going to start in on his ass with a knife and see how
he fucking likes it."

CHAPTER NINETEEN

THERE is no longer trip than driving to a hospital. Especially when a little girl I'd just met lay on a table somewhere in the building with surgeons' fingers inside of her guts. I stopped on the way to pick her up something to make her smile, blindly looking for something to stave off the wild dread running like a nightmare through my brain. All I could see in my mind were her tiny little flip-flops sitting on the porch and her little hands on her father's face when she leaned in for a kiss.

I parked and wondered if I needed to hit reception up to see where Abby'd been taken, but I spotted her father first, his waxen face a spot of white in front of the building's blue-gray stone blocks.

Hong Chul was standing in the large cement smoking circle outside of the hospital where his daughter, Abby, fought for her life. If I'd had any doubts of his love for his little girl, they were swept away when I saw the broken young father fighting to keep his hands from shaking as he lit a cigarette. I wanted to tell him I knew how he felt, but the hard look I got through a plume of menthol smoke told me he didn't want to hear it.

So I didn't say it.

Instead, I pulled a head-sized fluffy gray thing with ears out of a plastic bag and handed it to him. "Here. It's for Abby. It's called a Totoro. The lady at the store in Little Tokyo said kids love it. Thought she might like one."

"Thanks." Hong Chul made no move to take the toy. Instead, he took a long drag on his cigarette and stared up at the sky. Even in the orange-fizz glow of the parking lot lights, I could see tears forming in his eyes. A taint of pain-filled water, then they were gone, lost in the wispy streams. I put the Totoro back into the bag, paying close attention to fitting its body in past the handles to give him a bit of time to pull himself together.

Mouse-sized moths played death-tag with the lights overhead, creating fuzzy Batman symbols on the asphalt below. A few hundred feet away, the hospital's ER did a brisk business. The automatic glass doors barely had time to kiss before they were flung open again by someone hurrying in. Several scrub-wearing men and women hung at the edge of the smoking area, fatigue draining their faces to a lifeless gray. Blood and gore stained their cottons, making them look more like hapless butchers than healers.

Personally, seeing how tired they all looked, I'd sooner trust them with a Q-tip than a scalpel, but the hospital had other plans for them. One detached from the pack, then another. Others came to take their places, less splattered but no less tired.

Hong Chul and I were the only civilians. Almost made me want to light up just so I could fit in. As it was, Hong Chul's pulls on his cigarette seemed halfhearted at best. Nothing compared to the frantic inhale and puff assembly line next to us.

"How's she doing?" I had to ask. Even if I didn't want to hear the answer, I had to ask.

"Okay," Hong Chul grunted. "I guess. Fuck, no one's saying she's fantastic, but she's out of surgery. Fucker nicked her liver. We've got to watch her turn fucking yellow and get sick on top of worrying she'd die."

I knew nothing about the side effects of being stabbed in the liver, but it was never a good thing when an organ got punctured. I couldn't imagine how small Abby's organs were. A knife made serious damage in an adult. I'd be surprised if Abby's insides *didn't* look like they'd been put through a blender.

"How'd it happen?" His daughter was maybe three feet, tops. Someone would have had to squat down and stab her. It's not a motion that would have gone unnoticed. "Where'd it happen?"

"My mom took her to one of the Korean malls—I don't know—for a purse or something." Hong Chul's hands clenched into fists at his sides, and I took a step back. Even if Wong had told me Hong Chul was a nonviolent man, keeping out of arm's reach still seemed like a good idea. "There's this grocery store on the first floor, and I guess they were having a huge half-off sale. My mom put her in a cart so she wouldn't get stepped on, then grabbed a bag of rice. She turned around because Abby was screaming, and that's when she saw all the blood."

"What did the cops say? Any suspects?"

"Shit, no one saw anything. There were too many people." He sniffed and looked away. In profile, he seemed more like a lost little boy than the hardened thug Madame Sun made him out to be. His lower lip trembled, and he pulled his mouth in tight, desperately fighting to keep control of his emotions. "Who the fuck does this to a kid? *My* kid?"

I'd done calls with Ben where we'd found a kid in the middle of some of the worst shit imaginable. It always amazed me how brutal people could be to children—especially their own. Just when I thought I'd seen it all, some other monster would crawl out of the pits of hell and show me a new way to carve childhood and joy out of a kid. I wouldn't want to see that dead-soul film build up in Abby's innocent eyes.

From the way Hong Chul chewed on the end of his cigarette, he intended to find out who'd hurt his baby girl and God help them.

He pinned me in place, his face desperate with pain. "You think whoever killed Vivian stabbed my kid?"

"Dude, I don't know, but it's not something we can ignore." I wished I could give him some solace, but that kind of hope was too pie in the sky. "What did the cops say?"

"Fucking nothing. There's a woman cop upstairs. She's still talking to my mom." He cleared his throat. "It's one of the cops who came by earlier. She's the one who thought I killed Vivian. Told her what I told you, and fuck her if she thinks I did something to Abby."

"Is her name O'Byrne?" He nodded once, and, belatedly, I wished I'd called Bobby up so I could use him as a human shield if she started in on me. She'd caught Vivian's murder and Hong Chul was a one degree of separation from that case. It made sense for her to come around to sniff out anything about the assault on Abby. "Yeah, she's a bitch, but she's a hardass cop."

Then, out of the night, I heard her voice "Well, if it isn't the man I thought I'd have to hunt down tomorrow morning."

And I was pretty certain she'd just heard me call her a bitch.

There really should be an international warning signal that all evil people should wear. I'd probably catch some shit about freedom of speech or some crap like that, but really, a jester hat with bells would go a long way in keeping people—mainly me—from making an ass out of themselves. At the very least, the scrubs standing between us and the door should have scattered like pigeons when a cat strolled through them, but no such luck. Plastering a pleasant look on my face, I turned and gave her a nod hello.

"O'Byrne." I kept it short and businesslike. Maybe I was hoping she'd hop on the nearest broom and fly off with her monkeys, but she didn't deliver.

"McGinnis." She smiled, her hyena teeth turning a ghastly tangerine in the off-putting light. "Good to know you hold me in such high regard. Especially since I don't hold *you* in any."

"Calling them like I see them, Detective." I made another attempt to hand the fat gray ball over to Hong Chul. This time he took it. The bag crinkled loudly in his fist, and his knuckles turned white, pale even under the citrus glow.

Finishing off the rest of his cigarette, Hong Chul let the verbal ping-pong pass over his head and put the stub out on the cement. Exhaling the last of the smoke out of his lungs, he nodded at me but gave O'Byrne one of his hard looks. It didn't look like he was any more fond of her than I was.

"You done with my mom, or are you going to be harassing us some more?" The thug Madame Sun had told me about was suddenly evident in Hong Chul's furious glower. I would have stepped back, but O'Byrne was next to me. I'd have knocked her on her ass, and she'd probably shoot me in retaliation.

"I'm just doing my job, Mr. Park." O'Byrne used the patented cop soothing voice they'd taught all of us at the academy. "If you're done here, your mother hoped you'd head back upstairs. Your daughter was beginning to wake up when I left."

"Fuck, and I'm not there." Hong Chul swallowed any bile he had left in his throat, and I slapped his shoulder. "I'll talk to you later, dude. If you find out anything, let me know, okay?"

"Yeah, sure." It was a lie. O'Byrne and Wong would both have my ass if I told Hong Chul I found out who stabbed his daughter first. The detective practically snarled at me when Hong Chul headed inside.

"What the hell are you doing here, McGinnis?" She didn't even wait until Hong Chul cleared the doors before she turned on me. "And why are you hanging around one of my suspects?"

"He called me. We do yoga together." I stepped out of the bounds of the cancer-summoning circle. She dogged me, her legs long enough to match my stride.

Once clear of the smoke ring, O'Byrne grabbed my arm and tugged me around. I let her. She was friends with Bobby, and I never knew when I'd need him to hit her up for some info. It didn't mean I liked it or even wanted her to think she could push me around. O'Byrne pulled every subtle intimidation tactic we'd all be taught. She squared her shoulders and tucked her hands on her hips, pushing back her jacket and exposing her gun.

I knew she wasn't doing it because she needed to prove she was one of the guys. O'Byrne didn't play the gender game. She was a *cop* and probably bled blue. I bled red. I'd liked being a cop, but it hadn't been my entire life. Cops like O'Byrne cut their milk teeth on handcuffs and badges. I'd told Hong Chul the truth. She was a bitch and would stab at me in any way she could if she thought it would get the job done, but the bottom line was O'Byrne was a damned fucking good cop.

And I was glad she'd pulled Abby's case. Even if she was only on the fringes of it.

I looked down at her hand on my arm, and she released her hold, letting her arm drop to her side. "You really think Hong Chul stabbed his kid? That's fucked-up, even if you're in full paranoia."

"No, I don't think he stabbed his kid, but he might know who did. I was hoping he could think of someone who was pissed off at him." O'Byrne's frown was on me for a moment before her attention flicked over to the ambulance arriving. Something had her on edge. If I were a betting man, I'd have said it was me. "Did he tell you anything I could use? You know, since the two of you go play Frisbee together on Sunday."

"No, mostly we talked about who could have done it. You got any ideas?" I took her disgusted grunt as a no. "Look, if I had anything solid, I'd tell you. Or maybe Wong. I'd get at least a six pack of beer out of it from him. All I get out of you is attitude."

"Is this all fun and games for you, McGinnis?" She'd been primed for action when she'd first come downstairs, and I'd apparently tossed the last straw onto her back. "You know, they told me you were a joke, but I thought I'd give you the benefit of the doubt. Now, I see they were right."

"If you think I give a shit about what some cops say about me, then you're screwed in the head." I took a step in, pushing back on O'Byrne's personal space. She didn't flinch, facing my body full on. I kept my voice low, but it cracked under my anger. "Madame Sun came to me because the cops blew her off. I went to Wong with whatever I had because he was on the Choi case, and I'd have tried talking to Jenkins if I'd thought it would do any good. So don't accuse me of thinking this is a joke."

"I didn't know you'd gone to Wong before." Her eyebrows scurried together over her nose. "What for?"

"Gangjun Gyong-Si might be pulling a fake sexual therapy scam with his clients. Eun Joon Lee was one of his clients. I think he got Eun Joon Lee pregnant before she was murdered. Maybe even back in Seoul. I *know* Vivian Na and Hong Chul are both his. I don't know how May Choi fits into this, other than Gangjun was her maiden name. She might be related to Gyong-Si, but he says no." I ticked off everything I knew on my fingers, connecting the dots for her. "But then he plays up this campy fortune-teller gig to make himself 'safe' for women to see him. And I only have hearsay to go on about the sex thing, so there you go. That's pretty much everything."

"I knew Sun had clients dying but didn't know about this Gyong-Si guy. He's definitely somehow tied into this, then." She mulled over what I said. "If he is pretending to be gay, that's not a crime, per se. Might be fraud but I don't think it'll hold up. Abuse of authority if someone talks about it. I'll see what Wong's got on him."

"Doesn't matter if he's gay or bi or whatever," I replied. "The point is someone's pissed off about it. Maybe he has a lover out there who's mad Gyong-Si's sleeping around or a ticked-off husband who found out his wife got knocked up by her fortune-teller. Wong was supposed to see if Lee's husband knew she was pregnant—"

"They arrested him this afternoon for her murder." O'Byrne tapped her foot. "I don't think he did it, but the captain was pushing Wong for it. He'll be bailed out, pretty sure of it. Everything against him was circumstantial."

"Jenkins did a shitty job on that case. No way in hell someone climbed over the balcony to get into that apartment."

"I'd ask how you knew Jenkins put that in his initial report, but it sounds like you've got Wong in your back pocket." She'd sneered when she said it, but I could tell her heart wasn't in it.

"Nah, found that out before the case became Wong's." I didn't bring up how I got the information. As far as she knew, Jenkins could have told me over a bottle of vodka and a box of Krispy Kremes. "Look, I don't know what to tell you other than I'm trying to stay out of your guys' way, but I've got a case to run. Sun's the one who hired me. I work for her. She wanted to find out why her clients were dying. Now, she's got a dead daughter, and there's a baby girl upstairs someone tried to put on a skewer."

"Well, do me a favor—"

"Because you know, we're so close," I cut in.

"Don't be an asshole, McGinnis," she growled. "We've got a couple of witnesses who came forward to say Darren Shim was the shooter but someone else drove the car. If Hong Chul tells you who it is, I want you to let me know. Immediately. It could be the driver's the one who stabbed Abby. This could all be a warning for Mr. C-Dog to keep his mouth shut."

"Detective, if Hong Chul knows who was driving that car, you won't need me to tell you who it is. By tomorrow afternoon, you're going to be finding his body cut up and smeared all over Koreatown."

THE next morning after much too little sleep, I discovered I was out of coffee. The cat had lots of food, but somehow I'd let my bean supply dwindle. Grumbling to myself, I got dressed and braved the slightly chilled morning air. I bundled up the papers I'd left on the chest and dashed through the misting sprinklers toward the office. Bolting up the steps, my wet boots hit the fresh paint, and I skidded to a trembling stop. Shaking off as much of the damp spray as I could, I tried to wrestle my keys out of my pocket when it dawned on me I was smelling freshly brewed coffee, and the heavy wooden door was not only unlocked but swung open.

The coffee scent I dismissed. The granola sisters were early risers, and the masochists who jogged before dawn usually stopped in at the shop across the street for their morning hit. But the office door was quite another matter. I dropped the folder I'd carried up from the house onto one of the Adirondack chairs, edged open the screen door, and quietly slid halfway into the office.

Only to find myself being stared down by a large older black woman sitting behind her desk, her handsome, round face twisted into a skeptical frown.

"Boy, what the hell do you think you're doing? You're too old to pretend you're a ninja." Claudia'd mastered the evil eye before I'd drawn my first breath, and she used it indiscriminately, searing the skin off of my bones. "Either get your ass in here or stay outside. You're letting all the cold air in."

"Oh, fuck no," I exhaled hotly. "You *cannot* be here."

"Did you just cuss at me?" She stood up and grabbed at the cane leaning against her desk. If I wasn't careful, she was going to lay my head open with what looked like a master pimp stick from the 1920s. "I swear I just didn't hear that. Now close the damned door."

When life hands one a fierce Southern-born woman who'd whipped eight boys into adulthood, one does what she says. Even though one's death was on the horizon once said woman's eldest son found out she was sitting in one's office. I wouldn't admit to trembling when I retrieved the folder from the front porch, but my hands were definitely shaking from the cold.

Except for the cane and a faint stiffness in her walk, my office manager looked good. Claudia came in ready for a battle. She'd obviously been to the hairdresser while she'd been off work. Her head of loose curls were now a dark sienna without a trace of the silver hairs she'd earned. Girded in a Sunday-go-to-meeting deep purple dress and black camisole, all she was missing was a horned hat and a halberd. Although, taking a good look at the heft of the cane she wielded, she could have had a spear hidden inside.

She toddled over to the coffee machine and refilled her cup, then carefully stirred in a packet of sugar and a dash of cream. The cane made a hard thump on the polished floor when Claudia turned back to her desk. I noticed she didn't bring me any coffee, but I wasn't going to say anything.

I was too busy trying to figure out a way to call Martin and still sound like a man when I threw myself on his mercy.

"Martin's going to kick my ass," I commented as I tried to casually skirt her to get to my desk. "Just so you know, when he's done with me, Jae'll get the house. He'll probably turn this place into a photography studio, but he'll need an office manager. I'll put in a good word for you. Probably right before I use my last breath to tell him I love him."

She was about to say something, probably something strong enough to wither my manhood, when Bobby breezed through the front door. The surprised look he had on his face when he spotted Claudia was priceless. I would have laughed if I hadn't been trying to figure out the last time my will had been updated.

"Damn, Cole, Martin is going to have your fucking balls. Yep, he's going to take them and hang 'em off the back of his truck hitch right after he skins you alive."

He'd brought a bag of plain bagels with cream cheese, dumping them on my desk before heading to the rapidly disappearing pot of coffee. Unlike my beloved office manager, he actually brought me a travel mug of coffee, then proceeded to make another pot so there'd be plenty on hand for my wake.

"No one is killing anyone," Claudia proclaimed loudly. "Leastwise not until I finish watching that damned show Hyunae got me addicted to."

"How'd you get here? You didn't drive, right?" I hadn't spotted her sedan outside and then remembered the doctor had forbidden her to drive while she was convalescing. "Shit, tell me you didn't have one of the kids drive you. They're too young to die."

"I'll have you know, mister, I took a cab." Claudia leaned over between our desks and stabbed me with a sharp fingernail. "The kids can take me home this afternoon when they're done. I'll hold down the fort until then. I even brought my own lunch so I don't have to leave to go get something to eat."

"How about if I drop you off before I head out to where I'm going?" I suggested. "That way, I can... oh, I don't know... see if I can maybe bribe Martin with college scholarships for Mo and Sissy."

"Good idea," Bobby piped up. "He might only break your back then. You know, Bane-style."

"You two are chewing on my last nerve." Her tone remained steady, but there was a thin edge to it, and I knew we were dancing on the edge of disaster. "I was bored. At least I can be bored here without someone trying to get me to eat soup or nap. Swear to God above, you'd think I'd died and crawled back up out of the grave, the way those kids are."

"That's 'cause we love you." I almost flinched when she turned in her chair, but instead of a slap across my head, I got a wistful, teary smile. "And you were shot."

"Pffts, boy, you have more holes in you than a colander and you're like that stupid pink bunny on batteries. I can take one." She settled back into her chair and turned on her computer. "If I get tired, I can go catnap on that couch in the conference room. Besides, I left Martin a note. If he's got any issues, he can take them up with me."

"It's good to see you." I wheeled over on my chair and gave her a kiss on the cheek. She smelled of baby powder, home, and a faint hint of violets. I kissed her again, just to see her cheeks go bright pink, and Claudia slapped my thigh, pushing me away. Her system finished loading, and I heard her gasp, catching a glimpse of what looked like a sample model for silicone implants plastered over her desktop.

"How come there's a half-naked girl on my computer screen?" I didn't know her office chair could turn around fast enough to create a cyclone or how she could make it seem like she'd had lasers installed in her eyes during her hospital stay, but it could... and it seemed like she had. "Cole, what kind of perverted things have you been letting Mo do to my computer?"

I was saved from responding by the phone. A glance at the ID screen told me all I needed to know. I grabbed a bagel, my coffee, and Bobby, headed out quickly, and let Claudia deal with the call from her oldest son. Running had served me well in the past. I wasn't going to give up a tried and true method of keeping my neck in one piece, especially if Claudia started talking to Martin about Mo's choice in eye candy.

We'd gone five blocks in Bobby's truck before he asked the obvious. Sipping from his open mug of coffee, he battled through a left lane tangle and came out the victor. "Okay, Princess, where the fuck am I going?"

"I thought I'd see what Gyong-Si was up to today." I'd appreciated Bobby making me coffee, but it needed more sugar. I caught him up on what I'd been working on, and he grunted at the salient bits. "I don't know who else I can shake out of the trees. Maybe

Gyong-Si can think of someone from his past who's a crazy, possessive bitch or has an insane husband."

"Think he'd give a shit?" Bobby asked sarcastically. "That guy pisses me off on principle. Not just the whole pretending to be batting for our team—which is some sick shit already—but because if he *does* know who could be behind this crap, why the fuck isn't he at least trying to cough up some names for the cops?"

"He struck me as the definition of selfish," I answered. "And to be honest, after my talking with O'Byrne last night, I kind of expect someone in blue to be knocking on his door."

"You think he knows?" He cocked his head at me, keeping his eyes on the road. The morning traffic hadn't quite thickened to insane yet, but it still was tight in places. "About the kids he's got, I mean."

"Yeah, Bhak confronted him about Hong Chul. I guess he wanted to warn Gyong-Si off after Abby was born. Supposedly, the guy sent Bhak a letter saying he'd leave the family alone if Bhak invested in his fortune-telling business here in Los Angeles. I don't know if Hong Chul's grandfather actually coughed up any cash."

"How the hell does someone invest in a fortune-telling place? What is he going to pay for? Crystal balls? How much fucking incense can the guy get?" Bobby snorted. "What a piece of shit."

"Yeah, that's pretty much what I thought too," I agreed. "So did Jae. Ichiro too."

"Speaking of Ichiro, how about if you tell me the truth about something, Princess?" Bobby's face curled up with a wicked smile. "How much crying are you going to be doing once I get that tasty little brother of yours in bed? And how much of that is going to be sour grapes 'cause you wished you'd slept with me first?"

CHAPTER TWENTY

THERE were certain times when one wished they had a gun on them. Most notable of those times were being caught on the wrong side of the glass in a lion's exhibit, being trapped in an elevator during Christmas music season, and when a supposed best friend not only tells you what he wants to do with your baby brother but suggests you join in.

Luckily, he was parking in front of Gyong-Si's place or I would have gotten us into an accident by punching him while he drove. Slamming the truck door was the closest sound I could make next to an actual shotgun blast to Bobby's guts. It wasn't as satisfying, but still, rattling the windows gave me some sense of satisfaction.

"Not funny, dude," I told him over the roof of the truck. He smirked, and I slapped my hand on the painted metal to get his attention. "Bobby, I'm serious. Don't give him any of your shit. Just 'cause I told you he dipped his toe into the pool doesn't mean you can go take him skinny-dipping."

"Shit, okay." He held his hands up in mock surrender. "I will not in any way hit up your sexy little brother for anything other than a smile. Promise, Princess."

"Just once, Bobby, stop thinking with your dick." The last thing I wanted for Ichiro was Bobby sniffing around his ankles. "I love you, man, but you're kind of a whore."

"What if he approaches me first?" It was a masterful leer, suited to Bobby's craggy, handsome face. It spent a lot of time there, usually pulled out only when we caroused at clubs, bars, or the gym.

"Then you tell me so I can set him straight, in a manner of speaking." I went heavy on the sarcasm, but Bobby nodded. "Now, you want to come in with me or lurk out here like Mange from Powerpuff Girls?"

"You watched the Powerpuff Girls?" He trailed after me, working toward the back of the complex where Gyong-Si's bungalow squatted in its full rainbow-hued glory.

"Dude, I was laid up for months. The Powerpuff Girls were safe," I warned him. "Don't *ever* turn on the Teletubbies. It'll suck you in for hours. Worse than playing WoW. You in or out?"

"I'll lurk. He could take you out and make a run for it." Bobby's eyes widened when we turned the corner and he took in the spectrum of Gyong-Si's place. "Holy shit… that's… wow. What's the inside like?"

"Calmer. He went for the peaceful Zen spa look inside." The stairs creaked a bit under our feet, and the flyers and pamphlets by the door were organized neatly, a few spots of neon next to buttery pastels. A breeze picked up the ends of the chimes, trilling harpsichord-like tones over us when we approached the door. "If he comes outside, just try not to look directly at him. I think he's a hugger."

I went in, leaving Bobby outside on the porch. The front room was empty of people. Terry wasn't in, but the pack of cigarettes on his desk was the same brand I'd seen him with before. A nearly empty plastic cup of iced tea or coffee sat sentinel near a pile of papers meant he'd probably stepped out for something. Either that or he'd thrown in the towel that morning and stomped out without his caffeine and smokes.

There was a shuffling coming from down the hall, and then Gyong-Si emerged from behind the beaded curtain, throwing it back like a fake wizard failing to intimidate a little girl and her dog. When he spotted me standing in the front room, his first reaction was to utter a heartfelt, "Shit."

Whatever Gyong-Si had been up to over the past few days, it'd eaten him alive. The flamboyant counselor was gone and in his place was an old man who looked like he'd fought a homeless bum for the stained dull-blue tracksuit he was wearing. There was no trace of the finely applied makeup he'd worn the last time I'd seen him, and in the harsh daylight, every small crater and line on his face stood up and shouted for attention. A scraggly graying stubble started someplace on his chin and worked its way up his jaw to wrap around the back of his head. Spotty patches hopscotched along the top of his skull, turning his dome into a monochromatic knockoff of Twister. The only spots of bright color on him were the fire-engine red Crocs he wore over a pair of dirty white socks.

He also smelled. Like a fifteen-day-old gym sock left in a closed-up wet locker reek.

"You!" His lips peeled back, and I inhaled a whiff of cheap alcohol on his breath. Gyong-Si reached for me and slapped his hands on my chest. He couldn't get his feet under him, and he tilted, skewing off balance. "Get out of—"

I caught him before he stumbled to the floor. He must have been close to three hundred pounds of drunken pain, because my arms strained under his nearly dead weight. Close up, he reeked even nearer to high heaven than a six-week-old dumpster of trash left out during a heat wave. Sharp bites of pain erupted along my side and across my shoulder, and I must have squealed because Bobby was through the door before I had the chance to dump Gyong-Si on the carpet. He hesitated at helping me once he caught wind of the man's odor.

"Dude, grab his arm," I hissed. Gyong-Si twisted, his eyes rolling back far enough I could see their whites. He gurgled, and I began to worry he was either having a fit or was about to toss his stomach out. "Help me get him to the back, at least."

Bobby ducked down and hoisted most of Gyong-Si's weight on his shoulder. "Grab that curtain out of the way. Show me the way to the bathroom and we can dump him into a hot shower."

"Man, I don't think a volcano's going to be hot enough to burn the stink off of him," I muttered, but I held the beads back so Bobby wouldn't get tangled up in them. Gyong-Si's foot wasn't as lucky, and his ankle got caught, dragging a few strands down when Bobby moved forward.

"Not Mardi Gras," Bobby grumbled. "Get those off of him—"

"Stop fucking moving, then," I muttered back. After loosening the strings from Gyong-Si's leg, I tossed them aside and followed Bobby's staggering progress down the hallway. "Go straight. I think he lives in the back."

We found the bathroom, a fairly large retro-styled space with a shower big enough for us to toss Gyong-Si in on his ass and turn the water on. Bobby sniffed at his hands, headed to the sink, and stole some of the hot water supply to wash up. Gyong-Si came to life after a full minute of being under the spray. Sputtering, he flung his arms about, slamming into the glass walls, and from the way he was yelling and pounding, I was halfway afraid he would break through the shower enclosure.

Bobby finished drying his hands with a hand towel embroidered with pink seashells and tossed it onto the closed toilet seat. "That's your mess there, Princess." He jerked his thumb toward the floundering Gyong-Si. "I'll be outside. Maybe I can catch a game on that TV in the front office."

"Really? Fuck it." I was already talking to Bobby's back, and I opened the shower door, rolling up my sleeves in preparation for battle. Drawing the line at Gyong-Si's pouchy briefs, I got him mostly stripped, then worked some of the stench off of his skin with soap and a rough scrub cloth. I left him under the pounding water to find him something clean to wear.

It took me a few minutes to go through the carnage of his studio apartment, but eventually I found another tracksuit—a green and orange monstrosity—left in the dryer. After digging out a pair of clean underwear from the wrinkled laundry in the dryer drum, I returned to find Gyong-Si precariously balanced on the toilet. He'd gotten one leg out of his briefs, and I was hailed with a full view of his shriveled cock and balls when he spread his thighs to get the other side off.

"Jesus Christ." I held up the track suit to block my view. Turning my head, I tossed the clothes in his general direction, not caring if they landed in the puddles of water he'd managed to track all over the black-and-white hexagon-tiled floor. "Get dressed. I'll see if I can find some coffee in this shit hole you live in."

He took long enough in the bathroom that I was not only able to start a pot of coffee but also dig out the living room area. I tossed an armful of clothes into the wash, measured out soap, and began a holy reckoning on the sweat-and-beer-soaked fabrics. Collecting the various bottles and trash around the place took me another few minutes, but by the time I was done, I could more than likely sit on the couch without either catching a disease or getting pregnant, and the soured-onion smell of unwashed man had faded a bit from the air.

Thankfully, Gyong-Si hadn't found the Crocs again or I would have beaten him with one of them.

Despite the soaking, he was bleary-eyed and worn when he sank down onto the futon next to me and picked up the cup of hot coffee I'd left for him on the table. He hadn't shaved, and the scruff on his head sparkled in places where he'd missed it with the towel.

At least he smelled better.

I let him drink a few sips of the coffee before I started in on him. "Okay, let's talk about why you tried to kill me with your stench."

"You told me you were a cop. Then I find out that *bitch* sent you to spy on me." It was a bitterly flung accusation and one I easily punted back to him. "But then the real cops came by. That's when they told me about… my daughter."

"Vivian? That daughter?"

"So you knew?" he said accusingly. "Did *she* tell you about her? Park Hyuna Sun? She told you before the cops told *me*?"

"Probably only by a few hours, if that," I replied, leaving off the details of being with Vivian when she died. It was Madame Sun who'd needed that comfort. I wasn't sure how much of Gyong-Si's tears were as crocodilian as his shoes.

"Then you came here to what? Gloat?"

"I came over here to ask you who else you got pregnant, if you even kept track. Hong Chul's grandfather, Bhak Bong Chol, kept some records of other women you slept with."

"Ask anyone. That Bhak Bong Chol was crazy." Gyong-Si twirled his finger by his temple. "He would stand out in the middle of the road wearing only his underwear and scream at the cars parked too close to his house."

While I might have agreed a little bit with Gyong-Si after reading some of Bhak's notes, that wasn't going to get me anywhere. "Look, I already know about Eun Joon Lee. Can you think of anyone who might have wanted to hurt you by killing Vivian? Maybe one of those women? Or their husbands?"

"Eun Joon Lee? What are you talking about?" Gyong-Si spluttered, flicking coffee drops from his fleshy lips. "I had nothing to do with Hyuna Sun's daughter because I didn't *know*. Not until the police told me. If I'd known—but that doesn't matter either. It is too late. What does it even matter?"

"Because last night, someone tried to kill Park Hong Chul's little girl, and I think that person is trying to lash out at you."

My words seemed to shock Gyong-Si, and what little color he had left in his face drained out, leaving him waxen. From the red splotches and broken veins on his cheeks, his most recent drunken binge hadn't been his first. His hands shook, and I took the mug from him and set it down on the table before he upended its contents onto the floor.

"I didn't know—" he stuttered. "I don't know who would do that. I... when the police came here, they wanted to talk to me about Vivian, and... they said they would be investigating me... because I'm having sex with my clients, but I told them I am not!"

"Isn't that what happened in South Korea? Isn't that why you left? Because that's what Bhak suspected, that there were too many women you'd violated and you were chased out."

"I violated *no one!*" His Korean slipped over his words, blurring their edges. "The women I had sex with... back home... you don't understand what I—"

"Why don't you tell me?" I angled myself on the couch to face him. "Tell me what's going on, and maybe I can figure out who's trying to kill the people connected to you. Let's start off with May Choi. You knew her, didn't you? Was she your niece or another daughter?"

"She was my cousin, my father's sister's girl," he mumbled. "I never met her. I promise. I tried to talk to her when she moved here, but May wouldn't meet with me. I am dead to my family. That's why I told you I didn't know her. Even to someone that young, I'm nothing."

"Because you pretend you're gay? Why didn't you tell them the truth?"

"Pretend?" Gyong-Si's fleshy wattle flapped when he shook his head. "I am not pretending." He caught my sidelong glance and cleared his throat noisily. "Yes, I act more... colorful when I am with a client, but that's to put them at ease. Most of my customers are women, and it makes them feel safe. Korean women—more traditional women—are uncomfortable if left alone with a man. If they think of me as harmless, they will do business with me. I have to make a living."

I didn't know what to say to that. I honestly didn't know how to feel about how a man portrayed himself in order to gain business or even if I was qualified to judge. Even though I knew I couldn't live a lie on the scale Gyong-Si did, neither could I condemn him for making that choice. In some way, he was doing what Jae did, covering up who he was in order to survive.

"I left Seoul because I couldn't live as a man there—the kind of man my family wanted me to be." The broken look I'd seen on my lover's face was mirrored in Gyong-Si's expression. "I tried. There wasn't a woman around me I didn't try to seduce, but even as I had sex with them, I knew it wasn't what I wanted... what I needed. I left to come here because I thought I would be free, but instead I'm still living a world of lies. They are just different lies."

"Couldn't you just be... who you are?" I saw the answer in his eyes before the question was even fully out of my mouth. It was the same question I'd posed to Jae time and time again. While I believed life would be easier if he—and Gyong-Si—were honest with themselves, I knew that wasn't the case. "Okay, what about Eun Joon Lee? She was pregnant when she was killed. You telling me that baby wasn't yours?"

"I haven't touched a woman since I left Korea." His insistence was hot and furious. "I counseled Eun Joon Lee because she and her husband wanted children but they were unsuccessful."

"So this was a miracle birth?"

"No, she had an affair," Gyong-Si muttered under his breath. "I told her not to. I knew what it is like to live a lie, but she wanted a child, and, well, she was not getting any younger. She slept with a man she met at church. Eun Joon wanted to give her husband a child. I told her that it was wrong of her to cheat on him when there are other ways to get a child."

"Is that what you fought about that day? The day she was killed?"

"Yes." The wattle shook vigorously this time. "I told her she had to tell her husband the truth. Or...."

"Or?" I pressed.

"Or I would tell him." He dropped his gaze to the floor, turning his face away from me. "It was my fault she left early. If I'd only spoken to her more calmly, Eun Joon would have seen reason and those men wouldn't have been there when she returned home. It is my fault she is dead. Both Eun Joon and... her baby."

"What about in Korea? When you slept with her there? Bhak wrote that she got pregnant then too. What happened to the baby?"

"I never slept with Eun Joon. Not here. Not in Korea," Gyong-Si protested. "She became my client here. I knew her mother. She came by to visit, and I gave her a reading for free, only because of our connection. She liked what I had to say and became a client, but there was nothing between us beyond that."

I wasn't sure if I believed him, but I was going off of the words from a dead man. I didn't know Bhak Bong Chol's state of mind when he wrote down his suspicions. There was a distinct possibility he'd been driven more by outrage and revenge than anything else. Gyong-Si's hurt was palpable. I was going to have to readjust my opinion of the man blubbering on the couch.

"Who besides the family knew Hong Chul was your son?" I shifted gears, hoping to find something to chase down. From what I could see, Gyong-Si truly was broken up by the women's deaths and Abby's stabbing. If the murders were connected to him, I was going to worry about his mental health. Already unstable from alcohol abuse, he didn't look like he could take much more. "Who out there wants to hurt you?"

"I don't know." Gyong-Si pursed his mouth in thought. "I would have said Sun, but she never would have killed her own daughter. I was surprised she gave Vivian away. That doesn't... sound like her."

"What happened between you two? Could this be connected to her husband? Maybe someone from her past? Do you know?"

"Her husband was a friend of mine." He picked up his coffee again. His hands were steadier this time, and he cupped the mug tightly. "We... she and I... were both students when we... made Vivian. I was trying so hard to be *normal*. We got drunk one night after a session with our *sunbae,* and we found ourselves in a private room. I didn't think about her husband... my friend. Instead, all I could think of was trying to be a real man. I didn't know she got pregnant, but then I didn't know about Hong Chul either. Not until Bhak Bong Chol told me later. If I'd known, I would have married Hong Chul's mother. It would have made my family very happy."

"You did try to extort money from him after Abby was born," I pointed out.

"That Bhak Bong Chol—he was an angry old man," Gyong-Si scoffed. "Bhak tried to give me money to leave Los Angeles because he didn't want me around either my son or my granddaughter. I'd already told him I would not interfere with Hong Chul's life. He already had a good father. What would he want with someone like me? I told Bhak if he wanted to give me money, he could invest it in my business because I wasn't going anywhere."

"Jesus, this is a mess." If Gyong-Si was to be believed, I was back to where I started, spinning my wheels and chasing ghosts. "Did Bhak talk to you about any of the other women who had your kids? Well, except for Madame Sun. I know he didn't tell you about Vivian. What about Eun Joon Lee? Why did he think you got her pregnant in Korea?"

"I don't know. I didn't know her then." Gyong-Si chewed on his fingernail, thinking on something. "Wait, was he thinking about Joon Eun Yi? She was the only other woman I slept with besides Sun and Hong Chul's mother. We were lovers for about five months, right before I left. She wouldn't accept that I… changed at first, but eventually she was fine with it. I think. I don't know. I haven't seen her in years."

"So she's been in contact with you?" The name was familiar, but to be honest, most of the Korean names I'd come across sometimes blurred together.

"Terry, my assistant, is her son. It's why I hired him. She asked me to give him a job." He rubbed at his face. "I'm tired. I don't know how much I can help you."

"Wait, Terry's mother—" I suddenly remembered where I'd heard that name before. It was the name of the woman who'd spoken to me outside of Eun Joon's apartment. "Does she live next to the Lees? Next door?"

"Yes." Gyong-Si nodded slowly. It struck me the man never looked outside of himself and his needs. If he had, he would have realized what was just dawning on me.

"But Terry's last name is Yi," I pointed out. While Korean women might keep their last name, their children were named after their father. Terry's name shouldn't have been Yi. "Why doesn't he have his father's name?"

"I don't know." He scraped at his beard with his fingers. "Maybe she married someone with the same last name, as Eun Joon did. Do you know how many people are named Yi? I never thought about it. I only hired him because she called me up and asked me to give him a job. He complains a lot. Not my type. I like my men to be… more like you."

I knew when Gyong-Si set up shop in Los Angeles. Terry was—maybe—at most a year younger than Vivian or Hong Chul. After doing a round of quick math, I shook my head at the man's obtuseness. "Gyong-Si, *think* about it. Terry isn't just your assistant. He's your *son*."

CHAPTER TWENTY-ONE

"SON of a bitch." I slapped at the dashboard of Bobby's truck. "We read the name wrong. She even told me people got their names confused."

"Yeah, you said that already." He hit me lightly with his fist. "Stop beating up my truck, asshole, and tell me where we're going."

It was early enough in the day, and I wanted to talk to Joon Eun Yi again. If someone was stalking Gyong-Si's past conquests, she was going to be on the killer's list.

Bobby was easily persuaded to come with me. The promise of a cold beer and a hot hamburger went a long way in compromising any plans he might have had for the day. Right after his dick, his stomach pretty much ruled the roost. I'd pay for feeding him the burger and beer with a run around Los Angeles or going a few rounds in the ring, but it was a small price to pay.

I'd see how I felt about making that deal later when I was licking my wounds under a hot shower.

The main street fronting the complex was eerily quiet. Like most LA streets, all of the parking spaces were taken, including the half space people usually left behind a red zone, but no one was out walking. After Bobby drove up the street for the second time, I directed him to the small parking lot behind the apartments. He pulled into a space directly below the Lees' balcony and gave me the evil eye.

"If I get towed, you're going to be paying for it," he barked at me.

"You're not going to get towed." Looking around the lot, I gestured wildly. "There's, like, three cars here. By the time someone wants this space, we'll be long gone."

"Shitty things happen to my trucks when I'm with you." Bobby continued to grumble as we walked to the pass-through leading to the complex's courtyard. "I should be happy if all that happens to *this* one is it getting towed."

"*One* truck gets blown up and it's all my fault? *One!*" Pointing out the obvious—that I'd not been the one to blow his truck up—had no lasting effect on Bobby. His derision continued when we found the passage to the courtyard blocked by a locked security gate. Someone was certainly serious about keeping out the riffraff. Grabbing the heavy chain wrapped around the door handles, he rattled the padlock to see if it could be opened.

Much like Bobby's mind about my involvement in his dead truck's demise, the gate remained closed.

"Okay, so we walk around," I said to Bobby's disgusted hiss. "Come on. It'll help you work off that burger I'm going to buy you."

Not much had changed in the complex since I'd last been there. The trees were still tall and bushy, their tops reaching the upper floor roof, and the courtyard resembled an ancient rainforest. Someone'd gone wild with the fertilizer, because a pungent organic-fishy smell hit us in the face once we got past the front archway. The patches of lawn interspersed between the flower beds glistened from dew, and a butterfly dive-bombed my face when I stepped out into the dappled rays coming through the trees. Despite the cloudless sky, the morning was still bitter, and the wind whistling through the archway and pass-through cut down to the bone.

"This is kind of nice," Bobby murmured, looking around. Cocking his head, he frowned. "And kind of too… quiet. No toys or anything on the walkways. Mostly adults?"

"I think most of the people who live here either are retired or work during the day. Kind of feels like one of those places." I pointed to the stairs near the pass-through to the parking lot. "That's the only way up. Yi said she has the place next to the Lees. Let's see if she's home."

He sidestepped a sprinkler head that had popped up suddenly. A few feet down, the dirt beside the sidewalk sprouted a row of black spigots. "Those things better not go off. These are new boots. What exactly are you hoping to get from her?"

"Stop worrying about your delicate feet." He slapped my back with the flat of his hand, and I reached back to rub at the sting. "And I don't know. Maybe she knows someone who wants Gyong-Si to suffer? They were close, and he seems kind of self-absorbed—"

"Kind of?"

"Okay, very," I corrected myself. "She's one of those women who collects gossip. If there's any dirt on someone, I think she might have it. Especially if it's about Gyong-Si. I'm hoping she knows about someone like that. Or at least we can warn her to go to the cops if someone suspicious comes around."

The sprinklers went off full blast before I could go any further. The water was fucking cold and, for some reason, shot out in hard, pounding sheets. Dodging against the outside wall of the apartments didn't do us any good. The blasts of water coming from the popped-up heads were like being bombarded by fire hoses. I felt the sting of the blast through my jeans and tried to skip out of the way, only to fall prey to the next shot arcing toward my crotch.

"Shit, head to the stairs, kid." Bobby took a shot of water to his chest. The water continued to ratchet upward, leaving welts on his cheek and jaw. "What the fuck is—"

We never made it to the stairs. A shot came out of the shadows above us, scoring a groove into the cement by our feet. Another followed, then, like the sprinklers, a line of blasts cut us off from the archway.

Braving the beating lines of water, Bobby and I dove toward the center of the courtyard, both of us looking for cover among the tree trunks. Cowering behind one of the smaller palms, I pressed my back to the striated trunk and looked around for any sign of the shooter, catching the last bit of a water stream on my shoulder. Bobby somehow ended up farther in, a few feet away behind a eucalyptus.

"Can you see him?" Bobby shouted above the chunking sound of the sprinklers and loud gushes of water. I shook my head, and he bared his teeth in frustration. "Tell me you brought your gun!"

Shaking my head so the shooter couldn't hear my response, I grumbled to myself, "Who the fuck would bring a gun to talk to a fortune-teller?"

I dug my phone out of my pocket and sighed at its flickering screen. Soaked down to the chips, the screenshot I'd taken of Neko for my background glowed a demonic red before being cut through with blue dots and lines. Holding my phone up for Bobby to see, I lifted my eyebrows and pointed at him, asking him if his was any better.

His mouth turned into a sour fish kiss and he shook his head, then pointed back toward the parking lot.

"Really?" I grumbled over the water noise. "You fucking leave your *phone* behind and you give me shit about a gun?"

He shrugged and took a peek out from behind his tree. Our gunman must have had a better view of Bobby's hiding place, because the second his face popped out from behind the trunk, another shot went off and pieces of papery bark flew into the air.

We were a lot closer to the back of the complex than the front. Making it to the stairs would be tricky, especially since I couldn't guarantee we could get to the shooter before he cut into us. From the looks of things, the first floor was either deserted or filled with people with more common sense than Bobby and I had.

The water pouring out of the sprinklers was freezing, and I shivered, feeling a ripple of ice starting to kiss my blood. Rubbing at my shoulder to get my circulation going, I took another look around the trunk, trying to spot a way to get to safety. Short of getting inside one of the lower floor apartments and then smashing out through a back window, things did not look good. There didn't seem to be anyone to hear the gunshots, even if they could over the gushes of water, and the gunman wouldn't have to wait long for us to either begin to stiffen up under the cold water or float in the lake forming in the complex's courtyard.

I was about to damn myself and dash to the archway for help when a man's voice called out to me from the upper floor.

"Mr. McGinnis?"

I rolled my eyes at the *really?* face Bobby gave me. I wasn't surprised the guy knew who I was. Chances are, we were on the same road map, circling around Gyong-Si's offspring. Thing was, he and I had totally different reasons for doing so. He wanted them dead, and I took offense to that. Sticking my head out a little bit, I shouted back, "Yeah? What can I do for you?"

Scintillating conversation at its best, but there wasn't much else to say, short of begging him to let us go. Considering he'd just spent the last minute or so trying to blow our heads off, I didn't think it was going to be an option.

"You know I'm going to have to kill you and your friend." He sounded almost delighted, a flippant slant to his voice. Like Jae, he had a smooth roundness to his English. I didn't recognize his voice, but he sounded vaguely familiar. "You might was well come out and get it over with."

"Dude, I don't even know who you are." If anything, the water got colder. Either that or my core body temperature was beginning to drop. I'd lost feeling in my toes, and from the blue splotches creeping into Bobby's lips, he wasn't doing much better.

"Really? I would have thought you'd have figured it out." A shadow emerged from the stairwell.

The light hit him, and I saw Bobby frown, struggling to put a name to the face. I had no such problem. Even distracted by the Beretta he held pointed at my head, I recognized him straight off.

I'd only really seen him twice. Once when he picked his mother up at my office and when he'd been in the conference room after Vivian's death. He'd mastered the dutiful son look then, in his dress slacks and polo shirts. Now, he was working on serial killer and doing a damned fine job. Even as shitty a dresser as I was, I knew green khakis did not go with an orange Hawaiian shirt.

"James Bahn—fuck." He'd seemed like a decent kind of guy. It'd all been an act put on for his mother—an act that probably also included him being the loving older brother to his wayward illegitimate sister, Vivian Na. Bobby ducked back behind his cover, but not before he gave me a *who-the-fuck* look. "Madame Sun's son, right?"

"Good to know that, for some of you, we don't all look alike," he sneered at me. I scuttled around the trunk, carefully aligning myself so he couldn't get a clear shot.

"Pretty fucking shitty thing to say there, James." The numbness was eating away at my feet, and my fingers joined the party, tingling when I flexed them. "Kind of racist, actually. Especially since I'm half Japanese. What do you want to let us go?"

"Let you go? I can't do that, Mr. McGinnis." I heard him shuffling in between the shots of sprinkler sprays and strained to figure out if he went left or right without getting my head blown off. "Or should I call you Cole?"

"Whatever makes you happy." I caught a glimpse of Bobby's shoulder emerging out from behind the eucalyptus. Shaking, he came into view, curled up onto his haunches and balancing on his toes. He motioned toward the next tree, pointed to himself and then again to the tree. I shook my head, hoping to keep him in place, but Bobby frowned furiously, negating my concern. I took a deep breath and shouted at James, hoping to keep his attention on me. "What are you doing here? Besides trying to kill me?"

Bobby took off before James could answer, and suddenly, the bushes around Bobby were peppered with two shots. I heard Bobby's pained grunt and toppled over, trying to sprint toward him. My legs weren't responding, and I shook from the cold. The sunlight coming through the trees wasn't hot enough to warm us up, and I was struggling to get some feeling in my limbs when Bobby rolled under a stand of thick hibiscus bushes, their yellow pollen dusted over his short hair.

He was clutching his left arm, and a trickle of blood seeped out from between his fingers, soaking into the cedar mulch chunks around the stand's roots. Making eye contact, Bobby mouthed at me, *I'm okay.*

Nodding in return, I went back to shouting at James. "Let me guess, you're here to kill Terry Yi."

"Smart man." His laugh was loud, telling me he was closer than I'd have liked. "You're not as stupid as you look. I thought I'd kill his mother too, since I'm here. You, on the other hand, are becoming a problem I sorely need to get rid of. And now your friend too. Such a shame. Especially after everything you've done for Mother."

Cursing the water spray leeching the warmth out of my body, I dug around the tree, hoping to find a rock or something to throw at his head. "Want to give me the five minute evil villain monologue, or should I just guess? It has something to do with Gyong-Si and your mother."

"Gangjun Gyong-Si? That bastard?" Any calm in James's voice melted away under the heat of his furious reply. "For a gay man, he's ruined a lot of lives by sleeping with women he should have left alone to begin with!"

Across from me, Bobby smirked and jerked his head toward the archway again. I snarled a silent no at him and cut my stiff hand down, telling him to stay put. If James had a clear shot, he'd probably take it, killing both of us if he could. The water spray arched toward me again, and I ducked before tossing another question at James.

"Why now? If you're so pissed off at him, why not just kill him? Why go after innocent people like your sister?"

"Vivian? She was never my sister. My mother gave her everything, a family back home, money and education, and what did she become? A whore. She was so much of a slut she fucked her own brother." James's fury escalated, and he sounded like he was popping a vein. "It was never enough for her. Why didn't she go to that faggot father of hers for money? It was bad enough she ruined my family in Korea. She had to come here to get between me and my mother?"

"So you went after Gyong-Si's kids?" It was a stretch of the imagination by anyone's logic. Claudia told me once, sometimes it doesn't pay to argue with crazy, but in this case, I needed to argue. Anything to buy us time to distract him. "That doesn't make any sense!"

"It would have been too easy if I just killed the whore. Gyong-Si deserves more than that." Another loud crunch of mulch sounded next to me, and Bobby's grimace deepened.

Holding his hands up a few feet apart, he tried to tell me how far away James was to my hiding place, then pantomimed jumping with his closed fists. I nodded, hoping Bobby was telling me James was hopscotching around the courtyard, probably to avoid stepping directly into the punishing blast of the high-powered sprinklers.

"I wanted him to know what it's like for his family—every damned child he's ever made—to be taken from him. Just like what he did to us back in Korea. My father left us because of him. And don't worry, I'll deal with Gyong-Si last."

I didn't know if that meant he'd already killed Terry Yi or still had the kid on his hit list. Even if Terry were dead, there was still Abby and Hong Chul. Bobby and I needed to get out of there and take James down with us.

A thin river of blood ran down Bobby's arm, and he'd begun to shiver uncontrollably. Huffing to control his breathing, he turned over onto his side, tucking himself farther under the bush to get away from the sprinkler heads pointing straight at him. The water was pooling up around my feet, and small bits of foamy mulch were floating around the sides of my Doc Martens.

My boots.

They were black leather and hefty, meant to take a pounding. I'd worn them while doing the renovations to the house, and they'd shrugged off hammers and power tools being dropped on them. Once, after a two-mile hard run to chase down a runaway I'd been hired to find, I actually took them off because it was easier to walk without their weight. Steel-toed and thick-soled, they were as heavy as shit.

They were going to have to do.

I quickly yanked them off, then hastily pulled at the shoestrings until I had enough hanging to knot them together. Using the tree trunk for cover, I crept up to my feet and called out to James. "Tell you what, how about if we talk about this?"

I looked at Bobby and pointed behind me, hoping he could tell me where James was. The tips of his fingers were nearly bleached white, and the beds of his nails were a sickly blue. A smear of blood covered his hand, and a trickle of red ran down his wrist toward his elbow. He was bleeding too much for a flesh wound, and his arm shook when he held up two fingers then made an *L* before pointing behind me.

"Why don't you come out so I can shoot you?" James's sneer leaked through his voice. "I'm pretty sure I've already killed your friend."

"Like you killed Darren Shim?" I could sneer back with the best of them. "Nice how you killed him so no one could trace Vivian's shooting back to you."

"That asshole came to her office! I had to get rid of him. He was going to hurt her."

It was easy to put together now I had the missing piece. He'd probably run into Shim when Hong Chul was around. From what little I knew about Shim, he'd gladly have done some dirty work for cash. I wasn't going to waste any tears crying over a man who shot up a café and killed a defenseless woman, but he probably hadn't known he was walking into his own death trap. If James hadn't bashed Shim's head in then, he still would have killed his hired gun later to cover his tracks.

I wasn't graceful. Other guys brag about how they pounce on a guy during a fight, and they make it sound like a ballet. The only ballet I could have been accused of doing was the "Dance of the Hours," and I was a pink-tutu-wearing hippo named Hyacinth. Still, at least I had some element of surprise when I stumbled out from my hiding place swinging my jury-rigged nunchucks.

One caught James across the throat and slapped the back of his head. He pitched forward, nearly doing a face-plant into the mulch. He grabbed a handful of the bark chips and flung them at my face, trying to blind me. They were too wet to do much more than fall a few inches from his outstretched arm, but James unknowingly gave me an opening.

I didn't spend time in the boxing ring with Bobby for exercise. Since the only person I'd ever gotten into a real fist fight with had been my brother Mike, I'd thought it would be good to learn how to actually punch. JoJo was a good teacher. Bobby was a good opponent, and the various men who'd ducked under the ropes to go a few rounds with me never gave me any quarter. So I felt pretty confident that I could hit… and hit hard. After rearing back my arm, I laid one out, planting my curled fist into the middle of James's face. He reeled back, his head bouncing on his neck in a loose bobble, and I got a satisfying crunching noise and a fountain of blood streaming out of his nose.

He also dropped the gun.

I wasn't going to waste time going for the Beretta. I didn't know where it had landed, and James was standing right in front of me. Kicking up as much mulch with my feet as I could to hide its whereabouts, I moved in, intent on doing some damage with my bare fists. With more than a few inches and about forty pounds on the guy, it wasn't going to be much of a fair fight unless he had some martial arts moves I didn't know about. From the way he threw his arms up to protect the top of his head, I was safe.

The trick to hitting someone effectively is putting weight behind each punch and having a good, firm stance. My problem was I couldn't really feel my feet, and my arms were deadened from the icy water. I was slower than I'd have liked, and the mulch slipped around under me. The fight was still more mine to lose, but I was going to have to work for it.

James swung at my head, an open-palm slap I would normally have avoided easily if I wasn't frozen down to the marrow of my bones. The smack of skin against skin was something I preferred to have happen in the bedroom, and only with a naked, sweaty Jae-Min. James's ill-aimed cuff brought me no pleasure. Only a ringing sound when his cupped palm forced a burst of chilled air into my ear canal.

The rush of pressure against my eardrum hurt more than the slap, and I bit back a grunt of pain. James floundered, losing his footing. He made a grab for something to steady himself, then screamed when the palm's serrated trunk dug into his hand. It wasn't the best distraction, but I was going to make the most of it.

I tackled James at the knees, wrapping my arms up around his midsection. We went down into a bunch of shrubs, shaking out a shower of tiny purple flowers. He fought me, punching at my shoulders to get free. Hooking my legs around his thighs, I heaved up and drew back, blocking one of his flails with my arm. He struck at me a few more times before I found an opening I could take.

That's when I broke his nose again, driving as many bone shards up into his sinuses as I could.

Concentrating on his face, I hammered at James's cheekbones and jaw. His nails scored lines into my neck during one of his passes, and the cold air bit into my now burning skin, leaving behind a painful sting. The blood on James's face splattered, then ran when a blast of water hit us from one of the churning sprinkler heads. The spray caught me unawares, tearing into my mouth. It tasted nasty and with a suspicious iron-metallic aftertaste that had me wondering if I'd torn my lip. I spat out the foul water, and James struck back, delivering a soft punch to my side. I would have laughed off the strike, but when he punched again, a searing pain erupted across my ribs and I caught a flash of glittering metal in his hand.

He must have had the knife in his pocket. Only a few inches long, it was a wide, strong steel, easily cutting through my soaked shirt and into my side. Grinning up at me with a maniacal smirk, he dug his elbow into the ground and twisted the blade, catching its tip on my ribs. The pain was intense, and I doubled over, nearly puking from the ache coiling around my abdomen. I rolled off, taking the blade with me. Clutching at the hilt, I was trying to pull it free when I heard a gun blast echo through the courtyard.

Tensed, I curled up onto myself, quickly working through the numbness and pains I already had. A moment later, Bobby's hand yanked my sliced shirt up and pressed against the deep, bleeding cut on my side. A few feet away, James Bahn lay still and pale. There was no mistaking the stippling of gunpowder on his skin. At some point during our fight, Bobby'd found the gun and fired it, nearly point-blank, into James's neck.

"Is he dead?" I coughed, and my wound leaked, the flaps of skin gulping like a dying goldfish.

"Don't know," Bobby grunted at me, pressing harder on the cut. "Don't care. Probably. Now shut up. I've got to get you to stop bleeding."

To tell the truth, he didn't look much better than James. The cold had set its hooks in deep, and I was pretty sure we'd lose a toe or two from frostbite. Bobby hooked his arm under me and dragged me out of the landscaping. Not stopping until we were in the relative safety of the dry stairwell, he gripped my shoulders and stared me down.

"What the fuck is it with you and crazies? It's like you're not happy unless someone insane is chasing you down." He wrung his shirt out as much as he could and used it to staunch my wound. The hit he'd taken from James's gun looked like it'd taken a chunk of meat out of his arm, and it began to bleed freely now that we were out of the deluge. "Think you can stay out of trouble long enough for me to go get my phone and call 911?"

"Out of trouble, sure." I grinned up at him, probably looking stupid from the pain. "Hey! One good thing—"

"What the fuck could be good about this?" Bobby growled, grabbed my hand, and put it firmly on the damp shirt to hold it in place. "You tell me, Princess... what the fucking hell can be good about this shit?"

Pointing at the knife wound in my side, I replied, "At least I didn't get shot this time."

CHAPTER TWENTY-TWO

BY THE end of the next afternoon, I was sucking down handfuls of ibuprofen and wishing I'd taken the doctor's offer of painkillers. Hearing me hiss in anguish for the twentieth time that day, Claudia gave me the evil eye over her granny glasses and pursed her mouth.

"You're going to kill your liver there, boy." Mo looked up at her, and she shooed him back to his studying. "Not you, the idiot over here."

"I'm fine. Really," I lied.

It ached a little bit, but I wasn't going to let the slight pain bother me. Or so I told my manly self. The knife went in a bit sideways, and other than a bone nick and minor muscle damage, it was mostly okay. I'd had worse. Hell, I'd have taken worse if it meant Bobby escaped unscathed, but I didn't and he hadn't. From the way he'd bitched at the emergency room when they'd begin poking him a local sedative, someone would have thought he'd been gutted by a Tyrannosaurus rex instead of getting a 9 mm slug into the meat of his upper arm.

Three hours of his complaining, and when the doctor announcing the inevitable overnight stay to watch his vitals turned it into a full-blown typhoon of rage, I played the coward and let Claudia take a verbal strap to his ass.

"Besides—" I smirked back at her, rocking back in my office chair. "Why do you keep coming in when the doctor told you not to? You got shot, you know."

"Boy—" Claudia inhaled hard, and I braced myself. Mo stepped in to save my ass, once more reminding me that one did not poke a simmering dragon with a look that clearly assessed me for mental stability and found me wanting.

"Nana, it's time to go. We've got to get going if we're making dinner at Uncle Mace's." His backpack was already bulging with electronics and books. She huffed, and I slipped him a twenty, mouthing a thank you behind Claudia's broad back. He palmed it like a pro, tucking it into his jeans pocket while I handed Claudia her cane.

Then dodged when she tried to hit me with it.

"Hah!" I almost stuck my tongue out, but she caught me with her backswing, smacking my calf. "Shit!"

"Don't think I can't beat you down, Cole McGinnis." Claudia shook her cane head at my nose. "Mo, help me down the stairs before I stay here and knock some sense into this man."

Detective Dexter Wong was climbing the steps when I opened the door for Claudia. He was sporting a new haircut, shorn nearly down to his scalp on the sides with a pouf of chunky spikes on top. It looked a little silly on him, but by the way he strutted up the stairs and gave Claudia a jaunty wave, I figured I couldn't really give him shit about it. The gray polyester jacket, however, was fair game.

"Man, you're dressed like a bad seventies cop." I followed him back into the office, dogging his steps. "Where'd you hide the Gran Torino?"

"Fuck you, McGinnis." His rejoinder lacked bite, especially compared to Claudia's skilled cuts, but I wasn't going to point that out either. "Sit down. I'm here to figure out what the hell you did yesterday."

I got Wong a soda from the fridge and handed it to him over the desk. Slumping down into my chair, I popped open my Diet Coke and sipped at the froth bubbling up over the tab. "What's there to say you didn't hear last night at the hospital?"

"You were in the ER for what? Five minutes before Jae dragged you out of there? How much could I ask you?"

"I wasn't that hurt. He was happy to see me whole and hearty. Very happy. He even showed me how happy he was in the parking lot."

"I didn't need that image in my head," he moaned. "Also, I'm hiding from O'Byrne. She thinks I let you run all over this case and didn't do anything to stop you."

"You didn't." A staple remover came flying at my shoulder, but it went wide, clattered across the floor, and came to a rest against the far wall. "She wasn't too happy to see me when I stopped in at the hospital to see Hong Chul."

"Yeah, unhappy is an understatement." Wong sighed. "James Bahn didn't make it, you know. He was alive long enough to talk a bit to his mother and the cops but seized up on the table. They couldn't resuscitate."

"Sort of figured that out on the scene. Bobby got him close range." I'd seen too much bloodshed over the past week. Vivian's death would haunt me, but I'd sleep better at night knowing James was dead.

"Madame Sun's packing up shop and heading back to Seoul. Guess Gyong-Si's going to corner the market on fortune-telling around here."

"She lost her daughter *and* her son. Do you blame her?" I'd liked the *ajumma*. She seemed like a nice woman who'd been dealt a shitty hand in life.

"No, it's a pity, though. Bad enough her daughter was murdered, but to have her son be the killer?" He shook his head, the spikes on his head bobbing in waves.

Thinking of Kim Hyun-Shik, I said, "I've seen it the other way around too. Sucks either way. Did James say anything about killing Shim?"

"Yeah, I got to the ER when they were prepping him. He spilled his guts to his mother. Guess he knew he wasn't going to make it. Amazing how many people find God when they're knocking on Hell's Gate." Wong rested his elbows on his knees, gesturing with his soda can. "Shim popped Choi in her car and was waiting for Lee at her apartment. James paid him five thousand each for those hits. Vivian called him because she was going to be late for a dinner they were supposed to go to. So James knew where she was going to be and figured he'd take the chance to take her out."

"With not a damned thought about what it would do to his mother?"

"Nope. When she told him she was going to be at that coffee shop, James drove and parked his car on the street outside the window. Since the entrance to the place is inside the courtyard, he figured no one would connect his vehicle to what was going on. Shim met him there, sat in the passenger seat, and waited for a clear shot. Then they took off into traffic when the shit hit the fan."

"Shim didn't wait for a clear shot. He lit the fucking place up," I reminded Wong. "It was like Elmer Fudd at a bunny ranch."

"Darren Shim was not known for being a stable young man," Wong drawled. "Or for being very patient. James apparently didn't have the money on him, so Shim decided he'd go collect it in person. James denied telling Shim to come to Madame Sun's place of business the next day. I guess Shim decided he was going to show James he was dealing with a badass and collect what was owed him."

"So James bashing his head in with the urn to protect his mother was real?" If I sounded skeptical, Wong's expression bordered on intense cynicism. "Really?"

"That's what James told his mother," Wong replied slowly. "She seemed happy to hear her son wasn't a total bastard. It might have gone down the way he said. The attack on Madame Sun wasn't planned. Shim did it on his own. James killed him defending his mother."

"Huh. Maybe," I conceded. "He had a deep hate for Gyong-Si. Blamed the man for his parents' divorce. I guess when Vivian showed up out of the blue, it pissed him off. His mother was bending over backward for the daughter. When Vivian wasn't appreciative enough, James was done. He did say killing Gyong-Si was the ultimate goal. Hurting Gyong-Si by killing off his kids was just a bonus."

"We're guessing Hong Chul's grandfather, Bhak Bong Chol, told James all about Gyong-Si's children. He must have let his own hatred of Gyong-Si slip out when he was having a consultation, and James pounced on it." I'd turned over Bhak's papers late last night, along with the notes we'd taken from them, but most of it was nonsensical.

"No word on if James had something to do with the grandfather's death. He was cremated, so there's nothing to run tox on," Wong supplied. "Captain said to let that one sit. Not worth pursuing. Well, not without causing the family a lot of unnecessary pain."

"Yeah, probably best. Some of his notes were kind of crazy."

"His daughter said Bhak was suffering from some sort of dementia. I'm surprised you guys got anything out of what he wrote down. Good job working it out, though. Even though it almost got you killed." He made a face, mostly apologetic, but I wouldn't put money on it. "Bobby doing good?"

"Yeah, I picked him up this morning. Half of the guys in his little black book are fighting over each other to take care of him." Sipping my drink, I snorted out at the carbonation tickling my nose. "Right now, his apartment probably looks like No Cover Charge Twink night at the Slip-n-Slide."

"Got word Abby Park's going to be okay. Her liver's responding to whatever meds they put her on." Wong made a show of flipping through his notebook, crossing things off with a pen he'd stolen from Claudia's desk. "And I got a hold of the Yis. The mother apparently broke her tooth on something and Terry took her to the dentist. That's why they weren't around when James showed up."

"Good. Honestly, I went over there to see if she knew anyone who hated Gyong-Si. I was hoping for a lead."

"She's a trip." He chuckled. "She's the one who told Terry to get a job with Gyong-Si. Thought it would be a good way for him to get to know his father. Of course, she didn't really believe Gyong-Si was gay. First thing she asked Terry when she found out was if Gyong-Si hit on him."

"God, don't go there." I shuddered. "Terry's a good kid. Wonder if he and Hong Chul are going to get together now that they know they're brothers."

"Don't know. It'll be nice for them. Brothers are good to have."

Even knowing Mike as well as I did, I'd want to have him around. Ichiro was easier to like, but we were still in a honeymoon stage of sorts. Or maybe it was just easier to get along with someone if you were too old to fight over the toy from a box of cereal.

"Yeah, they're good to have." Nodding in agreement, I gave the chair a few squeaks. "Although mine seems not to be as good at reading because he got Lee confused with Yi."

"Was it in English or Korean? The writing?"

"The writing? Probably both. The guy really had shitty writing, so I've got to cut Ichi some slack. So what now? O'Byrne going to nail me for impeding an investigation?" I wouldn't have put it past her. When she'd shown up at the ER, I was lucky to have survived, with her shouting at me until a nurse kicked her out. "Last time I saw her, she was measuring my head to hang above her desk at the station."

"Yeah, Captain's not too happy with either of us. If I'm lucky, I'll get a bright, shiny patrol car to tool around in when I'm giving out parking tickets. We'll see." Wong sighed mournfully. "Okay, I've got to get home to the girlfriend. We're supposed to go out to dinner with my parents. My mom's already hinting about grandkids. I think I'm going to tell her we're going to get a dog and see if we can't keep it alive first. *Then* I'll think about having kids."

I WALKED Wong out after locking the office up. Someone in the neighborhood was prepping for the cooler weather from the sounds of wood being split nearby. Rubbing at my injured side, I gave myself permission to be lazy and order in a few stacks of seasoned eucalyptus.

Seeing the white Explorer parked beside my Rover made me smile, and I forgot all about any aches and pains.

Jae was waiting for me on the stoop, sitting on the cold cement and smoking a *kretek*. The aromatic clove smell drifted toward me, greeting my approach with a fragrant kiss. He'd dug through my clothes again, unearthing a dark green fisherman's sweater Maddy brought back for me from Killybegs. Jae swam in it, and he'd pulled down its hem until it covered his knees, probably hoping it would keep his legs warmer than his torn jeans could. A box of groceries sat on the cement behind him, the end of a large butternut squash and a bunch of leeks peeking out over the top.

"Hey, that co-op thing you joined dropped stuff off?" He didn't look up. Instead, his eyes were fixed off into the distance, not even focused on the popsicle-stick-slat fence separating my long lot from the neighbors. I leaned over to kiss him and got a chunk of hair instead of the mouth I'd been aiming for. "Jae, you okay?"

"Babe?" I got no response so I tried again. "Jae?"

"Where's Tiffany? Do you know? She's not answering her phone." He turned his face toward me, but his eyes were still unfocused, pinned to anywhere but my face. It was a dead look, as if something inside of him was withering away in front of me. "I thought she was here with you."

"Maddy took her and Sissy out for a girl's afternoon. She was supposed to tell you. From what I heard, they're buying up LA." I touched his cheek, finding it chilled from the wind. It stung when he flinched, but when Jae leaned into the cup of my palm, I sighed in silent relief. "Talk to me, honey."

"They're moving here... to Los Angeles. I told you, *ne*? My mother and Jae-Su." He sounded worse than numb, his lips barely moving as he spoke. "I guess Ree too. I... don't know. She—fuck, Cole-ah. I don't know."

"Yeah, you told me." I sat down next to him. He looked too brittle to touch, but I slung my arm around his waist. "Did your mom call you to tell you when?"

"No, she called to tell me... I'm no longer her son." He broke in front of me, his control shattering under the weight of his words. I tried to pull him closer, confused and unsure about what to do, but Jae pulled away, keeping a bit of distance between us. "Cole-ah, she knows. She *really* does know this time. She—"

Any pain I'd ever experienced, even grabbing at Rick in those final moments between us, didn't *hurt* as much as seeing Jae crumble.

Whatever he had going on inside of him was devastating, an emotional massacre he didn't have a chance in hell of surviving.

"Babe, I need you to talk to me." I scooted closer, pressing tight against him. "What happened? What the fuck happened? Did Tiff talk to her? I thought she was cool with us. She said she was going to be okay with us!"

"My aunt, Hyun-Shik's mother, called her. She told my mother *everything*. That she'd found me with *hyung*... having sex with him, and that I'd been at Dorthi Ki Seu. *Everything*, Cole-ah... including... us." Jae's chest hitched, a sob caught somewhere in his throat. "All because my mother is coming to Los Angeles with Jae-Su... because Uncle wants his *son*. My aunt... had to hurt her... hurt me."

"Your *aunt* told her?" There weren't enough foul words I could come up with. Rage filled every crevice of my being and spilled out through my mouth. "*Fucking bitch.* Why? What the hell would she do that for? You bent over backward for her. You did everything you could for that c—"

"She was jealous... is jealous." Jae finally looked at me, and I recoiled at the pain in his face. He was laid bare in front of me, carved up and left for dead by the woman who'd given birth to him. "So she told my mother I'm... like *this*. How I whored myself, letting men fuck me, and that's how I was supporting the family. By selling my ass to men like Hyun-Shik... or to you. My aunt destroyed me... my family... because she—"

"Because she's a fucking bitch," I whispered, reaching for Jae's shoulders to fold him into a hug. He didn't fight me, collapsing into my arms. Shaking, he began to cry, a noiseless weeping strong enough to send shockwaves through his body. Rocking him, I stroked at his hair and kissed the top of his head. "I'm here. I'm not going anywhere."

"I can't feel... inside of me anymore, Cole." He sounded scared, more terrified than I'd ever heard him sound before. Even in the grip of the bloodshed and death we'd slogged through, Jae'd been stoic, practically phlegmatic in enduring his troubles. Suddenly the shell was cracked, and a little boy with a broken heart poured out in a slithering, yolky mess. "I can't feel my heart anymore. It just… hurts too much to breathe."

"What did she tell you? Your mom?" I didn't even know the woman's name. He'd never told it to me. Right now, it didn't seem as important as what she meant to him. "Maybe you didn't hear her straight. Maybe she just needs time."

"No, she is done with me. She said that she'd always known I was… wrong, but she didn't care because I wasn't there living with her anymore so it didn't matter. *I* didn't matter anymore." He was tiring, too much energy spent on too little, and the bitch seemed to have sucked everything out of him. Bruised circles puffed up the skin beneath Jae's drooping eyes, and he sighed, unable to hold himself up anymore. "I was nothing to her. Nothing more than someone to feed off of. I thought… I wanted it to be different… I wanted her to love me. She is my *mother*—"

"You have me. And Scarlet. Hell, Jae, you've got so many people around you."

"But they're not family," he insisted softly. "Not *my* family. She's going to take Tiffany. I don't know if I'll ever see her… or Ree again. I can't… I can't let her take my sisters from me, Cole-ah. She doesn't care for them… forgets them and does things with men. I can't let my sisters live like that. Like I did when I was their age. It kills you inside. You're so *alone*, Cole-ah. I don't want them to be that alone."

"We're your family, Jae. *I'll* be your family." I didn't know what else to say. Trapped in the sticky threads of Jae's pain, I could only hold him tighter and rock him as he cried. "And you're not nothing. Babe, you are *everything*."

"Don't leave me, Cole." His arms tightened around my stomach, thrusting sharp tingles through the bandaged knife wound along my ribs. "You promised if I told you to never let me go, you'd be here."

"Hey, I'm here, aren't I?" I reminded him. Sliding my hand under his chin, I tilted his head up until I could see his face. "I'm not going anywhere, Kim Jae-Min. Promise to God, whatever it takes, wherever you go—I'm there."

"*Agi*?" Jae didn't cry pretty. His nose was red, but he was pretty. Beautiful in every way that mattered, especially when he bent his head down to kiss my fingertips.

"Yeah, Jae?" I murmured, stroking his lower lip with my thumb.

"*Saranghae, jagiya.*" He took a deep breath and whispered something I'd wanted to hear him say for a very long time. "I love you."

THE day was just beginning to kiss dusk when Jae began to shiver violently in my arms. I'd sat and held him close for nearly an hour and a half, letting him cry himself out at first before spending a long time kissing him better. I didn't want anything more from him than his mouth and body against mine, stroking his heart back open after it'd been stabbed through by his mother's rejection. We'd talked some, coming to the conclusion we were both freezing our asses off and the world would look a whole hell of a lot better if we had food and alcohol in us.

I reluctantly let him go and picked up the produce box. The leeks tickled my nose, and I pushed them to the side. Jae moved stiffly, his legs probably frozen from squatting on the cold cement.

"Let go. You're injured, remember? Go unlock the door." Jae sniffed with shuddering hiccups as he wrestled the box from me. "I want to talk about something besides... me. Is Terry and his mom okay? No one knew where they were, *ne*?"

"Yeah, he'd gone to take her to the dentist. She broke a tooth on something. It's why he lit out of Gyong-Si's, so they missed the whole thing." I snatched an escaped apple from the box as it rolled around near a bunch of celery. "Wong said Abby's doing well too."

"Did you talk to Bobby? How is he feeling?"

I didn't have a chance to give Jae an answer. Instead, my attention was drawn to a woman who'd stepped out from the back of my building and onto the walkway, her arms draped loosely by her sides. I barely recognized her, and when I did, my brain stuttered to a standstill, refusing to accept the reality of the skeletal woman shuffling across the cement walk.

Defibrillating my mind, I choked past the lump in my throat. I squeaked, "Sheila?"

The last time I'd seen Ben's wife, Sheila, had been the day of Rick's memorial, a hastily thrown together affair attended by a few of his friends and my family. When I'd called her to tell her about the service, she'd responded with such a dull voice, I'd wondered if she'd even heard me. I would have preferred the brain-dead zombie who answered the phone to the harpy who'd arrived at the chapel. She'd cornered me in the vestibule, told me she never wanted to see me again and she'd be damned if I ever came near her kids. That was the last I'd seen of her, and even then, she'd taken an emotional beating she probably couldn't recover from.

It'd been the final blow for me, and I'd walked out of the memorial mourning not only the loss of my lover but the disintegration of a family I'd thought of as my own. To see Sheila standing in front of me was a shock, but not as bone-chilling scary as what she'd become.

Sheila was nearly unrecognizable, more like one of those shrunken apple dolls shaped to look like her. Red lesions mottled her sunken cheeks, and the blonde mane she'd once been so proud of hung in brittle hanks around her too-thin shoulders. Even from a distance, she smelled rank, a sour, curdled odor with a hint of raw sewage. A soiled wifebeater hung on her skinny frame, but the thin fabric did nothing to hide the concave swoop of her chest or the slight bloat around her belly. The black of her teeth stank of meth use. Even without seeing their rotting, crumbling edges, the lesions were as good a sign of a meth addict as any.

Her parched, cracked skin flaked off in a dusty storm when Sheila raised her arms and leveled a wicked-looking Glock at us. It was nearly too heavy for her, and I recognized it as Ben's personal piece. I'd given it to him for Christmas once, and we'd spent time on the range testing it out, turning up very late for dinner that night.

I moved forward to grab at Jae, but Sheila warned me off with a wave of her weapon. When she spoke, her lips cracked further, and I could see the black rot eating away at her teeth. Holding up my hands, I slid slowly closer to my lover, and Sheila let a shot bark out, shattering the living room window. The shot-up glass blew out everywhere, pelting Jae and I with tiny sharp pebbles. The gun jerked up in Sheila's hand, nearly slapping her in the face, but she brought it back down quickly, its sight finding me again.

"Hey, come on, Sheila. You've got friends here." I was going to try talking. Hell, I'd try sucking the gun off if it would make her feel better, but Ben's wife had other plans. "What's going on, huh? Do you need some help?"

"They took my kids, Cole." Her tongue slithered around her mouth as she spoke, unfettered by her lack of front teeth. "You know that? Did your friends—*the cops*—tell you that?"

"Cole-ah." Jae began to speak, but I shushed him, wanting to keep Sheila's attention on me. He was still caught up in the savagery his mother had inflicted on him, and I could hear him try to catch his breath behind me.

"Sheila, honey… we can get someone to help you get them back, okay?" I nudged closer, trying to get closer to Jae. Seeing her strung out and wild-eyed, I didn't have any doubt the kids had been taken from her. She barely looked stable enough to be outside of a loony bin. "Why don't you tell me what happened?"

"What happened?" she screamed. "They took my kids! My parents took my kids! I've got nothing now, you fucking faggot. Nothing! No one!"

"Sheila—"

"Don't say another *goddamned* thing!" She was in full scream mode, and I took the chance to edge up against Jae's side. "Is this who you're fucking now? Does he know what a damned slut you are? You weren't happy with that faggot asshole you were living with? You had to go and fuck Ben too? You probably got him sick and that's why he killed himself. Because you gave him some faggot disease he couldn't live with."

"Honey, Ben never *ever* looked at me like that." I patted at the air, hoping the motion would calm her. "He didn't like men. Not like that. He loved you. Things were just too hard for him."

"You think he loved me? Then why the fuck did he leave me? What the hell was so damned hard that he killed himself? Huh?" More spittle flew from her mouth, and a speck hit my face.

"I can help, honey," I soothed. I was searching my brain for a way to get Jae out of there, but short of throwing him through the broken window, I was coming up empty. "Just tell me why you're here. What can I do for you?"

"You know what I'm doing here, Cole? I'm going to do to you what you fucking did to me. You took Ben. You took my kids. Rick was fucking *nothing*. You want to know how I feel? This is how I fucking feel."

That's when she lifted the gun up again and blew a hole right through Jae's chest.

EPILOGUE

WHEN I'd been under, consciousness slid up around me with an undulating lucidity. Once when I was floating on a river of painkillers, I listened to the whistles and beeps serenading me and wondered who was playing Pac-Man over my dead body. The machines wheezed and beeped and moaned, blipping out squeals in rhythms usually only found in video games or bad porno. Sitting with Jae-Min in the hospital room, I was again being sung to by the bells and whistles, and not for the first time I wondered who was in charge of the controller and when would he stop fucking with the man hooked up to the machines.

A shadow passed behind me, one of the nurses or orderlies tending to Jae, but I didn't really see them. The only thing I saw was the man lying too still under the bleach-scented white hospital sheets.

Over the past few days, the hospital staff had tried to move me from the room. I wasn't having any of their shit. I followed Jae from ICU to the private room they'd finally put him in, keeping an eye on him. Keeping my heart going with every beat of his.

There'd been an argument about letting me stay with him. A lot of swearing on my part and then some negotiating done by Mike and Scarlett's *hyung* convinced someone Jae and I were domestic partners. Either way, I wasn't moving. While everyone, including Ichiro, took turns sitting beside me, Scarlet kept me company most of the time. She and Tiffany were my constant shadows, while Maddy and Claudia provided a backup chorus for their nagging, sometimes even ganging up on me to take a shower or eat.

His mother never came. I called. God fucking knows I called. I fucking begged into her voice mail, promising her everything... *anything*... just so she'd come to her son's side.

Nothing. Scarlet told me to give up, that the woman wasn't worth it, and plied me with so much coffee I was beginning to wonder if I was fucking Tantalus.

Still, hot and bitter coffee was good. The hospital food, not so much.

He woke up sporadically, at first fighting the tube they'd shoved down his throat, then battling the nurse when they took it out. I'd held his hand, trying to soothe his fears, but Jae was too far gone... too far in the black to hear me. I wasn't even certain he knew who I was when he woke up the next time, his unfocused brown eyes trying to track my face when I leaned in to talk to him. He might have heard me say three words, and then he went under again.

HIS face was wet with tears when I came in, and the deep brown eyes I loved to stare down into were caught someplace off in the distance, staring at something outside of the window. It wasn't much of a view, mainly the ass end of the building next door, but something in the reflective windows called to him. I pulled the chair closer to his bed and picked up his hand before I sat down and held his cold fingers tightly.

"Babe?" I got no response, so I tried again. "Jae?"

"You're too far away. I need... to feel you against me."

I was going to catch hell for what I did next, but fuck the rules. Working down the bed guard, I slid in behind Jae, tilting him slightly forward so he could rest against me. Other than a wince when his stitches were pinched, he said nothing, but the shuddering sigh of relief was all I needed. Cradled in my embrace, he snuggled back, his breath snagging on his pain until he was comfortable. I was mindful of the drainage tube they had placed on his right side, keeping it as tangle free as I could.

"I am so stoned. No wonder you get shot a lot." His tongue sounded like it was two sizes too big for his mouth and a silly grin played hide and seek with me. "How is Neko? Where's Tiffany?"

"Trust you to ask about the cat, *then* your sister." I laughed, rubbing at his stomach. "Tiff's staying at Mike's house. I think Maddy likes having a full-sized doll to dress up. From what I hear, they're buying up LA. Ichi's at our house. He's Neko's favorite person right now. He cooks her an egg every morning."

"How bad was I hurt?"

"Not too bad." I grinned back at him when he gave me a sour look. "No really, on the scale of zero-to-Cole, you barely registered. She hit your lung, but other than that, you're doing okay. They just wanted to keep you under for a few days."

"Fuckers." It was odd to hear him swear. Most of the time he rolled with everything, but for that one second, it seemed like I was rubbing off on him. Which was a good thing, considering how much time I spent rubbing against him. "Did they catch her?"

"No, hon. They didn't. *I* didn't." I kissed the back of his head, grateful Scarlet had brought waterless shampoo for his hair. "They will. I'm not going to let this go."

I could have said more. I could have told him how I didn't give a shit about where Sheila'd run off to after she'd shot him or how I didn't chase after her, choosing instead to hold my hands over his wound to keep the blood in his body.

After sitting in the ER with Jae's blood all over my hands, I chewed through every cop's ass I saw until Wong was hailing down a doctor to tank me with sedatives. My own wounds hurt, scarred-over reminders of the last Pinelli who fucked with me and my own. Ben took the coward's way out. He took himself out before I could get a hold of his fucking life-destroying ass, and I'd feel cheated if I found out Sheila danced off to her karmic destiny without me helping her get there.

"Let the cops find her, Cole-ah." He tightened his arms around mine, and one of his elbows thrust sharp tingles through the bandaged knife wound along my ribs. "Remember when you promised you'd never let me go? Now is good. I need you here. *Now*."

"Hey, I'm here, aren't I? I've even eaten the shitty Jell-O they put on your plate so you don't have to," I reminded him. "I'm not going anywhere, Kim Jae-Min."

"*Agi?*" The time spent drugged out of his mind had taken a toll on his face. His skin was drawn tight across his cheekbones, and he'd lost some weight, sharpening his features until they were nearly vulpine.

"In case it was lost in all of this, *I love you, jagiya.*"

It was fantastic to hear. Despite the R2-D2 orchestra playing the salsa behind us, those were words I needed to hear... wanted to hear. Even sweeter was the kiss he gave me, a slow brush of his mouth, the chap of skin rough on my chin.

"I love you too," I whispered into his mouth. "But no more getting shot. I don't think I can take it."

RHYS FORD was born and raised in Hawai'i, then wandered off to see the world. After chewing through a pile of books, a lot of odd food, and a stray boyfriend or two, Rhys eventually landed in San Diego, which is a very nice place but seriously needs more rain.

Rhys admits to sharing the house with three cats, a black Pomeranian puffball, a bonsai wolfhound, and a ginger cairn terrorist. Rhys is also enslaved to the upkeep of a 1979 Pontiac Firebird, a Qosmio laptop, and a red Hamilton Beach coffeemaker.

Visit Rhys's blog at http://rhysford.wordpress.com/ or e-mail Rhys at rhys_ford@vitaenoir.com.

How the story started

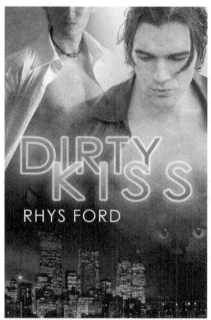

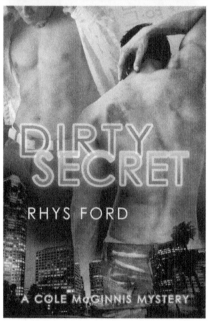

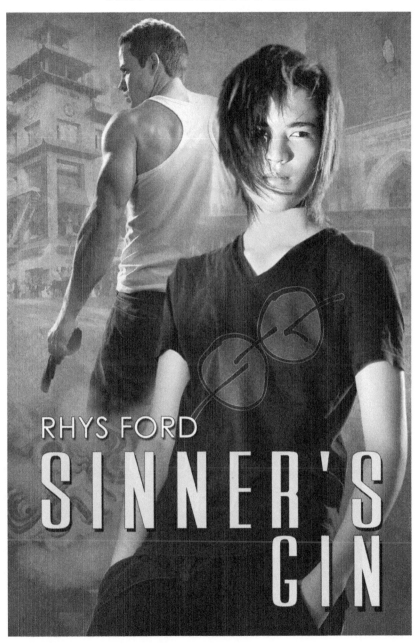

CPSIA information can be obtained at www.ICGtesting.com
Printed in the USA
BVOW08s0538110614

356049BV00011B/474/P